T0248040

DEAD WEST

ALSO BY LINDA L. RICHARDS

DEAD WEST

A NOVEL

LINDA L. RICHARDS

OCEANVIEW (PUBLISHING

SARASOTA, FLORIDA

ISBN 978-1-60809-512-4

Published in the United States of America by Oceanview Publishing

Sarasota, Florida

www.oceanviewpub.com

10 9 8 7 6 5 4 3 2 1

PRINTED IN THE UNITED STATES OF AMERICA

*"Perhaps home is not a place
but simply an irrevocable condition."*

—JAMES BALDWIN

CHAPTER ONE

I'M SITTING ON a beach. It's a ridiculous proposition. Fluffy white clouds are scudding through a clear, blue sky. Surfers are running around carrying boards, often over their heads. Then they plunge into a sea that looks deadly to my non-surfing eyes. Palm trees are waving, and the air is so neutral, you don't have to think about it. Soft, welcoming air. You just float right through.

The view is beautiful. It's like a movie backdrop. A painting. Something skillfully manufactured to look hyper-real. Textbook paradise, that's what I'm talking about.

I'm sitting on this beach, trying not to think about the reason I'm here. But it's hard. Difficult. To not think about it, I mean. I'm here, in paradise, because someone has to die.

Someone will die.

I got the assignment a few days ago. I flew to this island to pull it off.

My target is a businessman who lives on this island in the South Pacific. He is the kind of self-made guy who has achieved every goal in life and would seem to have everything to live for. Only now, apparently, someone wants him dead because here I am, ready for business.

So I stake him out. You need to understand at least the basics of who someone is before you snuff them out. This is the idea that I have. I'm not going all sensitive on you or anything, that's just how it is. In order to do the best possible job in this business, you need to understand a little about who *they* are.

His name is Gavin White, and I researched him a bit before I got here. He made his fortune in oil and wax, which is an odd enough combination that you perk up your ears. Only it doesn't matter: the source of the income would seem to have nothing to do with the hit. Would *seem* to, because there is only so much I can learn about that, really. On the surface, anyway, I can find no direct connection between Gavin White's livelihood and the death that someone has planned for him and that I am now further planning.

I follow him and his S560 cabriolet all over the tropical island. He makes a few stops. I watch what he does, how he moves, and who he interacts with. Some of it might matter. I'm not doing it for my health. I'm watching him so I can determine when I might best have advantage when I go to take him out. There are always multiple times and different places to fulfill my assignment and usually only one—or maybe two—that are virtually flawless. Sometimes not even that.

And it's more than an opportunity I'm looking for, though that can play a part. It's also a matter of identifying what will make my job not only easier, but also safest from detection. And so I watch. And I wait.

As I follow him, he stops first at a bank. Does some business— I'll never know what. After that he visits his mom. At least, I guess it is his mom. An older woman he seems affectionate with. From my rental car, I can see them through a front room window. There is a hug and then a wave. It could be a bookkeeper for all I know. But mom is what I guess.

After a while he heads to the beach. He sits on the sand, seems to contemplate. I think about taking him there; full contemplation. But it is crude and much too exposed.

More time passes before he takes off his shoes, leaves them on the beach, and walks into the surf. I leave my car and take up a spot on the sand, just plopping myself down not far from his shoes.

I watch him surreptitiously. It is obvious he did not come to the beach to swim. He is fully clothed and he hasn't left a towel behind there with his shoes. There is none of the paraphernalia one associates with a visit to the beach, even if this were one that is intended for swimming, which it is not. Signs warn of possible impending doom for those who venture into the water.

"Strong current," warns one sign under a fluorescent flag. "If in doubt, don't go out."

"Dangerous shore break," warns another. "Waves break in shallow water. Serious injuries could occur, even in small surf."

I don't know if Gavin White read the signs, or noticed them, but even though he is still fully clothed, he steps into the water anyway.

First, he gets his feet wet. Not long after, he wades in up to his knees. He hesitates when the water is at mid-thigh, and he stops there. For a while, it seems to me, it is like a dance. He stands facing the horizon, directly in front of where I sit. His shoulders are squared. There is something stoic in his stance. I can't explain it. Squared and stoic.

Waves break against him, push him back. He allows the push, then makes his way back to the spot where he had stood before.

Before long, he ventures deeper still. The dance. I watch for a while, fascinated. I wonder if there is anything I should do. But no. The dance. Two steps forward, then the waves push him back.

And now he is in deeper still, and farther from shore. I see a wave engulf him completely, and I hold my breath. He doesn't struggle, but then I see him rise, face the horizon, square his shoulders.

The waves are strong and beautiful. And they are eerily clear, those waves. Sometimes I can see right inside them. Careful glass tubes of water, I can even observe that from shore.

For a while he stands like that, facing the horizon—a lull in the action of the waves. And then he is engulfed once again. I hold my breath, but this time he doesn't rise.

I sit there for a long time, considering. And waiting. My breathing shallow. But he doesn't reappear.

After half an hour, I text my handler.

"It is done," is all I say, just as I know she will expect.

It was not my hand, but the mission has been accomplished regardless. No one knows better than me that there are many ways to die.

CHAPTER TWO

THERE ARE MANY ways to die.

I think I have died many times. Certainly, I've wanted to.

I died when I lost my child. Died later when I lost my husband, even though by then there was little love left between us. Still. I died.

I died the first time I took someone's life. At the time it felt like living, but I didn't yet know the difference. And then there was the time I had to kill someone I loved. I died that time, too.

Sometimes I believe I have died so much that I've forgotten how to live. That I should most correctly walk into a waiting undertow just like Gavin White did. I don't know what stops me, honestly. I don't. Though there are days when it's a very close thing.

This isn't one of those days.

When my phone rings, it tells me the call is coming from Kiribati, a place I've barely heard of before. All of her calls are like that. Routed through some other place. They might be chosen for their convenience, but I think they are also selected for the mirth they might provide. I'm not certain she has a wicked sense of humor, but I suspect it, pretty much.

She never used to call me. For a long time, it was text and email only, secure channels always. And then the calls began. I imagined that it meant we had developed some sort of connection. I no longer wonder about that now.

Whatever the meaning, the calls have never been from normal places; they don't come from the places one might expect. And none have been from the same odd place twice. They are chosen for some reason I don't understand. Some inside joke I stand outside of. She can be cryptic that way. Another reason I guess I imagined for a while that we belonged.

"That was efficient," is what she says by way of greeting.

"What do you mean?" I figure I actually know, but it makes no sense to admit that going in.

"He walked into the sea," she says. How does she know that? It makes me wonder, but not deeply. It would not be the first time I've wondered if there is someone who watches the hunter. It would even make a dark sort of sense.

"Yes," I say, unquestioning. She has her ways. "That's right. He did."

"Hmmm," she says. And then again, "Hmmm."

"There are many ways to die," I say, and by now it feels like gospel. Something sacred. And more true than true. "What I really don't understand," I say, sailing in a different direction, "is that you said things weren't going to be like this anymore."

"Excuse me?" I am put off by her tone. Surprised. It comes to me from a new place. Unexpected. And she doesn't back away from it. Goes on just as strongly, instead. "What do you mean by that?" It's a challenge.

"I'm trying to think how you put it," I say. "Something about how things have been wrong with the world. How we could . . . how we could make it right."

"Did I say that?"

"You did," I reply.

"I do maybe remember something like that. Maybe."

I feel my heart sink a bit at her words. And why? I can't even quite put my finger on it. It felt like I might be part of something. Again. And now? Now I'm not.

"You did say that." I say it quietly though. Almost as an aside.

"These things take time, as it turns out. One can't just flip a switch." I can hear her pushing on, rushing through. "Meanwhile, I've got another one for you," she says, and I'm relieved that she has tacitly agreed to leave the drowned man to sink or swim. Disappointed by how easily the hopeful words she'd fed me not so long ago could be pushed to one easy side. Disappointed and relieved all in one gulp. It's an odd thing to feel. I find I don't like it.

"So if you're ready," she says.

"Another what?" I ask it, but I suspect I know.

"Job," she replies, and I wonder why I wasted breath.

"I'm ready enough," I say, though I'm struggling. I struggle every time.

"Good," she says. "I'll send you the details, but I think the juxtaposition of these two will amuse you."

"How so?" And I try not to digest the irony around any aspect of a contract killing being amusing.

"Well, you've just been in the Pacific. Water, water everywhere. And now you're heading for the desert."

"I am?"

"You are. Right out into it, in fact. The target is in Arizona."

"Phoenix?" Which is all I really know of Arizona.

"You'll fly to Phoenix, but, no: the target is near a national park. Rural. A place you won't have heard of before, I'm betting. I'll send the details once I'm off this call."

When I first get off the phone, I try not to think about it too much. It's like my brain doesn't want me to pay attention. Or something. But I put off checking my email. I'll do it later. Right now, there are things that need my attention.

Okay. "Need" would be an overstatement. There are things. I choose to give them my time. Walks in the forest with the dog. Cooking succulent meals for one. And recently, I have taken up plein air painting, simply because it was there.

When I want to paint, I take the dog and my gear and we hike out to some remote spot and I set up my stuff and I paint what I see. Try to paint what I see. The dog, meanwhile, amuses himself—chasing squirrels, digging holes, sniffing his own butt. He's very skilled at self-amusement. I've never seen anything like it.

In less clement weather we hunker down and brave it out. I make a fire in the fireplace because it's beautiful, not because we need the warmth.

There is something idyllic to this life. Easy. After a while it gets even easier to forget . . . forget what? Everything, really. It gets easier to forget to remember.

I paint the dog. My online classes have gone well enough, and I have proven to be a good enough student—and the dog a good enough subject—that I end up with a pretty credible representation of him; something I am proud to hang. And even if I wasn't, it's not like anyone is ever going to see.

* * *

It's a sunny day, and after dealing with several things that are important to me even though I know they don't really matter, I take my laptop out onto the patio and get to work.

While I set out my computer, I get the foolish and unlikely feeling that I am being watched. And why is it unlikely? Well, that forest, for one. It is all around me, my house occupying a bit of clearing, but in other directions, there are trees as far as one can see. The trees are more sparse over by the lonely road that runs near my property. And, honestly, though it legally carries that title—road—it is ambitious to call it that. There is never much traffic, and on this day, I have observed even less than the normal share.

The feeling of being watched persists, so I observe keenly for a while. There is no motion, no anything to disturb that deep country peace. I glance at the dog, happily snoozing at my feet. He is as undisturbed as the peace. While I watch, a breeze ruffles his coat. He stretches out his legs, sighs contentedly, and slips into an even deeper slumber.

Looking out over my sad and desolate garden, I put that watched feeling aside because I know it has no merit. It can't. There is simply no one who would be watching. I focus instead on opening my laptop and loading the Tor browser that gets me onto the dark web. From there I check an entirely unhackable email account for the details of this impending desert hit.

The name of my target is Cameron Walker. A quick Google search reveals that there are more than fifty people of that name in the Phoenix metro area. And based on the name alone, the Cameron Walker I'm looking for could be a woman or a man, black or white, old or young. It's a name with a lot of possible outcomes. Fortunately, though, I have the latitude and longitude of the primary location of the target. And I surprise myself by wondering, for the first time ever, why they don't just send me the goddamned address. Why dick around with secret codes when there is a perfectly good civic method of sharing someone's location?

Instead of an address, though, I use the latitude and longitude to find the location, which proves to be a place so far out in the desert it barely has a name. Lourdes, Arizona, pop. 12. Twelve! The town rests practically within the Cathedral National Forest, which I have never heard of, but I don't doubt exists.

In a place with a population of—twelve—I'm going to have to give some serious thought to how I take him out. That is, I of course always give it serious thought, but with no one around, it's possible everyone and anyone might see. I feel as though I'll have to be extra careful and watch my front as well as my back.

I give the dog extra skritches that night. He leans into it, but I imagine he does so warily, like he knows something might be up. Especially since, between skritches, I toss things into a suitcase distractedly. I'm not expecting to be gone a long time, but with jobs like this, one never knows.

When I fly, my gun travels within its own special locked container that fits inside my suitcase, which will travel in the hold with all of the checked baggage. I never pack ammo because the stuff makes airlines even more nervous and it's always easy to pick it up on the other side, particularly when my destination is a gun-happy place like Arizona. Between the rattlesnakes in the desert and the scoundrels at the statehouse, there's plenty of hardware to go around.

Of course, flying means that I can't take the dog. Hence the extra skritches. Of course, I *could* take him—although it's more difficult to travel with a dog than it is with a gun, something I've never fully understood. And I've fixed things so that leaving him is no challenge at all. He has an automatic waterer that levels up when he drinks it down. And he has a special feeder, purchased at great cost on Amazon, that dispenses his proper rations three times a day. To take care of his most basic needs, a dog door leads out into my carefully fenced yard. My own property is twenty acres, but just at the house, he's got a whole half acre to go out and sniff around and do stuff. The yard is big enough that he can even run around or take himself for a little walk.

Even with all this doggy luxury, I feel guilty as hell whenever I leave him behind. Something in those golden eyes. No matter how comfy he is at home and how *un*comfy he'd be on a trip, I know he'd rather hang out with me. Always. It's just how he's built.

"Sorry, pup," I tell him during a particularly good skritch, "it's just better you stay here. I have a sense of things. This isn't going to be a ride for a dog."

He doesn't understand the words. I don't think he understands the words. But he feels them. And do I see reproach in those lovely golden eyes? I imagine I do. But I keep fixing to leave, just the same.

In the morning I drive away. Near town, I leave my car in a commuter lot, as I always do, and take the bus to the airport. I imagine I am untrackable/untraceable. I certainly work hard enough at it that I should be. Even so, I feel a shadow behind me. I find myself looking over my shoulder more often than I would have thought. More often than a shadow would warrant.

And then I'm at the airport and I forget everything else. Is someone following me? I can't imagine. And the airport is filled with people. I feel suddenly safe and lost in the moving mass of people. Secure and invisible in the crowd.

It's not a big airport, but this time I only have one hop. I go straight to Phoenix, as I always do. There's a difference this time, though. When I get there, I know I'll stop.

CHAPTER THREE

PEOPLE TALK ABOUT my name. It confuses me. Which one do they care about? The one I was born with? The one I carry now? They are not the same.

The name I was born with stopped serving me some time ago. It belongs to someone else. Someone who isn't me.

It must be said that I did not come by the name I use now honestly. I gave somebody money. They gave me an identity: all papers included and no questions asked.

If I'd thought about it closely, I would have realized that, money notwithstanding, things like this can never be unencumbered. How can they be? To truly exist in this world, the name—the identity—had to come from somewhere. But I did not think about it closely. And I do not think about it now. I handed over money. Papers were handed over to me. How could there be repercussions? The deal was honest. Straight. It was a good exchange.

That was the person I became. Newly encumbered by a name I had not been born with. A name that the former owner no longer had use for.

I googled it, that name. As soon as I got it, I sat down and searched.

Katherine Eveline Ragsdill. I thought it even sounded old-timey. Like a ghost. Like a James Joyce character. Like something that wasn't me.

Katie Ragsdill. She sounded like someone who would have the freckles I had when I was a kid. Someone scrubbed and clean. Scrubbed so well their skin tingled. So that is who I became.

But first I did the search, and I got nothing back. It was as though the person I became had never before existed. How could that even be? I couldn't imagine. And yet, I was the only one. Just me.

The blank identity is what my large amount of U.S. dollars purchased. And once I bought it, I could fill that identity up any way I wanted. Katherine Eveline Ragsdill got a license to drive. A passport. Credit cards. License to carry. All of these came to me with very little trouble, once I had the empty vessel to fill them with. It came to me perfectly clean, that identity. There was nothing attached to the name, until I attached it.

After a while the new person that I was became me, and I shed what had been before. She was damaged goods, that old me. I didn't need her anymore.

I didn't need her. I was Katherine Eveline Ragsdill, not whoever I had been before. Not that either of those names matter. I've given it all a lot of thought and decided that all of these things— names, identity—they are social constructs. They don't add up to much—not really—in the course of everything we drag through a life. We need the identity for a few reasons. First, we have to pass through life without remark. That means, we need the right paperwork to complement our physical trials. Without the paperwork, the trials may as well not exist.

We need the documentation. To get on a plane, for one thing. But for other things, as well.

We need the documentation, but—beyond that—does it matter? That's what I ask. But I don't ask it loudly. I've got thinking to do.

CHAPTER FOUR

I'VE BEEN TO the airport in Phoenix many times. Phoenix is a hub, so pretty much any time you're going anywhere in the United States that requires a stop, there's something of a chance that stop will be Phoenix.

On this trip, however, Phoenix is the destination, not just a place to stop on the way somewhere else. I surprise myself by feeling excited at the prospect of seeing a bit more of the desert city than what can be seen from a runway.

Signs throughout the airport indicate that this is the "friendliest airport in America," and as I make my way toward baggage claim I wonder how an airport gains that distinction. What does an airport have to do to be the friendliest one? Maybe more importantly, who decides? Who makes the decision about which is the friendliest? Is there a contest? And what does the runner-up do? Do they have different, slightly less enticing signs in their airport advertising that they nearly became the friendliest, but somehow Phoenix beat them out?

They're certainly the fastest in Phoenix, I discover, because my suitcase is already waiting for me when I hit baggage claim, something I don't remember having experienced before. And it makes me a bit apprehensive because this time there is precious cargo. I checked the bag because the weapon is snugged inside the suitcase in its little case. I have a gun. And, of course, no one is going to try to steal my suitcase. How often does that even happen? But what if they did?

I reserved a car in advance, and when my suitcase and I get to the rental center, I'm glad to see that the car waiting for me is a sturdy-looking SUV. It's not a four-wheel drive, but it looks pretty badass anyway, like it could get you places. And my target is a rancher, which means ranch country. Which means a big, badass truck will be just the ticket.

While I head out of town, I muse about the fact that he is a rancher. What could some rancher have done to so piss someone off that a hit had to be ordered? But that's the thing, isn't it? It's usually hard to tell from the outside what motivates a thing like this. Often, I don't know, but honestly when I do, it's usually about the damnedest thing. It can be money, but sometimes the hit is around matters of the heart or insurance or lineage. Business. In my experience, too, sometimes it's just best not to ask that question. Because—maybe—you just really don't wanna know.

It isn't difficult to find a gun store in Phoenix. Before I leave the airport, I type "ammunition near me" and my phone lights up with the possibilities. I choose one on the way and head out.

The stop I make is brief. A couple of boxes of cartridges for the Bersa and then I'm off again, following the thinning light of the day into a bright red and gold sunset. As I head toward Lourdes in the waning light, I discover I'm driving right into that sunset. And it's beautiful.

Once the city has been left behind, the desert sprawls out endlessly toward gray-blue mountains in every direction, illuminated this early evening in shadow. Between here and there, the landscape is dotted with cactuses—or cacti? Some of them are as tall as giants. Some even taller. Their spiked arms reaching out toward a darkening sky. I think back to my brief recent time in the Pacific, on a beach with pitching waves that seemed to be made of glass. That landscape was so beautiful. Welcoming. This landscape is beautiful, too, but it is not welcoming. The opposite, really. It is the sort of harsh landscape that looks like it could chew you up and spit you out without much bother. Harsh. Cruel. And beautiful. It sounds like those things might not go together, but somehow they do.

And then the sunset blinks out and I am driving in darkness. Lourdes is only half an hour more down the road, but even if my mission there is to be brief, trying to complete it in the dark on foreign terrain seems foolhardy, at best. I see a sign for a casino hotel flashing in the distance, and I don't take any time at all to think about it. A soft bed, a good meal, and time to make plans all seem like the right move.

Once checked into the hotel and up in my room, away from the cigarette smoke that drifts out of the casino, I find that I am pleasantly surprised by this desert oasis. My room is expansive and clean. A big soaker tub dominates the bathroom. Since my tub at home is elderly and scrawny and also seldom used, I decide to soak off the travel miles in the bath. It works. In no time at all, I'm feeling clean and more relaxed than I've been in a long time. I try not to think about why I'm there, in this lovely hotel room far from any place I can ever imagine wanting to go. Instead, I soak up the feeling of luxury and pampering all around me.

There are four restaurants inside the hotel. Three of them have good ratings, but as I walk through the casino to have a look at each, I again have that feeling of being watched. And that shouldn't be an odd feeling, I tell myself. There are hundreds of people here—a proper weekday crowd. Why should someone not be looking my way? Even as I compose the thought, I realize that's not what this is. My body is not sensing the casual look of interest from someone I've passed near. I can't quite put my finger on it, but I do know: this is some different thing. I look around, but I can't spot the watcher. Can't even determine if it's just pure paranoia: something my own mind is creating. It doesn't seem like an impossible thought. I try to put it out of my mind. Even if it's true, I can't imagine it will impact the outcome. I have a job to do. I think this watching can't be related to that. And if it is, it's because those who assign me have a hand in it, so there's nothing I can do or need to. I keep my eyes sharp anyway, but even though the feeling persists, I don't spot anyone.

After a while I've had enough of the game. I head back to my room and order room service. A large shrimp cocktail and a glass of wine. I know it's dumb, but it's also just what I want: a bit of quiet while I eat, and no looking over my shoulder required.

Once there I realize that eating in my room was the best choice. There are things I need to mull over. Consider. Over my desert-prepared shrimp cocktail, I mentally explore the possible scenarios I might engage in the following day.

I'm already figuring it will be tricky. Cities provide a certain anonymity. There is a splendid cover in masses of people. You can't just drive up to someone's ranch and start blasting away. Even if it *is* the west, it's not the *old* west. I'll need some kind of plan.

Cameron Walker. I plug the target's name into Google again, and though it's a common name, I'm able to isolate him fairly easily because of the location I now hold. The latitude and longitude have given up the address, and the address proves to be attached to a wild horse sanctuary—a registered 501c3—adjacent to Cathedral National Park, as I'd previously observed.

According to the sanctuary's website, the organization rescues wild horses when there is no alternative, no way to get them back on their own, but mostly they try to help keep them wild. It's all pretty intriguing. Also confusing. This guy, Cameron Walker, sounds like a horsey humanitarian. A hero, really. Who'd want to off a guy like that?

The Circle W Wild Horse Sanctuary's website indicates that the organization was created by Cameron's father on land that had been ranched by Walkers for four generations. Cameron is now the chairman of the organization. He looks out at me good naturedly from the website. He has a sort of noble brow, and in the photo, I see a smile that manages to be warm and commanding at the same time. He looks like the kind of guy you'd want leading something, for sure. The kind of guy that, if he were president, you know stuff would be getting done. Those are my first impressions.

One of the photos on the website shows him with a kid on one shoulder. A young male, I gather. His son? I can't tell, though the little steely jaw has a mini-me quality to it: the kid looks like Walker, that's what I figure.

Beyond that, though, Cameron Walker just doesn't look like someone anyone would want to kill. Even though I've learned those things are often not apparent to me and I shouldn't think about it, I do. I can't help myself. People are such a puzzle, aren't they? Do you see them as they are? Or do you see them as they want to be seen, or even how you want to see them? Plus, you can only observe what is on the surface. What the viewer wants to share with you. But who knows what goes on in anyone's house or mind? What I'm seeing might not reflect reality in any way at all.

Enjoying my meal, I try to put all thought of Cameron Walker out of my mind for a while. I nibble at my shrimp, then try to get some shut-eye. I know I'll have to get up early to roll out to Circle W first thing in the morning, before the heat starts to punch a hole in the day. In any case, there are times you just know when you've thought circles around a thing. You know when you've had enough. Once my belly is full, I catch that feeling straight on and, after a full day of thinking and traveling, I have no trouble at all getting to sleep.

CHAPTER FIVE

IN THE MORNING, the drive out toward Cathedral National Park is beautiful. It exceeds all expectations. The view from my hotel room had offered a taste of this classic southwestern landscape. But now I'm driving straight into a Roadrunner cartoon, only more so. It is lovely.

It's early and a weekday, so the roads are quite clear, and I blast along in my rental car, covering the miles smoothly. Not long after I leave the highway, I notice a sign that says, "Watch for horses on road." I smile, thinking how much I'd like to see one. So I watch for those horses very closely, indeed. But, other than the one on the sign, I don't see any signs of horses at all.

After a while it seems I've gone impossibly far. Just when I think I've totally miscalculated the route, my map app directs me to take a left onto a road I hadn't even noticed at first. It's unmarked. I bump along it dubiously, wondering if this can possibly be right, knowing that I won't truly get an answer until I get to the end of whatever this is and can't go any farther and my phone tells me I-told-you-so in whatever form it chooses—"Make a U-turn, make a U-turn, make a U-turn . . ."

But the electronic correction never comes. Instead, an impressive ranch driveway rises in front of me. It is so impressive and so unexpected it feels like a mirage. The driveway is wide, not paved, and a sign swings above it: CIRCLE W RANCH, it says. And then, in smaller letters, WELCOME TO SANCTUARY. There is something in those words that moves inside me. *Sanctuary*. Indeed. We all dream of that, don't we? We all yearn.

But I don't get much time to gather wool. I am processing what my next move should be when a big pickup comes barreling out of nowhere, twin twisters of dust kicking up behind it.

The truck circles around and stops next to me. It takes me a second to recognize him. In the photos I'd seen, he looked commanding. Impressive. In person there is a boyishness about him. He is clean-shaven though he looks maybe two weeks past needing a haircut. There is an engaging shagginess about him that only adds to the boyishness.

To my surprise, he gets out of the truck and heads toward me. I roll down the driver's window at his approach.

"Oh hey," I say, trying to think quickly, wanting it to seem as though my presence is a natural thing—that I'm not trespassing or spying. Then I have an idea that gives me the feeling I've come up aces. "You're Cameron Walker! How splendid." Did I just say "splendid"? I did. I try not to cringe while I move on. "I recognize you from the website. I think it's wonderful, what you're doing for the horses."

He looks maybe surprised to see me there, but not put out. I flatter myself, even, by thinking I see a light of interest in his eyes. And I think what I've said tracks: in the business his nonprofit is in, it's possible horse lovers appear unannounced just to pay their respects—and perhaps make donations—all the time. That's what I've banked on anyway. And it seems to play.

"Oh, thanks. You've come a long way to tell me that."

"How can you tell?"

"Am I wrong?"

I laugh. Shake my head. "You don't know the half of it."

He laughs, too. "Tell."

"I had business in Phoenix." I didn't tell him he was it. "So I thought I'd roll out here and see if I could see any horses."

"And did you?"

"Did I what?"

"See any horses?"

"Not yet."

"Do you want to?"

So that was how my target ended up giving me a tour of the wild horse sanctuary his family had created. In the time we spend together, I both learn and laugh a lot. It is fascinating and somehow soothing, and during those first hours together, I wonder again and again: Who could want this lovely and compassionate man dead?

CHAPTER SIX

BUT ALL OF that is later. At first, I am just following, trying to look like there is nothing on my mind beyond what he is showing me. In the meantime, while he gives me the grand tour, I see opportunities to complete my mission go whirling past me. I don't take them and I'm only kind of not sure why.

I follow his truck down the road, all the way to the house. He stops in a widened area, and I stop as well, and prepare to walk. We're going to see horses, he says.

He leads me past the main ranch house. It is large and low-slung, surrounded on all sides by paddocks. Just outside the first set of corrals, I see my chance. No one is around. We are out of sight and earshot of the main house, and there is no one near any of the corrals.

I'd come upon him unprepared, of course. Just thinking I was checking things out from a distance. So my gun is not silenced, or ready in any way. And he's larger than I am, so clearly I won't be able to have a physical advantage over him.

While I'm doing all of these quick calculations, he's talking. I can't tell if it's because he thinks I'm potentially a large donor, or a woman he finds attractive, or if he just likes to hear the sound of his own voice. Maybe he's just nice. Whatever the case, I try to take in at least some of what he is saying. He's talking about the importance of the foundation's work. How it has never mattered more. How the very future of the wild horse in America is currently threatened due to political and partisan forces almost beyond control.

The parts of what he's saying that filter through to me make it clear he is sincere and passionate about the work he does here. I try not to let that cloud my mission. I know what I see: a handsome, sincere man with gleaming goals for a better world for horses. Who knows what heinous thing he's done? Or who he's angered or offended or gotten in the way of? Someone wants him dead so badly, they have paid a fair amount of money to have him killed. None of that is my concern. It can't be. Not ever. I have a job to do. I try to inject steel into my spine. Never mind try. This is not my first rodeo. We move on with our tour, and I stay watchful for opportunity.

Meanwhile, he talks. He explains that the horses housed here used to be wild. That they still are to a certain extent. They don't live here the way they would in a show or race barn. He tells me that any type of horse housing near the ranch buildings leads to an adjacent paddock or field so that the animals living there can distance themselves from people if they feel threatened or even slightly unsure. His people aren't trying to gentle these horses, Cameron tells me. They are trying to make them as comfortable as possible while the humans who have appointed themselves their guardians work out what the next stage of their lives should be.

"It's gotten to be challenging," Cameron tells me as we walk. "There are so many forces against them."

I don't ask the obvious questions because, as an enthusiast so keen that I'd drag myself all the way out here, he probably would presume I'd know a lot of this stuff. I keep my lips buttoned and hope for the best.

The lack of questions doesn't stop Cameron from answering, though. I'm guessing he's so used to being in tour guide mode, offering up information about his organization is no effort at all. And so I make a mental note to watch myself. He appears engaged with what he is saying, but it's possible he is being as observant as I am without giving anything at all away.

The tour continues.

Some of the horses, Cameron tells me, came to the ranch because they were injured or ill. Depending on the nature of their injuries, these animals might be nursed back to health and re-released with the free-ranging herds in the national park nearby. Other animals have permanent injuries or other things that might keep them from being able to enjoy a life in the wild, and those would stay on at Circle W.

"We're lucky," Cameron tells me. "We have both the land and resources to make decisions like that. Not everyone does."

"What do you mean?"

"Well, it's a luxury. I guess that's what I'm saying. We are able to do what's best for the individual horse. All the time. Not everyone has that ability."

It occurs to me that, in all parts of life, that's true. There are those that have the luxury to do the right thing. Always. And there are those who cannot find their way clear to do the right thing no matter what. I imagine myself to be somewhere in the middle. And also, what is the right thing, anyway? Certainly, killing is always wrong. Taking lives, no matter the reason. But I figure, some of the people I have brought to the end of their life needed killing.

And you can take it all even further. For example, what, anyway, is right and wrong? Good and evil? And who makes those determinations? Are they made from above? If so, I figure I'm done for anyway.

As the ranch buildings fall away behind us, the enclosures we pass through become larger. Some small groups of horses have several acres to themselves, and it looks like even these enclosures can be opened up so that the horses inside them have still more land on which to range.

"How do you keep track of them all?" I want to know, though in some ways I already have the answer. Moving around the property, meeting the various equine inhabitants, we've encountered many people. From ranch hands to assistants of various types, even a few cowboys and others that seem as though they might be volunteers, there just to be near the horses. It is a big operation. And I can tell that it also means I can't just take him out. There are so many people around, plus by now a lot of them have seen me, and my rental car is parked back at the ranch. It's not like I could get away without anyone noticing.

"I get how all of this could seem overwhelming," he says at one point, and he has no idea how accurate the statement is, "but it makes sense to us in their context. For instance, the Kiger horses."

"The what?"

"The Kigers. You haven't seen them yet. Maybe we'll pop up there now. I haven't visited them for a few days. I'd like to check in with them. You can come, too."

Do I hesitate before getting into a vehicle with a man I've just met? I do. I couldn't have lived the life that I have without caution and hesitation. But I know I have a loaded Bersa Thunder in my purse. And the fact that it is currently not silenced would not matter if it was self-defense and in the wilderness.

In any case, all of my instincts are letting me know I am safe with this man. He is not safe from me, but that's a different story.

We get into his truck and, as we head out, Cameron shoots a look in my direction from under what I notice are super long eyelashes while he begins to tell me about the Kigers. He explains that they were all descended from a herd of horses, exceptional in their purity in terms of original Spanish blood.

"They're hardy and loyal and smart," he tells me. "And wait until you see them. They are so very beautiful, too."

We drive for a mile or so to a pasture that really just feels like a desert-based wilderness. Cameron tells me that we are still on his family's land. It is by now too hot out for much exertion, but he says he knows where to find the horses in the heat. Sure enough, it doesn't take long to locate them sheltering from the sun at a shady bend in a slow-moving river, some of them up to their fetlocks in the cool water, chewing on the harsh grasses that grow on the shaded marshy land near the shore.

"They tend not to stray too far from the river," he tells me, sounding pleased with himself. I get it. It's nice when things go as planned when you're showing something to a stranger. "It's like a lifeblood."

I think for a minute. "You mean the river?"

"Yeah. It gives life . . . to everything. The trees. The grass. The horses. Us. In the desert, you get a real strong sense of the importance of water."

"That makes sense," I say, not really sure what is expected of me. Then I realize that nothing is.

As we leave the truck, he pops on a cowboy hat and hands me a ballcap that can be easily sized down to my smaller head.

"It's okay," I say, thinking about my hair. Not wanting to mess it up. "I'm fine without a hat."

He keeps it extended in my direction. "Please," he says, a note of gentle command in his voice. "It's ridonculously hot out there. It's midday, and the sun is beating down. Wear this, please."

He's said it politely and in a tone that suggests to me he is genuinely concerned about my well-being. I've never lived in a hot
climate, so I hadn't thought about the need to protect my head
from the sun. I take the hat. Size it. Pop it on my head. He smiles.

"It looks good on you," he says. "You can keep it if you like."

I'm not used to compliments. Or cowboys. Or hats. I'm not
quite sure what to say. I grin at him uneasily and mutter something I hope sounds vaguely intelligent. I'm grateful when he pre-
tends not to notice my discomfort, though I wonder at myself for
the feeling. It's not as though there is a lot of time left to him for
his opinion to matter to anyone, least of all me.

We leave the truck and move in the direction of the herd. The
horses are wild, but you can tell they're not unused to people.
They watch us alertly, but they don't bolt. After a while, they stop
even being interested in us and go back to their lazy waterlogged
lunch. I notice that their attention never fully leaves us though,
and ears twitch meaningfully in our direction. Waiting, I imagine,
for any loud or sudden sound or suspicious move.

I look at Cameron with something like wonder. He just looks
back at me and smiles, appreciating that I appreciate what I am
seeing. All of the horses in our view are various shades of gold,
from very light to very dark. Most have black manes and tails and
many have black legs, some with striping. I can see that they are
obviously horses, but they are more than that, too. From my first
sight of them, I understand that they are special. I find myself
wishing for my paints, my easel, and time to record this with some
of my newly developed skills.

"There are differences," I observe after a few minutes of watching them, the silence between us companionable, "but they are all
just the same."

He nods. "Yes, they appear that way. That's well put. And they are. But they are all Kiger horses."

"Is that a breed?"

"Kind of, but not really. It's more like a lineage. They are connected by blood."

"Like a family?"

"Something like that, yes. Also, the color looks the same, but there are subtle variations—can you see it? And those colors all have different names. You can see the slight variants?"

"Yes," I say, surprising myself. "I can."

"That bluish one is called grulla," he says, pointing to a horse that, after he points it out, I recognize as a bluish gold. I would not myself have called it blue. "And that one there is a dun, while the one next to it would be described as a buckskin."

I shake my head. "Those two look almost the same."

"Yes." He smiles. "Almost. But note the black legs on the buckskin."

"I see them now that you've pointed them out," I tell him. "And there are markings on the legs of the dun. Kind of . . . black squiggles?"

"Yes. Good eye." And I feel myself warm under his praise. "There are other differences," he says, "but that's probably enough for today."

"You're right," I say. "It's a lot. My head is swimming already, and it hasn't been that long." I hesitate. Think further. And then, "You make it sound as though there will be other days," I say, cursing myself silently and delicately.

Why am I flirting with him? It's not as though he has a future. And flirting is not something I generally do, totally aside from the fact that there is almost no one in my life that I talk to on a real level. Oh, "do you have this book?" to the librarian and, "where are the kumquats?" to the produce vendor at my local market. But real human interaction. I don't get much of that. But here, with Cameron, I feel something beyond, "can you help me find the dragonfruit?" There is an easy companionship between us. I know it isn't real and that it cannot last, but it is such a rare feeling that I move into it and try not to think about what it means and where it can't go.

"Maybe I feel like there could be," he says, in answer to my question. He has felt it too, then, I surmise. That instant easiness between us. And there, again, that rush of warmth, something I have felt before but rarely enough that it seems worth remarking on, at least to myself, even while I acknowledge that it may just be because I don't get out very often anymore.

When he turns away from me to lead the way back to the truck, I have a moment of sublime indecision. It would be easy—so easy—right here, in the wilderness, with no one around for miles. I could reach into my bag, bring out the Bersa, and end things quickly, right here.

Practical matters stop me. At least, that's what I tell myself. There are a bunch of reasons not to kill him right here and right now. For one thing, he told me we were still on his land, so it's not really the wilderness, at all. Plus, my car is back at the house. If I were to take him here—which I could easily do—I'd still have to go back and collect my car. And how would I get back there, anyway? Drive his truck? There are so many reasons that wouldn't do. Walk? I feel it is walking distance, but the heat makes it a dodgy proposition, plus I don't really know where I am. And, again, a dead man and my car. None of it adds up.

No. Killing him out here is not the call. Not under these circumstances. But he seems an easy, unguarded sort. I know I'll get other chances.

"We missed lunch," he tells me when we get back to the ranch. It isn't all that's been missed, but I don't point that out. "Will you join me for a meal?"

I must not answer quickly enough, or maybe the look I give him alerts him to something that's deeper beneath the surface, because he goes on.

"Honestly, I won't bite," and then he smiles a broad and open smile. "And I'm enjoying your company enough that I don't quite yet want to let you go."

My heart skips a beat, which is a dumb and schoolgirly enough of a reaction that I still don't say anything. I am tongue-tied, which is startling. It's not something that ever happens to me. And I can't be, can I? Not considering where all of this must end. What purpose does tongue-tied serve in this scenario?

When I don't say anything, he fills in the space.

"Well, if you've got some place you need to be . . ." He lets his voice trail off and I finally find mine.

"No, no," I say, finally shaking my voice free. "It's good. It's fine. I'd appreciate some lunch. Sure. Thanks."

He looks at me speculatively over this sudden torrent of words, but he doesn't say anything right away. He smiles though, and it's like the world lights up. Things just seem warmer near him, and I don't mean the heat that is by now shooting off the sun.

"Oh-kay then," he says after what feels like too much time. "Come on in and we'll see what we can find."

He leads me into the house, where it's clear that this is a working operation. We pass an office wing. I can hear phones and voices in discussion floating to us from that direction. The Flying W Sanctuary is clearly a going concern.

"I left a sandwich for you, Cam," a young woman shouts down the hallway.

"Thanks, Belle. Will it feed two?"

The young woman smiles a welcome at me. "I think you'll manage all right," she says, before heading back to whatever work she had been going about.

I follow Cameron into a large modern kitchen that retains a ranch house feel despite its large size. Stainless steel countertops, a huge refrigerator, and a commercial sanitizer rather than a dishwasher are dead giveaways that the operation is beyond purely residential in nature. He leaves me at a big oak table, then heads more deeply into the kitchen and busies himself making our lunch. After a while he brings out a plate with what looks to me to be an impossibly large sandwich. He cuts it in half and puts each half on a plate, along with some slices of tomato and half an avocado for each of us. When he puts the plate in front of me, it seems expertly arranged, as though some chef had positioned it all just so, not some deep west cowboy.

"That looks great," I say.

"Thanks. I don't know what Belle made today, but I should warn you, it won't be meat."

"Warn me?"

"Some people just expect it all the time. Meat. And I have the feeling you and I might be spending some time together, so I thought I'd get that out of the way up front."

His words confuse me so profoundly. It's the second time that I don't know what to say.

"Get what out of the way?" I ask it, ignoring the part where we're going to be spending some time together. And I don't tell him that, considering my mission, he isn't making a good bet.

"I'm vegan," he tells me. "Is that a problem?"

"Why would it be?" I'm answering him, but it's as though he is speaking some different language or saying things in a way that doesn't make sense to me. He's speaking to me like . . . and here I can't figure out what it is he is speaking to me like. And then I realize: the words he's pushing in my direction are things you might utter to someone who has a say. And I don't, of course. Why would I? It's a question I can't even begin to answer.

"I'm not a vegan, but I've got nothing against them," I say with a smile. "And, anyway, I don't eat a ton of meat."

"It would be okay if you did, though. Well, maybe not a ton. People think it's weird, though, the vegetarian thing. Some people. Can you see it? A rancher's son who is vegan. To a lot of folks around here, it doesn't even make sense."

"Not eating meat?"

I take a bite of my sandwich. It's good. I taste something that bites like tuna but that I figure might be chickpeas. There's a hint of curry, too. And vegetables that crunch.

"Yeah," he answers my question. "Some people around these parts think of it as being against man and nature not to eat meat. Probably the law. And my dad? He'd just spin if he knew."

"Knew that you are a vegetarian?"

"Vegan," he says nodding while he takes another bite. "But, yeah."

Which makes me think his father is dead and the spinning has to do with graves. But I'm guessing.

"You have your reasons, I'll bet. For being vegan, despite the rancher connection."

"I do," he says. "And they're mostly about the planet. I used to love a good steak. But when you realize what the beef industry especially is doing to the environment, it makes it more difficult to enjoy."

"I never really thought about it," I say.

"Most people don't," he says without malice, "and there's a lot I could say, and given half the chance I will, but I think I've blabbed on enough for now." He grins a crooked grin. Self-deprecating. And I grin back. "Now tell me about you."

"Me?" I am startled. It's foolish and I should have been expecting it, but I wasn't. And I am.

"Yes, you." And there's that smile again. White teeth in a bronzed face. "I haven't given you any chances to say anything," he says. "I've just been blabbing on."

"Well, surely not blabbing..." I twiddle with a piece of crust on my plate.

"Tell me." He commands it warmly. Endearingly. I have an almost overwhelming desire to tell him everything. About everything. But, of course, that would never do.

"There's not much to tell, really," I stall, trying to think fast. "I'm out here to ... ummm ... lecture at ASU." There had been Arizona State University banners in the airport. ASU. Apparently, it had been left in high memory. "And I wanted to see the desert while I was here. And the horses. And so here I am." I wonder: now who is blabbing?

Even as I say it, I realize I haven't said anything at all. I used a bunch of words, but the end result would not have been particularly informational. Unsurprisingly, he doesn't miss that fact either. I can see it on his face. I get the idea that he doesn't miss much at all.

"What are you lecturing about?" He seems genuinely curious, not skeptical. But I still feel strangely awkward about answering. It's a reasonable enough question, but I feel guilty because he's looking at me so earnestly. And the guilt is because I can't tell him anything but lies.

"Not wild horses." I say it with a smile, and he smiles back patiently. But he keeps watching me intently.

"That much I'd figured," he says. Prompting without saying much.

"Mostly I'm talking about . . . trash." I'm just riffing now, grasping at straws and memories. "Trash and how there are methods—technologies—available that would commodify the things we throw away at present."

He looks at me for a full twenty seconds without speaking. He seems dumbstruck, which concerns me, of course. And then he says something that surprises me more completely than I would have thought possible.

"Like Virginia Martin's technology? The stuff she developed for Greenmüll?" He says it, and I am so surprised by the words, I again don't say anything for longer than the usual amount of time.

In the end I decide on the most honest response possible under the circumstances.

"Yes. Exactly like that," I say. "In fact, I worked closely with her before . . . "

"Before the accident?" he says.

"Yes," I say. "Before that."

"She seemed so charismatic. I was sorry to see it end the way it did."

"The principles were sound though. They are still ideas worth thinking about."

He smiles at me, seemingly pleased. "I just knew you and I had some points of connection," he tells me. "I think maybe we like some of the same things."

I smile back at him, willing him to not ask more about me. Not wanting to lie, but intrigued about what he's thinking and where he imagines this might go.

He changes the subject. "Where are you staying?"

This is a natural and neutral enough question. I just don't have an answer.

"Somewhere near campus," I tell him. "But I can't think of the name."

"That's okay," he reassures me. "I don't know the city well enough for it to matter. But listen: how about I come into town tomorrow night and take you out to dinner."

"That's a long drive," I say.

"And yet here you are," he replies.

"Yes." I nod. "Here I am."

CHAPTER SEVEN

I NEVER GIVE out my phone number. How can I, considering my occupation? It's just a really bad idea. Because of that I am surprised when I give him my phone number, in some ways too rattled to even fully consider what I am doing. And I couldn't think of any sensible way to deny his request.

A jumble of thoughts are rushing through my brain. One of them, of course, is that it will be easier to end him in the city, away from all of the employees I keep seeing running around the place. The other thought is that I have yet to leave his company, but I'm already looking forward to seeing him again.

But he asks for the number and I can't think of a lie.

"In case something comes up," he says.

"Yes," I say as I give him the number. "Just in case."

I know instantly that it's a dumb game. Yet somehow, I like it. Somehow, I don't want it to stop.

And I've never given anyone my phone number before. Not to anyone not directly related to the business at the core of my new life. Not intentionally. It's too dangerous. And yet.

Here we are.

As I wave goodbye, part of me is shutting down my brain. It just feels so odd to say goodbye to someone in this way. I haven't done it in a really long time. And what way is that? There is something regretful in our goodbye. And anticipatory, as well. And it's a fool's game, I tell myself again. To be regretful to say goodbye to someone you know has to die.

But he isn't dead. Not yet. And that's the part, more than anything, that I don't understand at all.

*   *   *

I drive for a while with no real clear idea of where I'm going. Discombobulated is the almost-word that comes to mind. The only thing I know for sure is that I'm heading back to the city. Why am I going there? Well, only because that's where I told him I needed to be and now—more or less—we have a date. Well, more, when I think of it. Not less. He's taking me out. Driving into the city, he said, with the express purpose of taking me to dinner. That's definitely a date. So I'm heading for the city, but I have no place at all in mind to stay.

After a while I pull into a rest stop and open a hotel booking site app on my phone. In a few minutes, and without thinking about it too much, I book a hotel. It didn't have to be near the main Arizona State University campus, yet I find a hotel that looks just fine that happens to be within walking distance of the school grounds, so I book it. It fits into my story, so that works, if for no other reason than it is one less thing for me to keep straight.

He's never going to see the hotel, so what does it matter where it is?

The voice of reason is late to the party. The hotel is booked, so that is where I'll stay.

It looks like an excellent hotel, too. The photos are tantalizing and there are plenty of amenities I have no intention of using. "Walking distance to campus," it says. Okay. I'm in. In for a penny,

I think. And I head my car in that direction, trying hard not to think about where all of this might lead.

* * *

As I drive toward Phoenix and my newly booked hotel, the sun is setting and the funniest feeling comes over me. It's like *deja vu*, in reverse, as though the whole last twenty-four hours never occurred. A dream, a mirage, something beyond what is real. I know it's foolish, but I just can't shake the feeling.

The cactus-studded desert stretches out all around me. It is painted in vivid pinks and purples and golds. In every direction, at the far edge of my vision, mountains ring the desert plains. I am driving through a huge valley and the colorful light makes all of it seem beyond real.

After a while, all of that beauty seems to seep right inside me, and I think beyond what I see and on to the game that I am playing. Or, really, the game I am thinking of playing. Cameron Walker should already be dead. And he is not. Not only that, we now have a date. I'd laugh, for sure, if I weren't so close to crying.

And why am I so close to crying? That's a question, too, isn't it? Something about him. Something about the total package that is him. I could kill him easily. I *will* kill him easily.

And yet.

CHAPTER EIGHT

I AM RELIEVED when the hotel proves to be as nice as advertised. The room is all taupes and beiges and browns. The view is marginal but acceptable: downtown Tempe and those mountains are out there somewhere. I figure I'll see them in the morning, but right now it is dark. The room is not as sumptuous as the casino hotel from the night before, but there is a wholesomeness about all of it that is unexpected. College town in a place that lives for golf and tennis and baseball. Sports. It is wholesome. And bright. The whole thing could be healing if someone had something they needed to recover from. Life. Living. A spot of light in the darkness. I work hard at putting all of that out of my mind.

When I settle in for the night, I wonder what I will do with my tomorrow. It's not as though there is an actual class waiting for me to give a lecture. I find myself wishing there were and at the same time I am glad that there isn't. It's such a funny feeling, odd juxtapositions everywhere. All of my life, suddenly, seems like juxtapositions that are odd.

I go to bed early, thinking I won't be able to get any shut-eye, then surprise myself by falling asleep instantly, only able to register that surprise in the morning when I wake and encounter my well-rested self. It happens so rarely it is almost as though I have let myself down: the unexpected at an unexpected time. If I can't count on my usual challenges, who am I, anyway?

* * *

Tempe is a college town and so it is easy to amuse myself on this day. The little city is crowded with charming shops and eateries and even a lake that looks like a river. It's an odd place.

One of the things I do is locate an art supply shop. I buy myself a very small and light plein air box—even smaller and lighter than the one I have at home. I buy a few palette cups and a tripod to hold the box. I select a brush holder for the tripod on which the box will sit. I buy a decent little palette of watercolors and a watercolor block. Purists classically paint in oil, of course. Some of them in acrylic. But I don't feel ready for either of those. At present I prefer the forgiving nature of watercolor. As a beginner, watercolors suit me. They allow me the freedom to make mistakes and correct them easily. It's all just water. It forgives. And it all comes off in the wash if you need it to.

After I've made these purchases and I'm back in my hotel room, I set up by the window and start painting what I see, though it could be argued that a hotel room is hardly plein air. Still.

From my window high in the hotel, I can see that the desert stretches out, raw and wild, just beyond the buildings at the edge of the city. At first glance it is all burnt umber and sap green, but when I begin to sketch and then paint, I realize that the desert holds all of the colors of the spectrum. Sometimes you just have to look really hard to see.

As I work, I find myself wondering at myself, even though I know that I'm partly painting so that I don't think. And here I am, thinking anyway. If everything goes as I'm planning, Cameron will end tonight and the horses—the Kigers—that I keep seeing floating in my mind's eye in powerful watercolor, will never flow from under my brush. With no Cameron in the picture, I'll have no reason to go back. So the reason I bought these paints—to bring the Kigers to painted life—will most likely never occur. Meanwhile, though, there is now. And that desert landscape. I only feel slightly foolish—pretentious?—when I sign the piece with a title as I finish: *Valley of the Sun.*

As evening approaches, I leave the painting on the easel to dry, put my paints away, and focus on getting ready for the evening. I find myself applying the limited makeup in my possession and fussing a bit with my hair and my clothes, even while I'm thinking it's a foolish exercise. Why expend any energy at all on my appearance? What does it matter what he thinks? What does it matter at all?

Then I brush my hair until it falls in smooth waves by my face, and I dust a pale rose blush onto the apples of my cheeks. Next, I examine the results of my brief labor. It is hardly an expert application, but it'll do.

In the midst of my preparations, I get a text. "I'm on my way. Will meet you at six p.m. at Cafe Trix."

I text back a thumbs-up and then I google. It turns out Cafe Trix is a well-known restaurant—though not by me. And it's within walking distance of both ASU and my hotel. At some point I had been told that Phoenix was a city of distances. "You need a car. Everything is forty-five minutes away." Who had said that? Maybe the guy at the car rental place. But that has not been my experience. Other than the ranch, every place I want to go is a short walk away.

And so I walk. Before I enter, though, I think about waiting for him a little distance from the restaurant. I could watch for his truck, then take him in the shadows as he exits the vehicle. It would be easy. I've done hits in just that way before. Yet something doesn't feel quite right about it, though I can't put my finger on what the wrong thing might be.

Because of this consideration of stalking, I get to the restaurant before the designated time. Right away, though, my being unfashionably early gets swept away by the beauty of the spot. A mostly outdoor restaurant under huge old trees, the indoor parts of the restaurant are inside a brace of old houses. The garden seems deliberately rustic. It is well-organized chaos, and between the two houses, tables are dotted throughout the whole. I note that, despite the restaurant's proximity to campus, it is peopled more with professor types than students. It's a sweet and lovely spot. Cameron has chosen well.

By the time he arrives, I am at a table for two under one of those large trees. I guess it to be an oak, but it is Arizona, so it seems possible to me that it is likely something more exotic that I don't know about. Still, if it were sunny out, the tree would be large enough to provide shade. But by the time Cameron arrives it is dark, and the tree still provides a sort of warm shelter. A psychological effect, I'm sure. But still. It is a shadowy canopy above the table. I feel protected by it. Oddly safe. The tree above. Candlelight. The scent of flowers, heavy on the air. He has picked a perfect spot.

When he wrangles his tall form into the chair across from me, I am sipping at a glass of perfectly chilled rosé. He looks at me for a few beats. I look back. And then both of us smile. It feels like tacit agreement, though I'm not sure about what.

"You look so good it hurts my eyes." It's the first thing he says. I find that all I can do is smile back at him.

All I can do is smile.

A server brings a menu. Cameron points at my glass. "I'll have what she's having," he says. There is nothing but comfort in his voice.

"Are you sure?" I ask. "It's just rosé."

"I'm sure," he says, and he smiles at me in a way that makes me blush as pink as the wine. It's an odd feeling.

"How did the lectures go today?"

I look at him blankly for a second when he says it. Before I remember. And then.

"Oh. Fine. Yeah. Fine."

And he looks at me as though he might say something, but he holds his tongue. And I'm glad. Whatever it is he wanted to say, I'm pretty sure I'm not ready to hear it. And so I barge on.

"The drive out was good?" Even while I form the words, I wonder why I had to head straight at something so banal.

He looks at me. Smiles. It's a languid look.

"Sure. Yeah. Yours?"

"Uh-huh," I say, knowing I'm being toyed with but not clear how. And then I decide to go all in and be totally honest. Kinda. "Look," I say, "I'll just come out and tell you this and then we won't have to pussyfoot around it anymore."

"Okay," he says. He looks interested and not intimidated, so I figure that's a good start.

"I don't want to talk about it a whole lot right now, but for various reasons, I'm not going to be able to do what I came out here to do."

"The lectures, you mean," he says.

"Right," I say agreeably. "All of that. The thing I came out to do."

Our eyes hold. I find myself hoping that he can't read me; read my thoughts, though I chide myself about it. Of course, he doesn't know what I'm thinking. And that's a positive, because what I'm thinking would not be a good thing for him to know.

"Okay," he says agreeably. I see the question in his eyes, but he holds it. I'm grateful.

"Honestly," I say, "the mood I'm in after today? I'd much rather hear about you and the horses."

I see him brighten at that, as I'd figured he might. The horses are clearly a passion. I'd already seen that on him and, truly, his whole life seems built around them. And now it doesn't take much to point him in that direction. He's being polite, but also, he is never far from wanting to talk about his greatest passion. I find I like that about him, too.

"Okay. I get it. We all have days like that. I'll tell you the story. Of the horses. It'll take your mind off your day, too. So that's where we'll begin." He hesitates. I see him gather some wool. Then he starts in.

"Where to begin. Beginning, I guess. My dad started the non-profit before I was born."

"That *is* the beginning. And I think you said something like that the other day."

"Yeah. He was one of a handful of people who hated the way mustangs were being treated. He vowed to do something about it. I figure my dad had a big hand in actually saving the American mustang."

"Did they need saving?"

"They did."

"Saving from what?"

While he speaks, I watch the smooth way the skin moves over his jaw, and how his hair curls to his collar. It's a bit longer than it should be, his hair. But it's not unruly. It just looks as though it's a few weeks beyond when he should have cut it, but he hasn't wanted to take the time.

"Full-scale slaughter." His answer brings me back from contemplations of his hair and jaw with a jolt. These matters are serious to him. They are what he cares about beyond all else, that's what I think. "Slaughter and inhumane treatment on the way there. At the time my father started the foundation, there were people profiting on rounding the horses up and selling them for dog food."

"That's awful."

"It is," he said. "It was. Legislature was passed to protect the horses. As a direct result of that, their slaughter became illegal in this country."

"So, they're safe now."

"You'd think so, wouldn't you? I mean, it sounds like it when I say it that way, but no. Similar problems now. Evil finds a way. Different sources."

"How so?"

"The slaughter of horses is against the law in the United States. The horses can be captured and transported, but they can't be killed for their meat. So now they're still captured, but they are shipped live to Canada or Mexico or sometimes even overseas to Europe or China."

"That's terrible."

"It gets worse."

"I don't see how."

"The government agency charged with the protection of the American Mustang is conflicted."

"Conflicted."

"Yes. On the one hand there is the protection of the American mustang. On the other are the cattlemen who get practically a free ride grazing their cattle on public land."

"Free ride," I chortle.

He grins.

"Yeah. We call them welfare cowboys."

"That's rich," I say. "So, wait—on the surface I don't see the problem. Horses and cattle can hang out, right?"

"Hang out." He smirks, but there is kindness in the look. Affection, even. And I like how we seem to be getting each other's humor. "How cute are you?"

I wave away his comment, though I'm not displeased. And I'm glad we're not in full light because I'm fairly certain that I blush again. What the hell is wrong with me, anyway? "You know what I mean, though."

"I do. And the answer is yes. Sure, they can. The animals can get along fine, or at least peaceably ignore each other. Sometimes more than that. The humans involved? Not so much. The cattlemen want the range to themselves. Cattle and horses graze differently. Sheep, too. And they're among the grazing customers on the rangeland. Sheep and cattle basically rip the land up as they forage. They eat practically everything in sight. Even bison have a way of eating that is more selective, less invasive."

"Buffalos?"

"Yeah. Buffalo. Sure. But horses are more selective. And with the horses, it has been proven that the way they graze actually helps the land heal: helps restore it to how it was before it was ravaged by livestock."

"That's amazing."

"They're pretty amazing animals," he says. "And they're different, you know? Special. And adapted to this land like no other creatures."

"They mean so much to you," I say. Seeing the passion he has for protecting the wild horses gives birth to something tender in me. Or maybe it is more like rebirth. Something that had lived warmly in me at one point in my life, but that I thought had died. The protective feeling I suddenly feel toward him makes me think of something.

"That conflict you described—horses and livestock—does any of that manifest in danger to you?"

He looks at me speculatively for a minute. He looks at me in a way that makes me think I have given too much away.

"That's an odd question," he says after too long a pause. There is no charge to his voice as he says this. No change, either. And no anger or even anything beyond mild curiosity. But the fact that he said it at all makes me wonder what he wondered.

"Yes," I agree. "I think so, too. It was just something that popped into my head."

"Interesting," he says.

"Really?"

"Yeah. Because a few weeks ago, I would have said no. But some of those ranchers have become kinda . . . let's call it unhinged. Just lately. Well, one in particular. He's even threatened me."

"Threatened? How?" I don't have to pretend to be wide-eyed with surprise.

"I have been working at the state board level to get livestock grazing licenses on public lands revoked. It's a non-working solution for an old problem, the grazing licenses."

"Explain what that is, please. A grazing license. Like, for the horses?"

"No. Sorry. For the livestock. The horses have a small level of protection. And they aren't owned, so no licenses. But the ranchers. They buy a license for each of the cattle or sheep they wish to graze. Or each cow/calf unit."

"Or ewe/lamb," I suggest.

He looks at me sharply for a moment, and then he laughs. "Hey! You're one sharp cookie, but yes. Exactly. Anyway, the governing body of all of this has a formula about how much traffic each chunk of land can take. And so that's how many licenses they sell. Theoretically. But really, some of the land is so overgrazed that native species—like elk and some birds—are threatened because the land is basically being ruined. But the ranchers blame the horses and buy politicians to also say it's the horses. It's gotten to be a real battle. Not only here in Arizona, but all over the west. We are told the land is overgrazed and the mustang herds must be culled. Once that is done and the horses are gone, more grazing licenses for livestock are approved. That can't be right."

"It doesn't sound right, no. But you said you'd been threatened."

"It was somewhat veiled, but the intent was clear. You know what I mean? Stuff like, 'if you keep this up, Cameron, there's gonna be trouble.'"

"So not exactly direct threats then?"

"Right."

"Why could any of this put you in danger?" I thought for a moment, then added, "Like what is it you could say that would make such a difference that they'd want you to shut up?"

"I've had some luck at the state level. I mean for the horses. Both the public and elected officials love them. Except the ones the ranchers have bought, of course."

"They've bought horses?" I am confused.

The way he looks at me I feel like maybe he didn't quite understand the question. And then he does, and his face splits into a grin and, once again, I am warmed by his smile. Who wouldn't be?

"Not the horses, silly. The politicians had been bought."

I laugh with him.

"That makes more sense," I say.

"Right?"

We had ordered a while before and our food arrives now. Something with chicken and cheese for me. Delicious. Something involving smoked beets and greens for him. It looks equally good. And we set aside talk of horses and threats and politicians and enjoy our dinner for a while. We observe the magnificent garden we sit in and the fine night desert scents as well as the remaining piece of sunset we have managed to capture.

"I'm enjoying myself," he says at one point. It feels like an admission.

"Me too," I say.

"Is this a date?" He asks it earnestly. I can't tell if he is teasing me.

"I'm not sure," I say honestly. "I think so. You drove a long way, after all."

"I think so, too. And, unlike you, I had no business in the city today."

"Just me?" Did I say it coquettishly? It's possible that I did. I hadn't thought I had that in me anymore.

"Just you," he says with another one of those smiles. He reaches out as he does so, touching my hand lightly. So light. I'm almost not sure it happened, except for the tingle that trails behind where his touch had been.

"Just me," I repeat.

"I want . . ." I see him struggling for words. It seems uncharacteristic. "I want to tell you something else."

"Shoot," I say.

"I'm a dad."

"A father?"

"Yes."

"Am I supposed to act surprised?" He is the right age. The right combination of things. Even the right type. When I think about it, I have to admit I'd be surprised if he was *not* a father. What I don't know is why he wants to tell me.

"I . . . I guess not. I only wanted, at this stage, to let you know."

"Thank you," I say. "I guess. I mean . . . you don't have to tell me anything."

"You are going to be important to me," he says. And though the words have a prophetic riff, he doesn't say them in a way that makes me think he imagines himself to be a prophet. It feels more like a prediction. And I like the way it feels. Warm somehow. I imagine what it would feel like to be cared about again. It's been so long, I'm pretty sure I don't remember what that feels like. "It becomes important, also, that certain things are known between us."

I look into his eyes then. Curse myself. Cared about, indeed. As though that can happen for me. What am I getting myself in for here? So much more than previously imagined. So much more than I thought was possible/available for me. At the same time, there's a part of me that wants to run screaming at these words. We've known each other, what? Two hours out of two days? And he's letting me know he has growing feelings for me? Who does that? Even if it were true, who tells you stuff like that?

I choke all of that down and don't let any of that show on my face.

"How old is your child?" It's the only thing I say, and my voice is neutral.

"Mason is twelve."

I digest this. It was an age I had looked forward to. With my own son. Anticipated. He died several years shy of that number. I try not to remember that anymore.

"Does he live with you?"

"No. He lives with his mother in Phoenix."

"You see him though?"

"When I can. Yes. The ending of the marriage wasn't terribly acrimonious. Still. Sometimes it almost seems as though she weaponizes him, you know? Keeps him from me to punish me for whatever didn't work in our marriage. And I don't play. I can't. I don't want Mason exposed to that sort of energy if possible."

"Parenthood from that place must be challenging," I observe, searching for something to say. "From a distance."

"Yes," is all he says, though I imagine I hear more.

"How long has it been?"

"Hmmm?"

"The breakup."

He hesitates so long, I imagine he is considering not answering. Then he says, "Long enough," with a smile. "We're divorced, if that's what you're asking."

"I'm not asking, but okay," I reply. "Thank you," I say after a while. "For letting me know."

He nods. Grunts. But I can already feel that we've moved on.

We don't talk more about horses that evening. Or sons. We talk about common things. Tastes/sounds/scents that both of us like. Things we share. And sometimes there is laughter. Great gales of it. So precious, I feel like grabbing some of it; pocketing it. Saving it for a time without laughter. But maybe that has ended. Now. I allow myself to think that.

By that point in the evening there is no question that we will see each other again. It is just a matter of when. We don't discuss it, but somehow, I understand we both know. And when we leave the restaurant, he begins to walk with me, as though to my car. I tell him I walked and he laughs.

"Of course you did," he says, and I know he means it with affection, not a proper tease. "You can walk with me to mine, then."

"Would you . . ." I surprise myself by stammering a bit, ". . . would you like to come back to my hotel for a drink? I'm not far from here."

He looks at me for what feels like a long time then. I feel like he is looking right inside me. It is a beautiful feeling and yet for me—who has been keeping the world at arm's length for so long—it is somewhat frightening, too.

He looks at me without answering for long enough that I have the feeling he isn't going to. Or worse, that he hasn't heard and I'll have to ask again. But just when the silence between us has drawn out too long, he moves closer to me and tilts my head up so I'm looking into his eyes. He is enough taller than me that it strains my neck, though not painfully so. He reaches out so that his hand is cupping the back of my head. Even though he is so close, when he speaks, his voice is quiet. I have to strain to hear.

"I would like nothing better." There is a cushiony tone to his voice. "But I'm not going to."

I find myself oddly—surprisingly—aroused. Something about restraint.

"Why?" And my tone matches his.

And then he moves away from me slightly and I can see his whole face, though the edges are softened by streetlight.

"We're going to have plenty of time." He says it softly, but with confidence. I'm not sure if he means it, or if it's yet another come-on line. Have I grown cynical in my isolation? I don't discount the idea. I also think it's all happening much too quickly. On the other hand, my bed is going to be empty tonight. That fact makes the idea that he is playing me seem like less of a possibility.

Before I have any of these ideas fully marshaled, he leans down, kisses me soundly, then turns toward his truck.

After he drives away, I stand there for a moment, looking after him. It is then that I realize how very derelict in my duty I've been. I'd spent all that time with him—so many hours—and I hadn't thought about killing him. Not even once.

CHAPTER NINE

THE BED IN my hotel room is very large. It looms. And it seems to me it could accommodate a whole family. Certainly, it could have handled the addition of one earnest cowboy very nicely. Me by myself? I float in that big bed. It feels lonely, but also it feels as though I am riding a fluffy white cloud.

I feel myself filled with gratitude and the goodness of giving. It is something about connection, I think. Or belonging. I am not part of a whole. Yet. But for the first time in a long while it feels like a possibility.

It is beautiful to feel as I lie in bed and wonder, how have I not owned more of this feeling? What have I not been doing enough of? How can I mark this, so that it happens again. And again? Or, maybe, what can I do so that this feeling never stops? Is that even a thing? Maybe not. Still, I lie there in the hotel bed and let it roll over me. This feeling. I lie with my hands over my heart in such a way that I feel my breasts thrust up and away from me. I feel, in that moment, hyper aware of where I am in the universe and within myself.

Gratitude. It infuses me. Every part of me. And suddenly I understand the words. Gratitude turns what we have into enough.

In this moment, I am enough, too.

I don't know what tomorrow will bring.

It had been a lovely evening. Beautiful food. Meaningful conversation. I feel complete. Maybe it was the most beautiful evening I have ever spent.

Maybe.

When I put my head down, I fall instantly into the deepest sleep I have had for a long time. Not at all like falling asleep. More like falling off a cliff.

And so I sleep like I haven't slept in what feels like years. I don't know how long I would have gone on like that, but my phone wakes me and when I wake, I have slept so deeply I feel groggy.

I glance at the time. It is three in the morning. I think about not answering. But then I answer it anyway, partly because it *is* three in the morning, and who calls at that time? Then I'm glad I answered, because it is him.

"You survived!" I exclaim, genuinely pleased.

"I did."

"It was a long drive," I say.

"It was," he agrees.

"You don't have much to say for yourself," I say.

"I don't," he says equitably and in the same dry tone. Then both of us collapse into the kind of laughter you feel all the way through.

"That felt good," I say. "Laughing with you."

"It did," he says. Then he laughs again. "Sorry. It's an easy mode for me to get into. Apparently."

"Laconic cowboy?"

"I guess so," he agrees, which somehow sets us off into gales again. "But, yeah," he continues after we've settled down. "Clearly we have to see each other again." And his voice is more serious now. "This kind of laughter is a precious thing. One needs to reach out. Grab it with both hands."

My heart turns over when he says it, and I wonder at what the hell I am doing. I can tell myself I am planning to kill him. And I can tell the handler that, too. But at this point I don't think I'm telling anyone the truth. And at the point when you discover you are lying to yourself, that's pretty much when you have to take a look around.

"That's a lot of words," is all that I say.

"That's true," he agrees. "But seriously: let's make a plan."

"Okay," I say.

"Do you ride?"

"I'm not sure," I say.

"That's not an answer," he points out. "Either you do or you do not. It's not a trick question."

"Well, I've never tried," I tell him.

"Okay," he says.

"But it seems to me I'd be good at it."

"Okay, again. Not really a thing, but . . ."

"But . . . ?"

"Let's just assume you're going to be good at it. We'll ride."

"Okay."

"You seemed keen to learn more about the wild horses. I thought that, if we got an early start, we could try and catch up with the Salt River band."

"Not music, right?"

"Correct. I'm talking about the Salt River mustangs. If we get lucky, you'll be able to see them in their element."

"Wait. What about the Kiger horses that you showed me."

"They're wonderful, but they're not local. And though we manage them as though they are wild horses, they really aren't wild. They're protected. They are sanctuary horses. They came to the Flying W as part of a bequest: money came to us along with the plea that we keep that bloodline pure in a way that it can no longer be found in the wild. The band I introduced you to are the result. But that's not what we're talking about here. The Salt River horses are as motley a group as you can expect to meet. Their backgrounds are indeterminate, but some of them are thought to be descended from horses that have been wild here since prehistory."

"But there are no horses in North American prehistory. They got here with the Spanish colonizers."

"It's a matter of some debate, for sure. But not by me. I believe there certainly were horses in North America in prehistory. For me—and not just for me—the only debate is around if they have always been here."

"I'm confused."

"You should be. I could write a book."

I laugh, because I know he's joking. But still. Something about his words has confused me. And so I ask. Late night pillow talk. Why not?

"Seriously though," I say, "I know I've read that horses were introduced by the Spanish Conquistadors in the 1400s or something. I mean, they teach that in school." I'm feeling like a teenager. Talking to a boy on the phone in the middle of the night. There's something refreshing in the way that feels. Something not wrong.

"You're correct. That was once the common belief. The problem was science. Equine bones kept turning up. More recently DNA has cast doubts on some long-held beliefs. And many indigenous people have said they had horses in their culture the whole time. Long story short, we now know with certainty that horses were at least part of the prehistory of North America. In fact, they evolved right here."

"In Arizona?"

He laughs again, but I can tell it isn't at me.

"No," he says. "In North America. And at this stage, there's no debate around that. There can't be: there's been too much proof. Where there *is* still debate—and it can get ugly—is around whether or not horses were here all along."

"All along? Like the Spanish didn't bring them?" I thought a moment, then: "Or rather, didn't bring them back."

"Oh, they brought them all right. But there's a very good argument that the indigenous Americans already had horses."

"Indigenous Americans," I repeat it. "Do you mean Indians?"

"I do."

"Do you believe that?"

"I do," he said.

"You've gone all cryptic on me again," I say. He laughs at my comment in a self-deprecating way, and I like him for it.

"Look, I'm sorry if I've bored you with all of this. It's a bit of a hobby horse for me."

"Hobby horse. Groan," I exclaim.

"Sorry," he says, but he doesn't sound sorry at all.

"Anyway, I wasn't bored," I say. "And it wasn't too much. You're very passionate about it. That's nice to see. Good."

"So our next date will be riding," he says, glossing over the praise and taking us back to where the conversation had started. "At that time I'll gauge my audience. See if you look interested enough for me to tell you more."

"Okay," I say.

"Okay," he repeats in exactly the same tone.

"When?" I ask.

"Whenever you like. I suspect my schedule is more flexible than yours. Lectures, et cetera."

"I told you, my work here is not going quite as anticipated." He's alive, and I'm not quite sure what to do about that, but I don't say that out loud. "I can make myself free almost any time."

"How about tomorrow then?"

"Tomorrow is soon," I reply.

"It is." Endlessly laconic.

"But still," I say. And, anyway, what the hell else do I have to do?

"Okay. Tomorrow then."

And by the time we hang up the phone, I'm still smiling when I realize that killing him is feeling more and more difficult. I realize something else, too, and the smile drifts off my face. He had said at dinner that someone had threatened him. And he still hasn't told me who.

CHAPTER TEN

AM I ACTUALLY contemplating not killing him? It's a dangerous proposition. One I've faced before. In those cases, though, in the end, I always did the deed. I had to. I weighed all the pros and cons and, not without some gut-wrenching and self-debate, I completed the assignment.

I think about it all on the early morning drive back out to the ranch. It's nearly a two-hour run, so I've got some time to think.

Before I leave the hotel, I transfer the gear I usually carry in my purse into a light backpack. I may not know much about horses, but I know I don't want to ride one carrying a Coach bag. I transfer my phone, sunscreen, Kleenex, hand sanitizer, lip gloss, mints, and the Bersa Thunder into the backpack. I don't bother packing additional ammo because I'm not planning on using it, plus I know I've left the spare box of cartridges in the glovebox of the rental car. The gun is loaded and the safety is on. I tend not to carry an unloaded gun because there just is no point. I'm hoping there is no point to carrying a gun today at all. On the other hand, I think again about Cameron saying he had been threatened, and I *am* on a job, so I decide I'd feel naked without it. And what the hell? There are just more questions here than resolve.

I leave the hotel just before dawn so that I can get out to the ranch in time to make an early start on our ride. As the miles disappear under the rental car's headlights, the day comes up over the horizon, painting the desert in the glorious pinks and reds and golds of the rising morning. It's glorious. Much more so than the dark turn my thoughts have taken.

When it comes to my assignments, it's not like I ever get a say. The assignment comes to me most often from an anonymous source. When the job is complete, an agreed-upon sum is deposited to my Bitcoin account. It's not like there's even someone I can go to. And it's not like I indulge myself in thinking I'm the only hired gun on the roster. I mean, I don't have any proof that I'm one of many—it's not like we have monthly meetings or an annual morale-boosting getaway featuring team-building exercises or anything like that. But you get a sense of a thing, and my sense has always been that I'm but one horse in a larger stable.

So, okay. Let's say I turn down an assignment. What happens then? Well, first, of course, I don't know for sure. I've never done it before. Never seriously thought about it, beyond the academic. But one can imagine what might happen, and the imagining isn't pretty.

Here's what I imagine: I turn down an assignment, and the handler turns that assignment over to someone else. And just to make sure it doesn't happen again, a hit gets put out on me. That seems like the worst possible scenario. Nobody wins. And me and Cameron? We're both dead.

But is this case not different? And if so, how? And how can a case be made to illustrate for the handler how an exception should be made here?

And then I gather myself again. Check my head and my position. Why do I suddenly want this? And I *do* want this: I want

Cameron to survive. I tell myself that's foolish. Even childish. After all, I barely know the man. We're not anywhere close to a place where I should be feeling any of this as strongly as I am. And yet. I'm not in love with him. Obviously. But what I guess I'm hoping for is the time to see if he is, in fact, someone I can love. I think he is. But I need time.

What if I tell the handler I can't do the job? What if I withdraw? Maybe I even tell her why. In that scenario I might even manage to get out of this alive. Cameron doesn't, though. That scenario has no good outcome for him. And, again, I realize: I've faced all of these decisions before. The situation was different, sure. But the outcome was the same. But it's that seemingly inevitable outcome, that's the thing. It wrenches at my heart.

One can't just not have a life taken when one is ordered. It doesn't work that way. I've never done this before: not in the end acted when an order was given. Sometimes I've been slow, but I've never just disregarded what was requested. You can't really. There's no provision for that.

But still. There must be a way. And so I continue to ponder.

Instinct is an astonishing thing in this life. Animals have it all honed down, but it is not only animals that have it. We all do. Sometimes we humans have to listen hard for that instinct; we have to work at what animals seem to have without effort, but it's there if we put in the work. And that's what I do now. I drive. And I listen to what my instincts relay.

Cameron does good in the world. I feel certain of it. None of his choices are about anything other than helping the world be a better place. I feel sure, also, that some of that helping has made things less comfortable for other people. And sometimes in life if we make things uncomfortable for people, we get dead. There might not be many people alive who have seen that as graphically illustrated as I often have, so maybe that can help me to untangle this. That's what my instincts say now. The key to saving Cameron's life so I can figure out if he is someone I can love is for me to figure out who wants him dead. And possibly—just maybe—take that person out.

CHAPTER ELEVEN

WHEN I PULL off the highway and onto the ranch road, he is waiting for me. I see his truck before I get anywhere near the house. The very fact gives me a fast rush of pleasure. Endorphins? Or something else?

"Here you are," I say when I pull up next to him cop style: driver's window to driver's window. I have no idea if he was heading somewhere when I appeared or if he is there just for me. I think probably the latter. He knew I was on my way.

"Here we both are," he says in return. And we don't touch—we're not there yet—but there are layers of oh-so-much between us.

"Indeed," I say.

"Follow me," he says through his window before he heads the truck off in the direction of the house and I wonder what it is—exactly—that I've let myself in for.

As we arrive at the large, low-slung building, I see several people peep out of doors and windows. They do it surreptitiously, and I have to smile: it's pretty clear they're trying to get a glimpse of me. What has he told them? I wonder. What has he told his staff—and perhaps family? What has made them all seem to be looking out for me? It's disconcerting, but also amusing. And it's not a bad feeling. But I do wonder.

"You hungry?" He asks it as we enter the house. And he asks it in a way that tells me this is a normal question on a ranch where hard work produces large appetites. This is a place where being hungry might always only be a short distance away.

"No, I'm good," I tell him. I'd gotten an early start and it's around nine in the morning: past breakfast and nowhere near lunch.

"Coffee time," he says with a lopsided grin. "Belle told me she made sticky buns this morning. That'll keep us going until we get somewhere else."

I feel my eyes widen, but I don't say anything. They widen further when he comes to the table with two sticky buns. Each one is half the size of a normal dinner plate.

"I can't possibly eat one of those," I tell him. "They're humongous."

That grin again.

"Go ahead. Do some damage," he says while he plops one onto a plate in front of me, then another on a plate for himself. "I'll clean up what you can't get to."

Then he delivers a large mug of coffee for each of us, along with huge servers of cream and sugar. I taste before I add, and my eyes widen again. At first taste, the coffee is thick and syrupy in a way that I initially figure is revolting. On second taste though—and once cream and sugar have been plopped—I find I actually like it.

"It grows on you?" And I'm not sure why I make it a question.

He laughs, like whatever I said is super funny, and I figure there's probably a joke I've missed. The laughter isn't unkind, though, and I decide to recline into the sound of it. It is warm, that laughter. Gentle even. I can't explain it, but it makes me feel good. Like the world is full of love and maybe even possibilities. It's been a long time since I felt that way. Laughter is medicine? There is that, as well. Maybe he is my medicine. A startling thought. Not unwelcome. What if that could be a thing? The world might be different then.

"It'll put hair on your chest," he says matter-of-factly, breaking my train of thought. Then he lifts his eyebrows a couple of times in a way that leaves me confused, though not offended.

"I hope not," I say.

"Me too," he says with a leer that for some ridiculous reason makes me blush. I turn my head away, but his grin tells me he didn't miss the color rise.

I divert myself by focusing on the food and coffee. It does not surprise me that the sticky buns prove to be extraordinary. They are like next-planet, next-level sticky buns, and I say so.

"Yeah, Belle is amazing with bread things," and then he adds, "though everything she makes is that good," as though he doesn't want me to doubt his loyalty. He arcs a finger at what is left of the cinnamony confection on my plate. "She says it's because she adds love."

"That'll do it," I say, trying not to reflect on this ingredient that has been missing from my life for so long now.

"She's pretty amazing, actually. You know, she even keeps a few goats around, so she can milk them and make this really special cheese."

I'm only half-listening, but the half that is is amazed.

"She makes goat cheese? From milk she's . . . procured herself? That sounds crazy. Shouldn't you marry that woman?" I realize as I say it I'm only half kidding. I mean, goat cheese. Come on. How can I even compete with a woman like that?

He laughs, as he was meant to, and says the words he probably knows I needed to hear.

"Yeah, she's amazing, all right. But marry? No. That isn't the nature of our relationship. If anything, it's more like she's kin.

Cousin/sister type of thing? We've known each other since we were kids."

To my surprise, I consume all of the sticky bun, despite having had an appropriate breakfast before I left the hotel.

"I'm disappointed," he says with a smile as he clears away my plate. "I was hoping I'd end up with a few more bites."

And I smile back at him in a way that is non-productive but that both of us understand as communication, nonetheless.

Before we head out, he asks if I have brought boots with heels. I tell him I haven't, so he searches around until he finds a pair of what he calls barn boots in my size, presumably from someone on his staff. The toes are blunt and the heel looks low and efficient.

"It's the only bit of gear you really for sure need for riding," he tells me when he hands them over. "The leathers protect your calves from chafing. More importantly, the heel stops your foot from sliding through the stirrup. I bet even Godiva was wearing boots."

"Pretty sure she wasn't," I say, in the same light tone as I take the boots he offers.

"We'll agree to disagree," he says, and the smile touches every part of his eyes.

"She was bareback. Heels not a detriment."

"Whatever," he says.

"'Whatever.' Now you're a teenage girl?"

"Shall we ride?"

When we head for the stables, the horses are waiting for us, groomed and tacked up and ready to go.

"I called ahead," he says, and now it almost looks as though he is blushing. He had taken some care to make sure things were ready for this riding date. He had planned ahead to make things perfect and easy. There's a warmth to that, for me. To have been thought of. And then actually interacting with the horses we'll be spending the day with drives all other thoughts out of my mind.

Cameron's mount is a fifteen-hand mustang gelding called Monty. Cameron tells me that's especially tall for a mustang, but not necessarily an aberration. I'm told that Monty has been in captivity almost since foaling, and so maybe good food and care his whole life has contributed to his height, as well as his genetics. Monty's coat is a bright gold and, as soon as Cameron swings into the saddle, it is apparent that together this particular horse and rider are two parts of a singular whole. You don't need to be told they've logged many miles together.

My assigned mount is an ancient gray gelding called Captain. I am not expert enough to guess his age, but I suspect that, even if I were, I wouldn't get it right. His gray is flea-bitten—meaning black flecks mar a perfect white. His back is slightly swayed, his mouth is tough, but he follows Monty as though he were the other's child. He won't let Monty out of his sight, and he does it stoically and without fuss. He was the right choice of a mount for me because all that's really expected is for me to hang on. And I do.

We've only been in the saddle for a few minutes when it becomes apparent—truly—that we are in the desert. With the ranch buildings behind us, we are faced with a definite but beautiful beige. It is the season of dryness and at first everything looks the same. Closer study shows some differences, but you don't see them at first glance. It occurs to me you have to earn the right to see beauty in the desert. If you are dismissive, it's possible to miss it altogether, this secret desert. It is possible you might look and see only brown. But there is more here, too. The sly flowers—yellow, purple, blue—the cautious rabbits and lizards. The occasional family of quail, their little plumes quivering decoratively above their heads. In the distance, but growing closer as we ride, slightly undulating hills that seem to morph, quite suddenly, into formidable mountains as we get closer.

Everything seems possible out here. I'd seen a cactus-studded landscape on both trips out to Cameron's place in my rental car, but to be on the back of a horse and traversing it directly is an entirely different feeling. You're part of it. And it seems endless.

"Doing okay?"

We haven't gone too far and so I understand he is just checking in, not yet knowing quite how green I am. Not knowing, also, if I'm hardy or delicate or much of anything about me, really. But I find I like the feeling of being checked up on. It has been a long time since anyone has cared about me enough to do that. Too long? Possibly. But here we are, and from the looks of things, we are perhaps both of us ready for caring.

"Yeah," I say lightly, trying not to show how much effort it is costing me to keep my mount afloat. I know Cameron would have laughed at the thought, though not unkindly. That was the thing I'd understood about him almost right away: he is kind. But I doubt he will understand the feeling of near loss of control, because I have never been around horses before. Not really. And so it feels as though my participation is required to get where we are going. It isn't, of course. In fact, I am pretty certain that if I fell off his back, Captain would keep on plodding along behind Cameron and Monty. That being the case, my only job is to keep hanging on. This thought reassures me. It makes me realize that there is a possibility of pockets in my life where my own surveillance might not be necessary. I try to imagine that: a life that does not involve constant vigilance. It's difficult, but thinking it is like a breath in my brain.

Or maybe there was something more to that thought, though the breath is refreshing. I have built every part of my current life.

Created it from scratch. And it's the sort of life that one must claw at the edges to keep it all holding together. It gets tiring. After a while.

A long time ago it had stopped even occurring to me that there might be another less vigilant way. But here on this desert trail with Captain lurching along beneath me and the reassuring breadth of Cameron's broad back up ahead, it strikes me that there might be some version of my life where things could be different. It's like I get a glimmer of possibility maybe. Thinking about what would it be like to not live always looking over your shoulder. To have real safety. It was something to think about. A life where you could be safe. I had given up thinking that was possible for me. And now I think again.

The first part of our journey is relatively flat. That's good because I need to figure out how all the controls work and get to feeling comfortable in the saddle. After a while, though, we start to climb. Here again it seems as though Captain knows the way and knows where to step. I realize these are this horse's home trails, and he probably does know exactly where to go. After the first few terrifying minutes, I relax into the rhythm of it all, giving the beast his head and allowing him full responsibility for our course. He picks his way carefully up the increasingly mountainous trail. He doesn't fall, and I don't fall off and, after a while, I relax slightly and allow the flow to carry me along.

When we arrive at the summit, Cameron pulls Monty around so that they are facing us.

"Are we there yet?" I ask, feeling like a child when I say it.

"No, we have about this long again to ride. Maybe a little less, because soon it will be downhill. But the views," he says, and he puts the reins in his teeth and spreads out his arms. I smile—how can I not? He is like some beautiful, dashing cowboy/pirate. I pull my eyes away from him and follow where his splayed arms point and I catch my breath.

And he is right: the view from here is spectacular. We are at the summit of a small mountain or a large hill—here again, perspective in life is everything—and the cactus and rocks are all around us and in all directions. But on the other side of the mountain, in the direction our trail is headed, is a scrubby desert forest. A river runs through it, and at its banks the vegetation grows green and lush. All of that would have been breathtaking on its own, but what pushes thought of everything else away are the horses. Tiny and barely distinguishable from this distance, but there is no mistaking what I see. Their coats are variously hued and their sizes differ. Mostly mares, I guess. Many with babies at their sides.

"How wonderful," I breathe softly.

"Yes," he says, smiling at me like I am an "A" student. It takes me a moment to realize he's been waiting for my reaction. Would I see what he saw? And I had. I understand that from the look he beams at me.

And then we are traveling again, down the mountain this time, a sensation I find infinitely more distressing than climbing had been. I keep having the feeling I might pitch forward. It is as though, if I'm not careful, I'll topple out of the saddle and arrive at our destination ahead of my mount. The feeling is compounded by Captain's occasional stumble. He recovers quickly and easily, but every time it happens, I have the feeling my life is about to end.

"You okay back there?" Cameron calls over his shoulder.

He is checking in, knowing the terrain well enough that the question is a courtesy only. He'd made a plan and remains confident that everything will be fine.

And he is right, of course. But he is wrong, too. Had he really not known how green I was? I look at his tall, confident back. He is straight and easy in the saddle. The sight of it calms me some-what. Had he known how little experience in the saddle I'd really had? Of course he did. He lived a life where potentially dangerous decisions have to be made every day. Different ones than the decisions I make every day—the life and death decisions. I know some of Cameron's are life and death too, even if the nature of them is very different than the choices I must make.

After a while, though, I am comfortable enough in the saddle that I can think beyond mere survival. I can let my mind wander to things beyond keeping myself from falling from Captain's back and thus encountering a fate worse than death.

As we ride, I feel myself relax enough to fall into a reverie. The rhythm of Captain's stride lulls me into a place of repose so peace-ful I can almost not remember being there before and then, much to my surprise, suddenly we are no longer descending.

"It's a valley," Cameron says needlessly over his shoulder. The fact that we have come down and there are mountains all around us is apparent. We are in a small, protected valley. Various types of cactus can still be seen here and there, but there is a core of green that overshadows everything. To me it seems like an oasis. Or maybe more like what I had always imagined an oasis would be.

"It's magical," I say.

He grins at me, clearly pleased. "It is, isn't it? I'd never thought of it that way. Magical. It's always been in my life. But yes."

"When we get down to the valley, will the horses still be where we saw them?" We've pulled off the trail to chat again, the horses both calm and impatient beneath us.

"It's hard to say for sure. Probably at this time of day. It's un-likely they'll have gone far."

When we reach the river, Cameron points out what he calls "horse signs": small dark piles he told me the horses leave behind. "They're not far ahead of us. You still okay to ride?"

"Do I have a choice?" I ask it with a smile, but certainly, parts of me are beginning to feel my time in the saddle. Beyond beginning.

He grins back at me. That grin. "No choice, not really," he says. "And prepare to be sore as hell tomorrow. For now, though, we'll follow the river for a bit. See what there is to see."

Which is what we do; the temperature is pleasant, the day ideal. There aren't many places I can think where I'd rather be. No places.

After a while the trail takes a sharp turn, following the river, and then there they are, right in front of us. They are scattered on both sides of the trail, some of them belly deep in the lush grass that grows in the shallows at the river's edge.

"Eelgrass," he says, noticing what I am taking in. "It's a big part of their diet."

"This is the Salt River?"

"It is," he said.

"Is it salty?"

He is riding in front of me again. His back is to me but I can hear the grin in his voice when he answers.

"No," he says. "Yes. Maybe a little." I imagine him thinking it through.

"You don't know the answer, do you?"

"It's complicated. But it's not salty like the ocean. It's a different kind of salty."

I watch his back steadily for a moment.

"You don't know, do you?" I've said it again. Pushing. But I know he'll hear the smile in my voice.

"No," he says calmly. "I don't."

"You should find out," I say pertly. "It's the kind of thing you should know. A man in your position."

"Maybe you're right," Cameron says, both of us smiling now. He had stopped and now dismounts; an easy slide off his horse's left side. He comes to Captain's left side, and I can see he is ready to help me get down if necessary.

"You're going to be stiff," he warns as I dismount. He sounds concerned, not patronizing. "You're not used to being so long in the saddle. Swing down. I'm here to steady you."

I do as he suggests and discover he is right: I *am* stiff. But all those hours walking in the forest have paid off, too. I have stayed fit. But I am unaccustomed to riding, so I find that I am wobbling a bit, but I am nowhere near to falling down.

His hand is on my elbow lightly, ready to steady me. I can smell the bright muskiness of him, hear the soft breathing and stamping of our mounts and the whisper of the salty river not far away.

I look up at him, so aware of his hand, still on my elbow as his head bends toward mine. I know what is going to happen next and I don't pull away. Instead, I can feel myself moving toward him.

And then—suddenly—we are not moving toward each other. A strange, electronic whirring fills the air. It rises like an angry insect: faint at first, but louder very quickly. I can't place it. It breaks our moment—diverts wherever we may have been going— and the horses, previously peacefully cropping their eelgrass at the river's edge, are stampeding toward us, around us, and then away from us and away from the now very loud sound.

"What's happening?" I just have no idea.

Cameron points to the sky.

"Helicopters," he says. "They're chasing the horses."

"Who?"

Cameron shakes his head. He clearly doesn't know.

"Why?" I ask.

"To capture them," he says, his face still, as though he's holding something back. "That's all it can be."

His voice is calm, but I can see and maybe feel the veil that has dropped over him. I can only guess at the strength that is holding him back. Whatever is going on with the horses and the helicopters, he doesn't like it. A lot.

"I thought they were protected," I say.

"You'd think so, wouldn't you? But no. And yes. They are not protected from this. Exactly. The agency charged with protecting them is conflicted." He's talking, but he's already in motion. Moving us back toward where our mounts are cropping at the sparse grass. They too have noticed the helicopters, and their ears twitch warily in the direction of the sound. "They have a mandate to ensure the welfare of the horses, but other interests would like to see the horses gone. Listen, I'll tell you more about all of that later. Right now, we've gotta ride. Can you?"

"I . . . I think so," I say.

"Okay, I'm sorry, but I've gotta head there, all right?" He's speaking rapidly, urgently. I can see he needs to go, to see what's happening and see what he can do, but he wants to be sure I'm settled in, too. That I'm okay. I'm touched by this simple thoughtfulness, even with the urgency now swirling all around us. "I've gotta get to wherever they are chasing those horses. And I've got to get there now. Stick with Captain. He's as dependable as anything. Just take it slow and steady. I'll see what's going on and come back after a while."

"I know. Just go. Captain and I will be fine."

With me sorted, Cameron practically leaps onto Monty's back and the pair head off after the panicked herd at full speed.

For a while I don't do anything but hang onto Captain, who is clearly displeased at having been left behind by Monty. I hold fast to the reins, but he tosses his head this way and that, impatiently stomping out with one front foot when I don't comply with his demands. I've been told he is a good and well-trained horse, but the way he is acting is frightening me as I guess the circumstance is frightening him. I realize if I were a more seasoned rider, I'd probably know just what to do, but he suddenly seems so very large to me. It feels as though there is more of him than I can handle.

"Stop it!" I say it firmly and with confidence and am gratified when he seems to settle a bit. "Good boy," I tell him, even though he's not a dog. I give him a skritch on his giant jowl, going on pure instinct now, but it seems to work. He calms slightly and I get a glimmer of how things can be with a horse. I glean it from the childish trust I see in those big brown eyes.

The sound of the helicopter has receded now. I can't tell how far away it is, but based on the sound I guess it is at least a distance of a few miles. I'm briefly wracked with indecision. Do I stay here and just hang on to Captain and wait for Cameron and Monty to come back for us? Or do I try to mount back up on my own and head on after them? The old gelding's restlessness keeps me from thinking the latter is a good idea. I'm such a newbie to this riding thing. Will I even be able to control him? I doubt it. On the other hand, what if Cameron is in danger? I think about the Bersa in my backpack. I might actually be of some use to Cameron right now.

My decision making probably doesn't take very long, though it seems as though it does. By the time I decide to try and mount up, long minutes have passed, and the sound of the helicopter has disappeared entirely, and there is still no sign of Cameron and Monty and no indication of what had happened.

"Bloody hell, Captain," I ask the horse, "what should we do?"

I can't decipher the look he shoots at me, but it sheds no light on his opinion and it's possible he feels my increased nervousness because he seems to get a little more antsy again. I curse myself for letting him in on my thoughts because he's obviously having trouble enough keeping his own feelings under control. Instinctively I try to present a face and voice of calm to him, as one would with a child. In a short time I am surprised when it seems to work. He needs reassurance, that's what it seems to me. When I drag up the gumption to provide it, he becomes visibly more calm.

I feel like I've wasted too much time vacillating. Who knows what's happening? The inactivity is grating on me. It's not my style or my usual way of going. I decide we have to ride out after Cameron and Monty. But though I approach the decision with resolve, there are obstacles to the execution of the resolution almost instantly. It turns out that the distance between deciding to mount up and actually doing it is greater than I had at first thought it would be. When Cameron was present, it had all been pretty easy. Cameron had given me a leg-up, which looked like him putting his hands out for my foot and me stepping into his interlaced fingers and pushing upwards. With very little apparent effort, he just kind of elevated me into the saddle and not much of my own strength or coordination was required.

Without Cameron, mounting a horse proves to be a different story. To get back into the saddle in the normal way, I have to put my foot in the stirrup and swing up. As saddle-sore as I am right now, that seems too much for me to even think about doing. Or maybe it wouldn't seem too much if I had more horse seasoning on me—more hours in the saddle. But I am just so very green, I'm not sure I can manage clambering up there *and* keeping the anxious horse who is missing his buddy under my direct control. I don't want to be half in the saddle and have Captain take off, and with all things just as they are, that seems like a distinct possibility.

I give it some thought, trying to think of another solution. I start leading him along the trail. It's slower going, of course, but at least we are in motion and headed in the right direction. After a while, we come across a fallen tree. I clamber up and onto the horizontal tree trunk, then launch myself—inelegantly but effectively—onto the old gelding's back and into the saddle.

Captain accepts the intrusion with a low "whoof" of sound, then heads off directly in the direction Cameron and Monty had disappeared and at a faster pace than I would have hoped. He's taking things into his own hands, as it were. I revert to my original strategy of basically hanging on for dear life while Captain works out the actual details of getting us there. It seems to me there are worse possible plans.

It is a western saddle that is on Captain's back, and I know from very basic reading that the purpose of that horn on the saddle is *not* to give me a handle. Yet as we go along the trail, Captain picks up speed and there's not much that I know how to do to slow him down. I hang onto that horn for dear life, not even thinking through the fact that—since it's attached to the horse—it's not providing much security at all.

Then Captain takes things up another notch. It is far beyond anything he was doing when he was following Monty. I don't know what to call the gait—maybe it's a canter, maybe it's a lope— but at one point it seems to me he is moving through the tight canyon as though he is a carousel horse. I feel I am hanging on as best I can, but the ride is bumpy and I lose my stirrups and suddenly I feel myself sliding off, though maybe I had something to do with that, as well: a voluntary releasing of whatever ridiculous control I feel I have.

Whatever the case, it seems as though in one moment, I am jolting along a rocky canyon trail with Captain increasing speed at every turn, and the next I am alone in a sandstone wash, the sound of his hooves decreasing with every passing moment. I know I have managed to land on the rocky trail unscathed and, even though I am alone, I feel relieved because I am upright, and nothing is broken. It all could have been so much worse.

It is quiet there, in the wash. Alone. Incredibly quiet. I assess my situation for what seems like a long time when I land there, though I realize it is probably not actually that long. Like disaster, near disaster has a way of making life speed up.

I am winded, though. That is what I come to realize that I did not at first notice. The falling from Captain's back has knocked the wind out of me: an expression I have heard often over the years but never truly understood. Until now. It's frightening, when I try to breathe but my breath does not come. But only for a minute. Maybe less. And then I begin to breathe normally again.

Looking around, I try to determine my location. I take note of my surroundings. Where am I? I really have no idea. I take out my phone and am relieved when I discover I have a cell signal: existent even if weak. It means I can make a call if I want to, and I ponder that. Do I want to? And I realize: I will, but maybe not yet. It strikes me that I will still be more effective on my own than whatever non-official backup I might reasonably call, because it's not like I can call the cops.

So my options. At this point they are not deep. Fortunately, the boots Cameron provided me with all those hours ago are a good fit and slightly ample: they don't pinch. Since I'm now walking, that seems like a lucky break. With everything else that is going on, at least my feet don't hurt. I point myself in the direction in which Captain disappeared and hope for the best. It's not my best bet, but it's the only one I see.

CHAPTER TWELVE

I LIKE TO walk. I like to walk so much that I've done calculations around it. Forgive me, though: I'm a purist, so those calculations are in metric. They just make so much more sense that way. The tens, you know? Deca. So here we go.

This: I know from long experience that if the road is clear and I don't get stuck at a traffic light, it takes me eleven minutes to walk a single kilometer.

It will take me on average four minutes to ride my bike that same distance. And the same distance again will take just a minute or two in a car.

These are the things I think about as I follow the trail Captain took when he headed out, when he took off after Cameron and Monty. I think about the fact that some distance has to be covered, and I'm doing it in unfamiliar boots. But the distance is not necessarily insurmountable. Plus, I have a large bottle of water. Not to mention lip gloss, a phone, and a very cooperative .38. It would maybe be better if I also had a sandwich in there with the gun and the gloss, but at least I ate way too much cinnamon bun back at the house, so I'm not in terrible shape that way. I tell myself that it isn't possible that things will not come out right, though I'm not quite certain of the source of my confidence. After all, impossible optimism has never been my strong suit. But I have all of these thoughts, and I trudge along.

After a while the wash clears, and I'm at the point where the river meets the valley. I'm sure that this was where we saw the horses nibbling on their eelgrass when we looked down from above. Then the helicopters came and chased them away. Presumably. But as I trudge, I tell myself that at least progress is being made. I'm getting closer to something that was at one point far away. What that point might be I'm not quite sure of. Yet. But I have the feeling it will all come together. Soon.

And so on I trudge.

*   *   *

The light is only beginning to fade from the day when I come upon Captain and Monty. They are cropping the thin grass at the outside edges of a roughly constructed corral, and they regard me with disinterest as I approach. Both horses are still fully tacked up: saddles and bridles in position; reins dragging on the ground. I go to one and then the other, pick up the reins. Neither resists capture, simply allowing me to lead them away. I am so relieved to have them back, I feel I could cry. But there is no sign of Cameron, which makes me feel like crying on a different level.

The horses follow me obediently, like giant, slightly embarrassed kittens. Captain had left me in the dust, after all. And who knows what happened with Cameron and Monty. But where I have found them there is nothing left to see. I can't tell what occurred here, other than knowing without question that this was the spot where something did, in fact, happen. There are tracks of many vehicles and horses, and I can see from the prints in the dust that some horses had shoes and some did not. And lots of pointy footprints that would seem to indicate cowboy boots. It all tells a story, I know, but I'm not quite sure what it is. Were the mustangs herded here by the helicopters? Were they then turned lose? Or taken away? The one thing I know: I can see no sign of Cameron. And I have the feeling that, if everything were okay, that would not be the case.

CHAPTER THIRTEEN

BEYOND HOLDING FAST to two sets of reins, it takes me a while to think what to do.

I am alone with Monty and Captain. And though I try to pinpoint my own location with my phone's GPS, in real terms, I'm not even sure where I am: the mountains and valleys and canyons are all meaningless to me, even if in some cases I have their names.

And there is still no sign of Cameron. Leading the two horses, I look everywhere around the site, but there is nothing to see. And though I fell off my horse and walked here myself, there seemed to me to be no chance that the same thing could have happened to Cameron. He's an expert horseman. From what he said, he was practically born in the saddle. He wouldn't just fall off. Something or someone took him off Monty, but I don't have enough information to even build a mental image.

I think back to what he had said to me in those first few panicked moments when we heard the helicopters. When I'd asked their purpose, he had said it was to capture the horses. Clearly one doesn't use a helicopter to capture horses. Perhaps they were used to drive the horses, I think. And the corral was where they were confined. If that were the case, would they be gone already? I really have no way of answering.

I wander back to the corral, examine things more closely. The corral seems roughly made, even temporary. And there are signs of horses everywhere, but the wild horses themselves are nowhere around.

I quell the rising panic I feel. I remember who I am, what I'm capable of. Remember, also, to breathe. I've been feeling a bit like a dizzy teenager in love, and that won't help me here. I need action. Strong, clear-headed action. I'm just not quite sure yet what that might be. An almost bigger problem: it will soon be dark, and I'm out here in the middle of nowhere with two horses who I have the feeling are only barely tolerating my authority over them. I feel like that could end at any minute if that's what they wanted.

There is no question of me riding back to the ranch. For one thing, I'm fairly certain that, for the moment, I've lost my nerve to ride anywhere, never mind that far and alone. More to the point, going back up and then down the mountain under perfect conditions had been difficult. Challenging. Doing it in the dark is, for me, unthinkable.

I'm fairly certain something illegal has occurred, even if I don't know what. But I don't even consider calling the police. For me, there are so many reasons not to.

In the end, with the darkness falling and a decision needing to be made, I decide to reach out to the only connection that makes sense to me.

At the ranch, it is Belle that picks up the phone. I'm glad it is her. Her obvious competence—milking goats, making cheese, managing all that she seems to manage—makes me think she'll either know what to do or who to ask.

I tell her quickly what has happened. She doesn't miss a beat.

"From what you've told me, I'm pretty sure I know where you are. But just to be certain, please use your phone to send me your location." I do it as soon as she asks. "Then sit tight until I get there, please. I'm on my way. I'll be there in under an hour, no matter what happens and no matter what anyone says. Stay. There."

She rings off abruptly in a way that gives me hope because it gives me the feeling that she's jumping into action immediately. I'm glad because my situation is dire. I'm out in the darkening desert, with only two bratty horses for company. And Cameron is still missing.

The bratty on the part of the horses seems heartfelt. They clearly don't understand why they are restrained. Why they cannot go about their business without me hanging onto their bridles. Still, I don't give in. They push and I don't give in. In the face of my firmness, their impatience seems to calm.

On a very real level, though, mine does not.

What can have happened? With the small amount of light left in the day, I lead the two horses around the clearing, looking for clues. Beyond tire tracks and hoofprints from horses with and without shoes, I don't find anything. Before long, the darkness is complete and I hold onto those reins tightly, keeping the horses near where I think help will arrive. The flashlight in my phone is the only real light source. In the utter darkness, it illuminates only a small circle near me, which includes the nostrils of the horses. There is moonlight and starlight, but in the full dark neither of these things seems to do much to add to the light.

The horses hear the truck before I do. I wonder if they recognize the sound of the engine because Monty raises his head alertly and wickers gently. Almost right away, I hear it, too. Then, perhaps a bend in the road and headlights pierce what had been complete darkness.

I see at a glance that Monty's guess was right: it is Cameron's truck that appears now, this time pulling a livestock trailer. The truck is driven by Belle, who is proving to be a woman of considerable and disparate talents. I am astonished she has reached us so quickly. Cameron and I had been in the saddle for hours. It was so long it had felt as though we were really far from the ranch, and I am surprised to realize that, as the crow flies and with a motorized vehicle, maybe we're really not that far at all.

"You find anything more?" Belle says as she gets out of the truck. She moves instantly to the back of the trailer, then lowers the tailgate to the ground where it forms a loading ramp.

She moves toward me with calm confidence, takes Monty from me. She slips off his bridle and puts a halter over his head, then loosens the saddle's girth just a bit before leading him into the trailer. It's obviously not his first car ride, because he climbs aboard without trouble. Then she repeats the process with Captain, who likewise piles right in. Maybe they're both just relieved that they won't have to spend the rest of their days with me leading them around pointlessly.

Just as she is finishing loading the horses, a Jeep pulls up. I go to pure instinct: feeling myself sling my backpack off in preparation for drawing my gun. But Belle greets the two men who clamber out in a friendly fashion, though the worry on all of their faces is clear.

"Anything?"

"Just the horses." She cocks one thumb at me. "And her."

"Who's she?"

"Friend of Cam's," Belle says.

The taller of the two looks me up and down.

"What did you see?"

I relate everything, from the moment we heard the helicopters, to Cameron's reaction, and then him heading out after them. I hesitate when I get to the part where I fell from the ancient gelding's back, but I tell them that, too. It seems important that they have all of the details.

"Seems funny," the shorter one says looking at me. I can't read his tone. His red hair pops out from under a cowboy hat. All of us are haloed in the lights from both vehicles. "You show up here and this happens."

"Arte, stop it," Belle quashes the line of questioning instantly. "It is certainly *not* her fault. I think you know it, too. She didn't even know where Cameron was taking her."

"How do you know that?" Arte insists, his eyes flashing from me to Belle.

"Cam told me she had no idea what they were up to today, other than riding." And then to me, "Where are you?"

I look at her questioningly. "Arizona?" Then I think better of my answer. "Cathedral National Forest!" I say it with a sort of triumph, feeling like I got it right, yet knowing I'm missing something vital.

Arte sighs. "Okay. Right. I see what you're saying."

"But wait," I say, looking at Belle. "You just said Cameron told you I had no idea what I was doing out here. I still don't. Did he tell you something different?"

Belle looks at me evenly. I expect her to tell me this isn't the time. Not the place. Instead she answers me with candor, the reflection of the light creating a halo around her curls.

"He was aware there might be an attempt to poach some of the wildies off the range. He wanted to ride with you." It's like she's reassuring me. I can't decide if it's patronizing. Or not. "For sure, he wanted to spend that time. With you. But I think he had more than a hunch about what else you would come across."

Her answer steals the wind from my sails. He wanted to spend the time with me. And I believe that. But there had been a bigger picture and, in the end, we had walked right into a waiting trap, or something like that. Had he known it was waiting? I had the feeling I'd never know.

I'm so frustrated, I want to howl at the skinny yellow moon. There are answers available. And they are very nearby. But it's like everything is just out of my reach, and I can't quite lay my hands on whatever it is that is happening.

Arte still eyes me suspiciously, but for the moment, there is more that needs to be discussed.

"I'm going to take her and the horses back to the ranch," Belle says. "And I know it's kinda needle in a haystack time, but I think we should organize some searchers."

I'm relieved when Arte nods. "I agree," he says. "I'll organize two teams."

"I mean, I guess you can't do anything but cover the area by vehicle in the dark, right?"

"Yeah," he says, "that was my thought, too. But I feel like we have to do something."

Belle nods. "I agree."

Because of my sore backside, I climb into the back seat of the truck with effort. Belle takes the wheel while Arte climbs into the passenger seat and the other guy drives away with the Jeep. I'm so tired, I don't even bother asking where he's going. I'm so tired, I don't even care. My muscles are by now so sore that it is all that I can handle to just keep moving. It is not a long drive, but I am exhausted, but if it's because of all the riding or the emotion I'm not sure. Probably it's both.

As we drive, I fall in and out of an uneasy sleep in the comfort of the truck's narrow back seat. In periods of wakefulness, I try to focus on the conversation between Belle and Arte, but the gentle rise and fall of the two voices in the front only pushes me further over, and I don't really get a fix on anything that's being said.

I come awake as we pull into the ranch. Night is falling. It makes me wonder how Cameron had ever thought we'd get back when our ride out had been so long. I realize I'll probably never know what he had in mind for the rest of this day, and that thought tastes bad in my mouth. I regret what I can't know. There might have been magic in there someplace. I suspect there would have been. And everything had turned out very differently than anyone could have imagined.

We unload the horses—that is, Arte and Belle unload. By the time they are done, another couple of hands have rolled up in a second Jeep. This one looks all business. It has lights and a snorkel mounted on the hood and a rack on the roof. Without wasting too many words, the three men pile into the Jeep and head back out into the night while Belle leads the horses into the barn. I stand there uncertainly, the yard lights casting shadows and crickets and other creatures casting their sounds into the night.

After a while, Belle rejoins me.

"You all right?" she asks.

I nod.

"You must be all in."

I shrug. Words seemed to have left me.

A gong goes off somewhere near where we stand and I jump. Belle sees the jump and smiles at me reassuringly. "It's just dinner," she says. "I forget how unnerving the sound of that gong can be. You up for it? Come on. Let's you and me relax a bit before we join the others, okay? It's been a crazy day, for sure. But we've gotta eat."

She indicates I should follow her into the house, but we don't take the right into the kitchen, a room I've now seen a couple of times.

"I mean . . . maybe? I think I want to just sit for a bit. Maybe clean up. If that's okay?"

"Yes, sure. Of course. Follow me."

We end up back in the kitchen, which I then realize is the only room I've seen so far. She directs me to the bathroom. Tells me I'll find everything I need in there and, when I explore, I do.

When I look in the bathroom mirror, I am astonished to see the dirt-streaked face looking back at me. I hadn't fallen in the dirt on my head or anything, so at first I don't understand. Then I remember sweat and fear and heat, and everything becomes more clear.

I try not to think about outcomes. I think instead about just dealing with the now: getting myself cleaned up and then moving to the next activity. Looking back at it and forward, this day now seems endless to me. A time ribbon that maybe I will be surfing for the rest of my life.

I wash my face, brush my hair, pick some burrs out of my clothes. When I feel as though I've done all I can without a shower and some sleep, I rejoin Belle in the kitchen. She is sitting at the table where Cam and I had shared sticky buns that morning. Could that have just been a few hours ago? By now, it feels like a lifetime. I think of that time ribbon again. There is a bottle of wine and two glasses in front of her.

"I realize this probably should be whiskey," she says, "but it's all I had on hand."

I feel myself smile as I take a seat.

"Honestly whiskey at this stage maybe would just have knocked me out," I say as she pours two glasses.

"Well, that thought crossed my mind, as well," she admits.

"Do you think they'll find him?" I can't believe how small my voice sounds. And I know I don't have to tell her who I'm talking about.

Belle shakes her head. "Not tonight, no. It's a huge area, and most of it is unreachable by car. Even with a tricked-out Jeep.

Maybe we'll have better luck by air tomorrow. Or maybe he will have turned up. No, I didn't think there was much to be accomplished, searching tonight."

"But you had to try," I say quietly.

She looks at me sharply. Then she nods.

"Yes. We had to try."

We drink our wine, never straying far from our subject, but not really getting anywhere, either. It's the fear, I think. We are afraid. And it's as though we certainly can't relax and enjoy ourselves, because bad news might be just one more phone call away.

"You ready for a bite?" We're done with our glass. I'm glad she doesn't offer more. I feel I'd probably say yes, and then promptly fall asleep. "You don't have to join the group if you don't want to," she says. "I could just fix you a plate and bring it to you here."

"No, thank you. It's fine. I'm fine. All good," and I try a smile, but it feels shallow and brittle, even to me.

She leads me down several hallways and into a long, low space, more great hall than anything else. It's been outfitted as a dining room that can accommodate a large group at an extended table. Beyond the huge table, there is a fireplace that is large enough to walk into; with a friend. It's too warm for a fire tonight, but I have no trouble imagining a winter blaze and everyone ranged close to the fire, holding out cold hands and getting cozy. But that isn't now.

We all sit around that large single table made of some dark wood—maybe oak—and the surface is scarred but beautiful. A big fan turns leisurely overhead. I count: there are fourteen of us at the table. Belle indicates I should sit next to her, and everyone looks at me curiously. Belle has the air of someone who is trying to hold the fort in a moment of chaos, though I might be imagining that.

She introduces me around. I try to remember everyone's names, but I'm certain I won't recall half of them before the meal is through.

Everyone is looking at us curiously, of course. Wondering what has been happening. Some of them will be holding some information. Pieces of things. Some of them won't know that anything has occurred at all. It's an odd feeling. Sitting there. Knowing. But, really, just along for the ride.

It is clear that, in Cameron's absence, Belle is running the show. She seems comfortable there, too. Like this is something that happens: Cameron gone and Belle at the head of the table. Though I'm guessing most of his absences aren't related to a disappearance.

"Guys, sorry, listen," she says, quieting the group. "Not to panic. And I'm hoping to have answers sooner rather than later *but*: Cameron is missing."

The crowd isn't large enough for there to be a buzz through those assembled, but at a certain level, that is what is felt. I watch the faces closely while Belle speaks. I am gauging micro-expressions. Assessing what I see. And I am relieved because I see nothing that would make me think someone knows anything that they should not. On the other hand, I'm disappointed because a glimmer of something would give me a lead.

"Tell us what happened." The young woman that speaks has a pale and serious face, dark hair braided simply in a single plait. She could be eighteen or thirty, but her concern is palpable. And I don't doubt that the emotion I see is genuine.

Belle tells them what has occurred, but the details are sketchy. Cameron had gone riding with a friend, there had been evidence of an unofficial roundup, he'd gone to investigate and had not been heard from since.

"That's incredible," says one lanky young man when Belle has finished speaking. I can't tell if he's a volunteer or employee, then decide that, around here, it probably doesn't matter. "Helicopters, of all things. A secret and illegal roundup. We have to find out who did it."

"It's Skeeter, isn't it?" It's the same studious-looking ageless woman.

Belle's face is blank. "We have no way of knowing. By the time I got there, there was no sign of anything. Plus, it was dark. We'll go back and check in the morning. See if there's anything we missed." But she doesn't look hopeful, and I get it. I had looked around in the dusk. I am certain that there was nothing left behind to miss. "Meanwhile, Arte and a few of the other guys are out there right now. Searching."

"Not much point in that. In the dark." It's the same lanky cowboy, only now he's looking surly.

"Probably not, Marty. But we had to try."

There is general agreement with that. In the dense darkness of the national park, it seemed unlikely anything could be found at night at all. On the other hand, with the trail fresh, taking a stab at seeing if they could find anything just made sense.

"We don't know if they actually took any of the horses." The same pale young woman.

"No, sorry. As I said, it was dark. No one was left. And there was no sign of anything. Or Cameron." Belle's face is still blank.

"Do you think Skeeter actually believes he is above the law? Beyond it?" A skinny cowboy says this. At least, I think he is a cowboy. You can see that his legs are thin and bandy in tight jeans and they end in cowboy boots that have the patina of age on them. There are hats on a stand nearby—I'm guessing one of them is his.

But that name he said again. I note it. Skeeter. Easy enough to remember.

"We don't know for sure Skeeter had anything to do with it," Belle reminds them.

"Of course he did," lanky cowboy again. "Who else would have the balls to even try to pull this off?"

"And, really—" this is studious girl again—"who would even *want* to?"

"Who would have the motivation," Belle says. "Is that what you mean?"

The girl nods.

"Not too many around here will get the payoff that Skeeter will if he can get the horses off the range." This from lanky.

"I mean, okay," Belle says. "All of that is possible. Meanwhile, where is Cam?"

To my disappointment, no one offers up some easy and obvious answer, and seeing the worry etched on every face lets me know that my fears are grounded in reality.

"I'm sure it's Skeeter," says the young woman who now looks as though she is near tears. "Who else could it be?"

"And maybe he thinks he has enough friends in Washington that he will be protected," says another young man, and this one I figure for sure for a cowboy. He has a hardened look about him, something I suspect hints at years beyond those he owns.

"Or maybe he just didn't think anyone would find out," Belle suggests. "And I agree: I don't know who this would be beyond Skeeter." She hesitates. I get that she is gathering herself. She is proxy somehow. She has the appearance of someone who is trying to remain strong for those who are watching for her to be. "This happened out in Dead Man Basin," Belle informs the assembled.

"No one from the agency would have ever known had Cameron not happened upon it. I mean, we don't know the outcome yet. But it seems possible Cameron might have broken up whatever was happening. The timing seems right." She hesitates, then adds: "Or wrong."

"But helicopters?" The young woman that has asked is a pale blonde with a scrubbed look. Pretty. Girl next door, if next door is Stockholm. I figure her for a volunteer. "In broad daylight."

"We were riding," I say, my voice not as strong as I have known it to be. I feel rather than see every head at the table swivel in my direction. If they'd been holding back looking at me before, they don't bother stopping themselves now. I feel twenty-six eyes focused at me.

"You got lucky," the wizened cowboy says. "You could be missing, too."

"I'm not feeling that right now," I say. "Lucky." I can't even fully articulate what comes up for me in that moment. But I see Cameron, in that desert forest, in the moments before we heard the helicopters. I smell the creosote and desert flowers. And something dry and intoxicating, like a blend of sandalwood, amber, patchouli, though I know it's not possible that it was actually comprised of those things. I see Cameron's face coming closer to mine. Feel the bite of the stubble on his chin. Hear the impatient stomping of our mounts. Feel the desert magic all around us. Then feel it shatter—glass on tile—at the first approach of the helicopters. And what do I feel now? Grief. And something very like loss. They are familiar to me, those feelings. I didn't want to encounter them again. Or expect to. Now. Here.

There is a murmur of chatter between various factions at the table.

"We've got to take this seriously." Randall is tall and slender. He reminds me of a greyhound, and I can't tell from his clothes or his bearing if he's a volunteer or a hand. "The roundups the agency stages are bad enough. At least they warn us."

"And we've been having some success with local politicians." This from a serious-looking young woman whose job I imagine it may be to work with said politicians. When we were introduced, I learned she is Polly, which seems an unlikely name for the serious-faced young woman I am facing.

"You convince them?" I ask.

"We try," Polly says, pushing her glasses back into position with her index finger. "The horses are legally protected, but not all of them. There are quotas. Advised numbers for each region."

"But the numbers are bullshit," says Randall, looking earnest, and I can tell this whole line of conversation is a well-worn hobbyhorse for all of them. Everything that is being said has a well-rubbed feel, the edges soft. Like they've gone over all of these points many times before.

"It's also difficult to get accurate counts," Polly offers. The glasses get pushed up again.

"Because the horses move all the time?" I venture. It seems logical.

"Right," Belle agrees. "They are in motion. And there are mountains out there. Valleys."

"I saw some of them today," I say.

"It can take a long time to get a full understanding of the herds and how they splinter," Belle says. She is speaking calmly, but there is a wildness about her. An edge. And not just her. I can feel the façade. Everyone is acting like business as usual, but I get the feeling I'm not the only one who is wondering if Cameron is dead.

"But with all of these things we are talking about," I wonder aloud, keeping a sharp eye on those assembled as I do so, "would any of it ever go so far as to endanger someone? I mean, everything you've described sounds a bit like bureaucracy. Regional politics. Local feuds. But Cameron is missing. The things you are describing. Do you think any of them might account for why he is gone?"

I try to move forward with delicacy. It's important and I've occasionally gotten it wrong. Sometimes it's difficult for me to remember who normal people are. How they act. Is what I've asked a reasonable thing to say? Would a normal—reasonable—person ask such a thing? And I kind of get my answer right away when every head there turns toward me with curiosity.

Randall looks like he's about to say something, but Belle beats him to it.

"If there was a way that Skeeter could get away with murder," she says, "he'd do it. No question."

And the energy that is released after she speaks makes it clear that there is no one in that room who is not afraid that Cameron is dead.

CHAPTER FOURTEEN

AFTER BELLE SPEAKS there is a steep silence, and I can't be certain who has gone too far: Is it Belle? Or is it me? And then it doesn't matter, because someone pushes a huge cauldron in my direction and indicates I should eat.

I find, suddenly, that I am hungry, despite all of the anguish floating around the dining room. Or maybe because of it. Grief can make people ravenous. I've seen it before.

But the meal.

In this environment, it would have been safe to expect slabs of beef, maybe swimming in pork fat and with a chicken chaser. At least, that's what I would have imagined. But there is none of that.

Instead, what I am passed is a massive cauldron of vegetarian curry. And there is another of jasmine rice.

"The protein in the curry is tempeh," I'm told. Which when I search proves to be fermented soybeans, but it is just so much more delicious than that sounds. There is also garlic naan and raita. It all smells wonderful and ends up tasting as good as it looks. I eat it around my astonishment.

"This is not what I expected," I say to Belle, sotto voce.

"I'm not surprised," she says, beaming back at me. "But you like it?"

"Very much."

Despite their worry, and possible grief, there is an easy warmth among those assembled. It is a working ranch as well as a sanctuary, and so both ranch employees—cowboys, I realize—and volunteers are taking their evening meal together. It becomes obvious quite quickly that there is an overlap between these positions, as well. The paid employees seem deeply interested in the conservational aspects of the operation, and one gets the feeling that the volunteers are sometimes pressed into working the stock. They seem integrated, that's what I realize. That whatever differences they have, they are connected by work and also by people.

I imagine, on a normal evening, this would be a vibrant and convivial crowd. But this is not a normal evening, and Cameron's absence—and the circumstances around it—produce a wake-like atmosphere.

"I told Cameron a while ago I was afraid Skeeter would try to kill him." This said by a pale young woman with dark hair. There is nothing unattractive about her features, yet what comes across is a stalwart awkwardness. It's like she's all knees and elbows, but she is trying to talk with us in a way we won't read as offbeat. I don't miss that note of awkwardness. I've been that girl. And it takes one to know one.

"What did Cameron say?" I ask. "When you spoke about it, I mean."

By now the room is getting close. Maybe it's all the people there. Dinner was good. The day was long, and we are worried. All of us. We are not restless, but we maybe are beginning to need rest. Even so, at my question, all of the eyes in the room swivel to me then back to the girl.

"He laughed," she says. "He thought it was silly. Said it would never happen."

"He still thinks that," Belle says. "We've talked about it. Skeeter may be an old buzzard, but their families have known each other for generations."

"He sounds like someone you shouldn't turn your back on," I say. Thinking again of that desert forest. Of Cameron hovering just above me. And the smell of him. Something rough and sweet all in one gulp. I swallow and continue. "Skeeter sounds like someone to watch."

"We're beyond watching now," Belle says sensibly. "The only thing that computes is that Skeeter has him. But I don't even know where to begin to find him."

There is some wine. Some of the cowboys drink beer. It is some local microbrew with cacti on the label that looks good enough that I wish I liked the stuff.

The evening is convivial and beautiful, made all the more precious by that edge of fear. Cameron. He is not with us, but we feel him all around us anyway. All of this is his doing; his energy. Yet we don't know what has occurred.

"We should call the police," Polly says at one point.

"Already done," Belle says, and I glance at her in surprise. I feel as though I have been with her the whole time, and I haven't seen such a move.

"You did?" I ask.

"I did," she replies, not missing a beat. "On the way to pick you up. I knew they would tell me they couldn't do anything for twenty-four hours. But it seemed a good idea to put them on alert. Start the clock ticking."

I nod. The wisdom of this seems undeniable. Then I glance at my phone when I feel the vibration of a text.

"Is the assignment complete?" says the text.

"N—" just that single letter is all I text back. If Belle noticed the interaction, she gave no sign.

There is not much hesitation before the call comes, not a ring, of course. But, for me, another vibration. I slip out, hoping no one notices, but by the time I am clear of the room, it's too late.

"I can talk now," I text, and then I wait for a while, but nothing happens.

It is the desert at night. I breathe it in, reminding myself that no one really gets this chance. As I walk around the compound, I hear night sounds. I know all sorts of beasts are out there, but I try to put them out of my mind, as well. Javelina, the wild pigs that aren't pigs at all. Scorpions. Some poisonous, some not. Coyotes, baying at an ever-receding moon. Large cats. And so on. The desert at night? It is alive. I don't see any of that, but I feel it. Hear the rustles of it, as well. Rustles of promise. Or threat.

I wait for as long as I can without the amount of time I've been gone appearing to be unseemly. But there is nothing. I tell myself I will try to get her again in the morning. I have a bad feeling, though. And I hope that whatever happens, it is not too late.

CHAPTER FIFTEEN

WHEN I REENTER the long, low dining room, the whole group goes quiet in the way things do when you know you have been talked about. I don't look at them, though. Not really. I'm not sure what to do. It's been a long time since I was comfortable in social situations. This isn't actually one of those, but I am answerless, just the same.

Belle saves me. I'm not sure if I expected that. Or not.

"You must be all in," she says to me. And her expression is kind.

"I am," I agree.

"Let me show you where you'll be staying."

And I nod agreement, because there is no chance that I want to drive back into the city tonight, and the thought of hanging out with all of Cameron's concerned acolytes any longer is beyond what I can take. It's been a long day, after all.

After we leave the dining room, Belle leads me more deeply into the house. There are more twisty hallways and finally we come to one which she opens for me to go in ahead of her.

"This is Cameron's wing," she says.

I stop and back up, but she motions me ahead.

"Sorry to be dramatic," she says. "I could have explained better. You saw the crew out there. As it happens, we've got a full house.

And please don't take this wrong? But I'm fairly certain this is where you would have ended up tonight. I'm pretty sure it's what Cameron would have been hoping. We're good friends," she says when she sees my look. "It's what I would have been hoping for you guys, too."

The friend seal of approval. I know it was given with intention. I decide to accept the gift of it, meanwhile avoiding dwelling on the tense she is using. *Would have been hoping.* It sounds as though she has already given up on him. I try to think about something else.

"It looks . . . it looks very comfortable."

"You should be able to find everything you need here. And if Cameron should show up, I feel certain he will be happy that you are right here."

Our eyes meet as she says this. But neither of us believes that might be a possibility. I can see that in her face as clearly as she can probably see it in mine.

"I've got to get back out there. Arte and the others will be back any time, I'm sure. I'll want to know if they found anything."

"Oh, me too," I say. "You'll let me know if there's anything?"

"I will. Also, we need to organize for a first-light search party. If he's out there," she says, the resolve clear on her face, "I plan to find him."

And then I am alone, but the scent and energy of Cameron envelopes me.

I walk around the suite of rooms, touching a trophy here, lifting a hat there, just getting a feel for what is real and significant to this man who had become so special to me so quickly. And is it possible I'm also looking for some kind of sign? If that's the case, I don't find anything anyway. At least nothing beyond a deep longing for what might have been the first time I stepped into these rooms.

I sit down at his desk, his computer in front of me. I swivel around in the desk chair, survey the room. There is a beautiful painting opposite the desk. I suspect it was sited there to be a good backdrop for virtual meetings. It is a large canvas, a desert landscape in an impressionistic style. It is lovely, and I suspect it is valuable—it is certainly distinctive, but it adds a sort of gravitas to the room. It belongs here and, after a few minutes exploring the edges and taking everything in, I get a sense of belonging, too. It's a feeling I haven't had in a long time.

Belong. I savor the word. Taste it on my mouth. It's been so long since I belonged anywhere, I'm not totally sure I remember what it feels like. And I'm not totally sure it's something I want. My heart wants it, sure. Don't all of our hearts want that? But my spirit. I don't know. I've been so beat up by it all. Sometimes it just seems easier to hide and live alone.

Belonging. I surprise myself when I discover I suddenly want to belong again. And for that to occur and for the picture to be complete, Cameron needs to be in it.

I have to find him and bring him back.

CHAPTER SIXTEEN

CAMERON'S BED IS large and comfortable and the room itself is tidy. The sheets are sweet smelling, and the bed is perfectly made. I wonder if he had stripped the bed and perhaps cleaned the room in anticipation that I might join him after our ride. I know these are not good or productive thoughts on my part, but I can't help it. I had felt lighter this last little while, with him in my life. I am suddenly overcome with darkness again.

After the accident, when my child died, I stopped believing in a deity. I stopped believing in God. My heart went dead, absolutely. And if I believed in a spirit, it was only mine, and I pulled it taut inside me.

But now I find myself beginning to believe again. After all, who but some intentional but fickle deity could be so focused on bringing misery into one small and unimportant life? Have I not had more than my share? Can he not just overlook me for a while? Leave me be? I'm maybe not asking for searing happiness, but can I please just not have so much pain? And tests of my strength. I feel like throwing my hands up. I'm not strong enough, damnit. I'm not strong enough. At all.

It doesn't surprise me when, once I get into that large and comfortable bed, I can't sleep. I might have been feeling somewhat dozy in the dining room after a glass of wine and an eventful day. Now ready for slumber, though, I'm wide awake and staring. It's not a brand-new affliction.

Sometimes, when I'm sleepless, I try to count. It's usually times like this: bedtime. When my thoughts keep me awake. At times like that, I think: How many people have I killed? In a way, the actual number could be seen to fluctuate. Do you count the ones who were terminally ill? Those could be seen to have been already dead, when it comes to pure counting: I just helped with the inevitable. Shortened the time frames. Maybe helped with the insurance. It's almost like those ones shouldn't count as hits, at all.

But what is the actual number? For one thing, it grows. And some of those people needed killing. I know that. Before I do the deed, I almost always do some research. I'm looking for background information that might aid in my mission or put me on alert to danger. But what I often find is that looking straight at humanity doesn't help with what I'm doing, at all.

It is not a universal truth that in order for someone to want you off the planet enough to hire someone to kill you, you have to have done something really bad, but it's maybe not far off the mark.

So a lot of those I have killed have been bad people (as much of a generality as that sounds, and I acknowledge that it does sound that way entirely).

Understand, though: I'm not trying to justify my actions. Killing people for money is unjustifiable. I know: I've wrangled with the idea quite enough. Even if you're only killing people you judge to be bad, well, who the hell are you, anyway? Judge and jury? You don't get to judge. How do you—or I—get to make that call? That's not really how it works in the real world. And yet—here I am.

Maybe that's why I can't sleep.

So when I'm done with counting, I sometimes dream about a different life with other goals and values.

Other times, while wide awake, I think something has happened that will make that different life possible. And then the other shoe drops and I know that life has lined up in such a way that I eventually discover that no matter what I'd like better, at some point, I'll have to kill again.

On this night, in Cameron's room, I count. Something in the counting hurts my heart. There's just no way back from it. I don't remember falling asleep, but then I open my eyes and it is morning. There is a table near the bed and while I slept, someone—maybe Belle—has crept in with a thermos of coffee, a plate of pastries, and even tiny jars of jam and marmalade. Butter. Someone has been looking out for me. It's a strange feeling and my heart plays, again, with the idea of *belonging*.

When I start to pull myself out of bed, my body reminds me of the previous day's activity. I extend one leg, feel the pain in my thighs and calves and rear, all of which are sensitive in ways I never thought possible before. My butt is so tender, when I press my fingers against the fleshiest part, I recoil from the pain. It's like a bone in there is bruised somehow. It feels weird. Those many hours in the saddle are having their say now. I feel as though a bunch of my muscles have all gotten shorter. And some other ones I didn't even know I had have been awakened. And they're mad as hell at being interrupted in their sleep.

It is just when I am exploring this mysterious new shortness of my muscles that my phone rings. The call is coming from Bumpass, Virginia. I pick up right away.

"Bumpass. Seriously," I say when I answer. "Can't you do any better than that?"

"Why would I need to?"

"Point," I say, conceding. But still. If one were pushing to be creative, Bumpass might not be the way to go. And still again. Maybe creativity is not the issue here.

"There's been a change of plans," she says without preamble.

I hold my breath, but I don't say anything. I have a feeling I know where this is going, and—if I'm right—the news will be bad enough that I don't want to rush it.

"Yes?" is all I say.

"If the hit has not yet been done, stand down."

"Stand down?" It's not a phrase she has used with me before. Ever.

"Correct."

"Do you know that Cameron has disappeared?"

There is a beat, and then. "I do not know this. No." And there is a tightness in her voice around it. It has me imagining that Cameron being missing might actually impact her arrangement with whoever made the hit. I don't even bother asking about that. Like so much else, it is above my pay grade and not my concern.

"But it's interesting?"

"Yes," she says as though considering. "It is interesting, but beyond the scope of this conversation. From your perspective: your assignment is to be considered complete. Put it out of your mind."

I look again at the painting. I look at a rodeo trophy from his high school days. A photo of him with a couple I presume to be his mom and dad. Pieces of a life.

I let go of a long breath I didn't even know I was holding.

"Okay," I say.

"You won't be required to return the deposit."

"I wasn't considering it. In fact, if the assignment is complete, I should be getting paid in full."

There is a pause so long that I wonder if she has hung up. And then.

"All right then," she says, as though the deal had been done in the first place, and she was just waiting for me to say the words.

"Okay," I say again.

And then the line is dead.

I sit there, in the quiet, with my would-be lover's beautiful rooms all around me and contemplate what all of this might mean and what my next move should be. If, as she said, the "assignment is complete," does that mean Cameron is dead? I feel the possibility of that roar around in my brain. Upon consideration, it even seems likely. I've been around these people for a while. Contracts just don't get released.

I have effectively been relieved of my duty. That isn't distressing. It means that, if I manage to put this right, that's one single layer I won't have to explain. On the other hand, it means that Cameron may be lost to me forever. Why else would the assignment be canceled? And with my luck? I figure that is likely the outcome. And then I push that thought away because we can make things real with our thoughts, can't we? What we think about is sometimes what becomes. I deliberately spend a few minutes imagining Cameron whole and hale. I see him at the end of a tunnel and he is walking toward me. And there's a smile on his face. That smile. And when my imagination tries to tug me down other avenues, I push the thoughts back. But they are so persistent—those bad thoughts—that the whole thing takes a lot of effort. After a while I give up and just lie there and try to still my mind. Breathe. Because none of this is getting me anywhere. I'm spinning my wheels and getting nowhere fast.

I sit back down on his office chair, my back to his desk. I lose myself in the crags and valleys of the beautiful painting. I memorize every cactus. Every trail. I settle back and allow myself to catch my breath.

He is out there somewhere. He has to be. And this? This is only the moment when things catch up.

CHAPTER SEVENTEEN

So I AM off the job, which might actually prove to be a good thing. As long as I can find Cameron alive, I now have no reason to kill him. That seems at least one good thing. A step in the right direction.

The not-so-good thing is I have no idea where he is. No one does. It's frustrating, because I can't even begin to guess.

I think about what to do now. What to do with myself. What to do. There is an urge to run and an urge to stay. Part of me wants to stay and see if he turns up. Another part thinks that's stupid. Since the time before, motion has always been what saves me. It's when I sit still too long, I think. That's when things come apart. I have to move. But then I strike a compromise with myself. There is the need for space and distance. And the desert calls to me. It's not, in any case, like I can help Cameron by hanging around the house, waiting for something to break. Plus, the night before, Belle seemed to have everything well in hand, or at least as in hand as things can be under the circumstances.

When I emerge from Cameron's room, there is no sign of anyone around. Are they all out hunting for Cameron? It seems likely. I look around the rooms closest to mine, but I don't see anyone. And I'd like to. If there has been any word at all, I'd like to get it. Plus, I feel as though I should help, but I have no clear idea of what that should look like. I feel brimming with excess energy. And I know I don't have the skills necessary to help look for Cameron in the wilderness. I'd be just as likely to get lost myself. Still, I want to do something, but I just don't know what. And then I get an idea.

In my car, I try to retrace the route Cameron had taken me on that first day. The Kiger horses. There aren't many roads, so it's not the most difficult path to reconstruct. Before I get to the ranch driveway that leads to the highway, I watch carefully for a few miles until I see a wide path going off on another left. I follow that path for a few miles until it widens into a clearing. I park there, grab my backpack, and get my painting gear out of the trunk and then I head off with it in what I think is the right direction.

My paints and easel are held together by a simple strap that is designed to fashion easily into a backpack. I sling it onto my back now and carry my actual backpack in my hand and continue in the direction of where I imagine I'll meet up with the river.

The walk is brief but breathtaking. And it's early morning, so the day is still cool, even pleasant. It's not a long walk—perhaps a mile and twenty minutes—and the trail is relatively flat, though a bit rocky. As I walk, I notice the vegetation change, the arid full desert landscape giving way to a more verdant feel as I get closer to the river. Water. The giver of all life.

When I reach the river, I am overtaken again by its beauty, but also nearly overwhelmed with disappointment not to see the horses. Seeing them would have—I don't know—provided some kind of sign. Something hopeful. Instead, there is only this pristine beauty, like a postcard of some desert oasis. It is unbelievably beautiful, but also desolate without life. There is a sadness to it, and as I set up my easel and paints on the shade-protected bank above the river, I start to think about that: about the colors and techniques I'll use to try and capture what I see and feel.

I set about it and soon I am so engrossed that everything else falls away. Hours pass. I don't really notice anything change until they are upon me. I merely lift my head for another glimpse of what I'm painting and encounter four horses looking back at me.

"Hello, honey," I say softly. I'm close enough to see ears twitch, noses quiver. They don't seem afraid of my voice. I see them assess me, decide I'm not dangerous, then carry on with their business. More of them come around a bend in the river, their bright coats gleaming in the sun. They don't pay much attention to me. They crop the grass at the edge of the water, moving through the shallows as though they themselves are part of the river.

I begin to include them in my painting, the moody work I'd been creating taking on a different tone with the addition of the colors of their jewel-like coats and the controlled motion of their muscular bodies.

As with the animals Cameron had identified as the Salt River horses, some of the Kigers are now belly deep in the river, pulling at the eelgrass on the banks. And I paint and I lose myself for a time in the spectacle and the emotion and the sheer joy of creating.

When the horses lift their heads and snort toward that bend in the river, then seem to pull themselves together and run off, I find myself once again witnessing a mini-stampede. This one has a different cause though. No helicopters today and so there is not the urgency I had previously experienced, but as though the horses I'd been watching peacefully cropping the grass in the river suddenly discovered they had someplace else they wanted to go.

I'm not alone for long, though. Two mounted cowboys come around the corner, moving at high speed. They are focused on their quarry—the retreating horses—and they are moving fast so they don't see me, perched with my paints in the shade above the river. Even so, I am close enough to see that I don't recognize either of them and, though they are moving quickly, I am able to take some mental notes. The larger of the two has straw-colored hair sticking out at all angles from under a battered dark felt Stetson. The other is riding a pinto, the white splashes on his copper-colored coat reflecting brightly in the sun. The rider has regular features and dark hair, but a livid scar is clearly visible down the entirety of his left cheek, from eye to jaw.

And then they are gone and all that is left are the echoes from the thunderous hooves. And my painting. I glance at it, so complete I can't even tell where the finishing touches I had been adding would have gone. And I notice something else: it is the best thing I've done.

CHAPTER EIGHTEEN

WITH MY GEAR and the new painting tucked into the car, I head back to the ranch and seek Belle out, anxious to hear if there is news of Cameron.

"I'm so glad to see you," she says before I get the chance to say anything. She leads me into the empty kitchen, an air of secrecy about her. I'm curious, but try not to show it. She looks around, as though making sure the empty kitchen really *is* empty. When she speaks, she pitches her voice low.

"I got a voicemail," she says indicating her phone, and I realize that the normally poised and competent Belle is wild-eyed. "It's from him."

She doesn't wait for my response, but begins to play the recording. I have to focus to hear his voice. At first there is some background noise. Traffic, maybe? An airport? I can't be sure. But then things quiet a bit and I can make his voice out perfectly. There is no mistaking it. It is Cameron. My heart soars. There is hope. The fact that he's making the call from some noisy place makes me realize he isn't still out in the desert someplace, either. Best of all, he's alive. Hope beyond hope.

"Hey, Belle," he says on the recording. I think his voice sounds tired. I allow that I could be projecting, but I feel as though I hear that he's putting on a brave face. I listen still more closely, hearing the words but also trying to pick up any nuance. "I've taken an unexpected trip—" a self-deprecating half laugh. "I guess you'll have gathered that. And it's difficult to explain right now. But I . . . I find myself in Washington on a . . . on a mission of sorts. Please look after things there for a while. And don't be too dismayed by anything you hear. And tell . . . just tell everyone I'm okay and that I hope to see them soon."

And that was it.

"He didn't really say anything, did he?"

Belle shakes her head. "I noticed that, too."

"And the call came from his phone?"

"I don't know. I guess so. My phone was off when the call came in."

"What happens when you try to call him?"

She meets my eyes. "Voicemail."

"But he's alive," I say. "We didn't . . . we didn't really know that before. Not for sure."

She meets my eyes and nods. Maybe the possibility that Cameron was dead had never entered her mind. Considering the reason I am here, it is understandable that it had never left mine.

"What do you think?"

"I don't know what to think," I tell her.

"What are you going to do?" Belle wants to know, and though a part of me wonders at all these questions, another part understands perfectly. She is usually so in control, but today she is lost. She doesn't know what to do. And maybe it's easier to show her vulnerability to me because she doesn't really know me that well at all, and I have no expectations of her.

"I'm not sure yet," I say, sorry to have to let her down.

"You know you're welcome to stay," Belle says.

"I do know that, actually," I say, surprising myself by discovering that I mean it. "Thank you. I have things to do, of course. But everything just seems small next to this."

Belle nods her agreement.

"What do you think it means," Belle indicates her phone, but I know she means everything, including what has become of Cameron. Apparently safe, but acting mysteriously somewhere far away and having disappeared in mysterious circumstances. None of it makes sense.

"I feel that you are in a better position to know than me," I say honestly.

"I'm not sure about this one," Belle says. "It's so far outside of anything that has happened before. And . . . Washington. Politics, right? Cameron was scheduled to attend hearings there next week. He had intended to speak out against proposed legislation that would weaken the protection of the wild horse on western ranges still further."

"He hadn't mentioned that," I say.

"I think he kept hoping to get out of it. And maybe, I don't know, maybe he was hoping that if he didn't get out of it, he could ask you to come along. Make a trip out of it. I don't really know."

"He'd said that to you?"

"Not really. But I know him pretty well. I would think that was on his mind."

"What are you thinking now?"

"I don't know what to think," Belle says. "He disappears while riding, apparently during a secret helicopter roundup, but the boys that weren't searching went out at dawn, counting head, and as far as they can tell, no horses are missing. I mean, we never know exactly how many are on the range, of course. That's the nature of the range. But we have an idea."

Which reminds me.

"I was just out by the Kigers and I saw a couple of cowboys chasing them down."

As soon as I speak, it's like watching a window close. Her face just shuts down.

"You were out with the Kigers? What were you doing there?" Her body language has changed, too. She has crossed her arms in front of herself, protectively. And her legs are slightly akimbo, as though she is bracing herself. I wonder what it is I'm seeing.

"Painting," I say, realizing it sounds lame and realizing, also, that she's looking at me suspiciously. "I was painting them. The Kigers."

"Maybe it's time for you to leave." She says it coldly and I find myself seeing what she sees and trying to understand how she's read the situation.

"Wait," I say, realizing even as I speak that I'm not going to get anywhere. I can see it on her face and the thrust of those arms. Knowing I'll try anyway. "I didn't have anything to do with this."

She is standing directly in front of me now, arms crossed.

"I don't believe you," she says in a tone that is flat and ungiving. I can tell I'm getting nowhere fast. She's made up her mind, apparently thinking I had something to do with Cameron's disappearance. I don't blame her. Not really. In her shoes, I might even do the same. "There appear to be secrets everywhere. I think it's best if you leave."

Looking at her face, I know there is nothing I can say. I head to Cameron's room, collect my things, all the while regretting not having done that before I headed out to paint. In the time between the kitchen and when I get into my car, Belle doesn't let me out of her sight. A part of me understands perfectly. And another part is filled with grief. Something lost. Or, at least, temporarily misplaced.

I don't understand it, but I also don't put up a fight; I can see that her mind is made up. I grab my stuff from Cameron's room—I don't have much—and head back to my car.

CHAPTER NINETEEN

I LEAVE THE ranch because I have no choice. Belle has solidly closed that door. I want to try and find out what has happened to Cameron, but my best avenue of information has vanished, and I just don't know where to start over.

There is a single cafe in Lourdes. I think to stop there and reassess; get my bearings.

Belle's rejection has shaken me. How could she be thinking that I had anything to do with Cameron's disappearance? The very thought makes me sadder than I can say. Sadder than the situation warrants, really. But that feeling of belonging. It had been intoxicating, in a way. It seems I had wanted to be part of something again even more than I knew.

When I enter it, Sam's Cafe reminds me of a movie set for a rustic, western diner. There is western art on the wall. A black velvet sunset. Old photographs of famous people I don't recognize posed with the same stout man. Bad paintings of big vistas and the stuffed head of a big bull elk that looks like he might have stalked the range when Reagan was president. The booths are clean, but the leather upholstery is cracked and the Arborite tables are yellowing. I can tell that the place has been here for a while. There is a long, low counter with swivel stools where a few people are drinking coffee and eating what look to be abundant plates of food. It's mid-morning and the place isn't busy, so even though I am by myself, I take a whole table so I can spread out my laptop and just hope that no one gives me a hard time. I feel the need to be alone to think about everything that has happened.

The man who approaches me once I'm settled in is an older and stouter version of the guy in the photos. It almost looks like the once-white apron he is wearing is holding him together; his mid-section strains against the ties almost humorously.

"Morning," he says. "Coffee?"

"You Sam?"

"Who's asking?"

"Your name is on the cafe. It was a guess."

"Ha. Okay." His response is jovial. "You got me. But if you're looking for the special, we're out."

"I don't even know what the special was."

"Croque monsieur," he says.

"Get outta here," I reply, deadpan.

"We're a fancy place," he says matching my straight face. I suddenly feel like we're doing a vaudeville act, even though I barely know what vaudeville is. He might, though. I smile at him and he smiles back. The mood is broken, but polite.

"I can see that this is a fancy place," I say agreeably. "But if you're outta the special, what's special now?"

"Well, sure, everything is special. But we got a southwestern grilled cheese sandwich that'll knock your socks off."

"What's in a southwestern grilled cheese?"

"You got some cheese. You got some ham. You got some egg."

"Isn't that pretty much a croque monsieur?"

"No, not really. It's all in the execution."

"So much is."

"And the southwestern grilled cheese also has avocado and just a touch of molé."

"Sounds bizarre."

He smirks back at me. "Pretty much. But good. Are you in?"

"Sure," I say, fairly certain I'm being sold leftovers.

"Great. You won't be sorry. You drinking?"

"Got coffee?"

"That, we're not out of," he says, then trundles off to put in my order and grab my joe.

"You know someone named Skeeter?" I ask him when he delivers the coffee.

"Sure," he says, and I wonder if laconic just goes with the desert. I'm going to have to work.

"So . . . you've seen him in here once or twice or . . ." I prompt.

"Skeeter Allaband," he says, which is nice because now I have another piece. "He's in here a lot. Maybe couple times a week. Maybe more."

"He lives near here?"

"Near enough. He ranches on the other side of Cathedral National Park, near Belly Up Springs." This time I just keep looking at him and he continues. "That's maybe fifty miles from here. Calls his spread the Allaband Cattle Company."

"That's quite the handle," I say.

"It's all right," Sam replies.

"Sounds like a long way to come for breakfast."

"Did I tell you we're *out* of the croque monsieur?"

"Touché," I say, laughing.

"When in Rome," he chirps, though I'm not quite sure why.

"He's a cattleman?"

"Who?"

"Allaband."

"Sure. Most everyone around these parts is. Or they work for someone who is."

"Cameron Walker is missing."

I really don't know if I should be saying that. Spreading rumors in a way, even. Especially blurting it all like that. And anyway, hadn't we heard from him now? So was it even really true? I filed these voices away. I hadn't personally heard from him, and he'd gone missing while he was with me. Something was definitely not right and I had to start someplace. And right now, someplace turned out to be here.

"I know," the fat man says. "A few of his hands were in here this morning for breakfast. Early enough to get the croque monsieur, too."

"What did they say?"

"They said the croque monsieur was excellent."

I just look at him and so he continues.

"They said that he went missing while he was out riding with some girlfriend." He stops as though a light has dawned. "Wait," he says. "That's you?"

I shrug.

"And you think it's Skeeter? What took him?"

"I don't know what to think," I say honestly. "And I also don't know where to start."

"So you started here," he says, nodding approvingly. "Good idea. I don't think it would be Skeeter though. I mean, Skeeter would have plenty of reasons to get rid of Walker. They've been at each other for years. But I don't think Skeeter would actually start something."

"I think Skeeter is mad at Cameron for speaking out about wild horses."

He looks at me appraisingly for a few long seconds, then speaks his mind.

"Skeeter has a lot to lose if they take his livestock grazing permits away. And that's what it ultimately would be about, though you didn't hear that from me. Like, he'd lose a lot. I would say his operation depends upon them. Especially since he sold off part of his land last year to a developer."

"Are you saying that he has more cattle than his land can support."

"I'm not saying anything," the restaurateur says. "But I *could* say a few things if I wanted to."

"I don't get it."

He looks around before he answers. I can tell that he's looking to see who is nearby and who might be listening. I guess he figures he's in the clear though, because he begins answering right away.

"It relates to grazing privileges. Skeeter has them. Not everyone does. That means he's only paying, like, a buck-and-a-half for every AUM he has a permit for."

"AUM?"

"Sorry. It stands for Animal Unit Month. And the number is actually a little less than that."

"So, wait: are you telling me it costs him less than twenty bucks a year each to graze his cattle on government land?"

"Each head. And yes. You're a quick study," he says.

"You can't feed a dog for that. And how many cattle does he have?"

"That I don't know for sure. But it would definitely be in the thousands."

I consider. I don't know anything about the topic, but the picture is starting to fill in.

"So you said he sold a bunch of his own land. Are there private lands you can lease for grazing?"

He looks at me with sharp amusement. "Like I said: quick study."

"So there are?"

"Yes. Sure."

"And the cost per animal is higher? Grazing, I mean?"

"A lot higher. I'd have to do a bit of research but, based on what I do know, nothing less than maybe nine bucks per AUM."

"And you said there were potentially thousands of head."

"Maybe thousands of thousands."

I let that sink in. It's a big number. "So yeah," I say after a while. "Okay. Skeeter has a motive. But is he capable of doing something like that?"

"I have to be honest. I personally would not have said so. But some of the guys who came from the ranch early enough to get the croque monsieur would not agree with me. But . . ."

"But . . . ?"

"Oh, nothing. Forget I said anything, really. What do I know? I'm just an old restaurant owner, talking out of my hat."

"You're not wearing a hat."

He guffaws.

"Anyway, I've got a business to run. And you've got a head to keep on your shoulders. It's probably best if we leave all of this to run."

I try to get more out of him, but the bank has closed and the drawbridge is up. Once he decided to quit talking, there was nothing to revive.

CHAPTER TWENTY

SAM'S SOUTHWESTERN GRILLED cheese sandwich proves to be fantastic. Perfectly toasted, and with just the right amount of dense, gooey cheese, I promptly decide it's the best thing I've eaten since I don't know when. Plus, it arrives with fries *and* a salad, and I can't even believe it when I eat most of all of my portion. Clearly if I hang around these parts I'm going to need bigger jeans.

While I eat, I do some online research to try and get a fix on Allaband. For me it's a natural reaction, and I don't even think about the fact that this is the mode I go into when I'm preparing for a hit. I gather information.

Over the last of my coffee, I locate the Allaband Cattle Company. In the way things are measured in ranch country, Cameron and Skeeter are practically neighbors. I read that Allaband's wife died in a mysterious accident some three years before, as did a business partner and his son a year later. It all makes me wonder.

I am reading about Skeeter Allaband and looking at his picture in a newspaper article that quotes him when Sam approaches my table. He points out the window at a burly green pickup truck that has just pulled up outside the cafe.

"Allaband," Sam says, pointing at the passenger. I would have recognized him from the newspaper articles, but maybe I wouldn't have noticed him. At first glance, he is unexceptional. I am almost disappointed: in my mind, I had made him so much more of a presence.

Skeeter and a driver get out of the truck and head inside. Other than a cowboy hat and boots, I don't notice much about the driver. Allaband himself looks older than photos I had seen had led me to believe. Possibly they were old photos. He looks close to seventy, though he moves with the energy of a much younger man. And there is a bandiness about him when he walks, as though he'd be more comfortable on the back of a horse than he is just walking around.

The two men plunk themselves down at a table near me. I admonish myself for the surprise I feel that he has shown up here. After all, this is probably the only eatery around here for miles. For all I know, this is their morning ritual. I remind myself that I am the interloper here, not him.

I make myself small and hunch myself over my computer, trying to keep attention away from myself, but after a while I can see I needn't have bothered: both men are too engrossed in their conversation to bother noticing me at all. Allaband does not appear to even see me.

"Heya, Skeeter! Terry. What can I get for you guys today?" Sam has one eye on me as he says this. Maybe gauging my reaction, or watching what I'll do, but I can't be sure.

Skeeter plunks his computer case on the table and addresses Sam. It's a leather briefcase so worn, it's a wonder it's still hanging together. While he talks, he pulls an equally battered laptop out of the case and puts it on the table, plopping it next to the briefcase.

"Breakfast burrito and coffee for me, thanks, Sam," Skeeter's driver says.

"I think I'll have a burger, Sam," Skeeter says. "With fries, too. Breakfast of ex-champions! I'm on my way to Boseman. And you know flying these days: I'll be lucky if they give me a bag of nuts."

"Boseman ain't a long flight, though, right?"

"Just over two hours for me. If I want a nonstop, I need to do it outta Mesa-Gateway, so that's where I'm heading. If I left from Sky Harbor, I'd need to make a stop at one damn place or another."

Sky Harbor, of course, is the "friendliest airport in America." The one in Phoenix I've been in many times. Mesa-Gateway is an airport I've never heard of. Because of that, I imagine it to be small.

"Don't you usually charter outta Mesa-Gateway?"

"I do. That's right, Sam. There was a screwup with the service today though."

"He didn't book soon enough is what he's saying," the driver says with a grin.

"Well, whatever. I guess that's so," Skeeter says. "Either way, looks like I'm flying coach today."

"Ha," the driver jokes. "You ain't never flown coach before—I'm guessing you don't start today."

I stop listening to their banter, plug "mesa-gateway" into Google, and discover it's a commercial airport about an hour from where we're sitting. A half-baked idea springs to mind. I don't wait to hear any more of their conversation. I already have the feeling there is nothing from their talk worth learning. But an airport stop. That's another matter.

I get the coordinates for Mesa-Gateway airport up on my phone. Then I finish my coffee, wave goodbye to Sam before I gather up my laptop, leave a twenty-dollar bill on the table for a twelve-dollar tab, and head out the door.

CHAPTER TWENTY-ONE

I SPEND JUST under half an hour on country highways until I hit the freeway. Six lanes for another twenty minutes, but I'm passing through the living desert all the way. Cactus, ocotillo, and sparse and thirsty-looking trees dot the landscape. I think the whole time I roll. By the time I get anywhere near Mesa-Gateway airport, I have a plan that is more than half-baked. But not much.

I don't know how much lead time I'll have—he has to eat his burger back there at Sam's, maybe shoot some shit—but I do know there won't be any minutes to waste. I double-time everything.

The airport is small and efficient. It's easy to find a parking spot in the large open lot facing the single terminal. I pop my laptop under the seat of the car and stuff my hoodie into the backpack so the bag doesn't look quite so empty. Then I head into the terminal, hoping I look like I'm going places.

On the way to security there is a ticket counter. I stop and buy a ticket for the next flight available to me, which ends up being Bellingham, Washington, a place I don't want to go. It doesn't matter though: I have no intention of being on the flight. It's really a ticket through security I'm buying, and I have to do it quickly: I figure Skeeter won't be far behind me and I need to be on the other side when that happens.

I imagine the TSA guy looks at me funny when he X-rays my backpack and sees basically nothing, but that's probably just my imagination. They look at so many X-rays every single day they probably don't care what they see. As long as it is none of the things they're looking for, their brains probably just shut down. After all, who knows what's in all those bags that travel everywhere every day? Aside from TSA, I mean. There's probably a lot of weird stuff on airplanes all the time that has nothing to do with contraband. We probably don't even really want to know.

At the security checkpoint, as I wait for my shoes to show up on the conveyor belt, I wonder about what I'm doing. My half-baked plan isn't much of anything. Or maybe my subconscious knows something I don't know; otherwise why would I have shelled out three bills for a last-minute ticket? I mean, does Skeeter even have anything to do with Cameron's disappearance? After all, we don't really know that for sure. But he's my only plan and I'm in the thick of things, so I roll with it. What other choice do I have?

Once my shoes come off the conveyor belt after going through the X-ray machine, I take them and my pretty much empty backpack to a bench nearby. While I tie my laces and watch the conveyor belt bringing people's stuff along while they're getting X-rayed, the idea comes to me fully fledged.

I don't leave the bench. From my vantage point I have a clear view of both the before and after of security and so I see it when, not long after I take up my post, Skeeter gets into the line. He pulls the battered laptop I'd seen at the cafe from the same worn briefcase and places it in its own tray. Next comes the briefcase in another tray, along with his phone. A third tray for his wallet, coat, and belt: obviously the trophy buckle wouldn't have made it through the metal detector. Cowboy boots take up their own tray last. And it's pretty obvious to me he could have fit all his stuff into fewer trays, but he seems like someone who wants to take up as much room as possible. I don't mind at all. I figure it is that very self-indulgence that will make my plan work.

What I'm thinking is dangerous as hell, but it might be the only move I have, and while Skeeter is in the body scanner, I see my moment.

The TSA agent tells him to raise his arm above his head and hold still, "real still," and Skeeter doesn't like his tone or something, because he balks a bit, which slows things down even more. Then he seems to have trouble with the idea of holding still enough. During this back-and-forth, and then while the machine whirrs around him, I saunter up to the belt where the usual melee of sorting shoes and bags and laptops is occurring. I leave the briefcase but grab the battered laptop I've identified by placement as belonging to Skeeter.

Once the laptop is in my hands, I'm in motion across the terminal. Brisk, but not fast enough to draw anyone's attention. Even while I move, I'm sliding the laptop into my backpack. By the time I am nearly at the gates, the bag is settled easily on my back, like the carry-on backpack of hundreds of other travelers. I reach the gates without being stopped and with no one shouting at me or trying to intercept me. Next I look around for the exit of the secure area. And then I just walk out.

Back at my car, I drop the bag on the passenger seat and as calmly as possible exit the parking lot.

And then I drive away.

CHAPTER TWENTY-TWO

When I get back to the hotel, it feels as though I have been gone a week. It doesn't seem possible that it was just yesterday morning that I left here, my heart filled with anticipation of a day horseback riding and getting to know Cameron better. I chastise myself. What had I been thinking? Happy, that was what I felt. When has that ever been a feeling that worked for me? Happiness. Some people are not meant to have that. I am one of those.

But I've got stuff to do. I force self-pitying thoughts aside and focus on the business at hand. Whether or not I am qualified for happiness, I feel prepared to give it a shot. Cameron is out there somewhere. Whatever else the future brings, I would like to know Cameron is among the living. Whatever happens—or does not happen—between us.

I turn my attention to Skeeter's laptop. As I'd noticed from the first, the computer is battered, but clearly functional. If I were to imagine the laptop that belonged to a grizzled old cowboy, it would look just like this. It has the look of a computer that's been around campfires, and banged around on the back of a horse. It looks like it's been used far beyond what was intended.

I open the clamshell and am more annoyed than disappointed when the computer demands a password. It would have been a bonus if the machine hadn't been password protected, but it would also have been a nice surprise.

I enter a couple of random passwords with absolutely no hope of success. After all, I know practically nothing about the man beyond some cartoonish details and so I am not disappointed when my feeble attempts accomplish nothing beyond getting the computer mad at me.

"Too many failed login attempts," it tells me after a while. "Try again in twenty minutes."

I sit there looking at it for a while. Just some dumb little password. I've got the same computer: MacBook Air, though mine is admittedly less battered: no campfires there. But because I have the same computer, I know that it isn't required to be a particularly sophisticated password, just for entry. No demand for mixed case or special characters. It can be the simplest little thing. Six characters, none of them special or case specific. Just some simple word or sequence of numbers. And that's all that is keeping me from the information I want and desire inside of the computer: the tiniest little firewall, if one can even call it that. I want in and practically nothing is stopping me, yet I realize I could sit there all day trying passwords and getting nowhere beyond annoyed.

And so, in my twenty-minute cooling-off period, I turn to Google, typing in various versions of a question to see if I can get some kind of answer.

It's not by accident that it is difficult to just hack into someone's computer. And, certainly, I discover very quickly, there is virtually no way for me to hijack an Apple computer of this era. Not without a lot more expertise than I currently have. I discover, for instance, that I can't just reformat it and make it my own, which fortunately is not what I want to do in any case.

With my time-out over, I take another run at it. Maybe I could get lucky? Maybe I'll hit something coincidentally? So I try various things, but before long I've had too many tries and the computer gets mad again and shuts me down.

In my next twenty-minute cooling-off period spent googling on my own computer, I begin to get the idea I might be able to bypass that pesky password by not even trying. I learn that I should be able to access Skeeter's computer by using my own. I learn that to accomplish this I will need a Thunderbolt cable, something I'd never even heard of before. Thunderbolt cable. It sounds magical. I see pictures of the thing on the web and it looks like a couple of the cables I always travel with. I try them, though. And then I try them different ways, but it turns out there is some slight difference that makes Thunderbolt cables be Thunderbolts. I need to shop.

After a while I go out and get some lunch. I choose a pizza place near the hotel because I know it will be fast and easy. I haven't been out of the hotel for very long when that feeling that had been missing since I'd left the city returned: the feeling of being watched or followed. Sitting in a cool and dimly lit Italian joint trying to enjoy a small pizza margarita, it's like I feel eyes on the back of my neck. When I turn around there is nothing: the server, standing in the corner talking to a friend. Some skinny kid chewing on his own pizza. A couple of old ladies, laughing hard and showing signs of maybe getting into the prosecco a tad too early. Just nothing at all. And yet the feeling persists.

When I'm done, I head to a nearby electronics store, where the feeling of being followed does not persist. In addition to the Thunderbolt cable, I also pick up some screen cleaner so I can get rid of the grime on Skeeter's computer before I attack it. All those campfires—or whatever—have left their marks. Then I'm

back in my room and ready to take another stab at being an amateur hacker.

The instructions I find in the online version of a respected computer magazine are clear and seem easy. I turn off Skeeter's computer, attach it via cable to mine, then turn his on while holding
down the "T" key. The instructions tell me this will start Skeeter's
laptop in something called Target Disk Mode, which sounds fancy
enough to offer some hope. Also, it's easy for me to do. In any
event, it all goes just as advertised. And that's it. From there my
instructions tell me I should be able to access Skeeter's computer
as though it was an external hard drive attached to mine. I can't
believe it will be that simple, but I follow the instructions closely
and, after a while, I am surprised when it works.

I catch my breath before I progress, still not quite believing how
easy it was; then I remember that everything is easy when you
know how. Just as the article said, I see the hard drive of Skeeter's
computer in the same way I see my own external hard drive on the
infrequent occasions when I remember to do a backup.

Now that I'm in, I don't even know what I'm looking for other
than everything and anything that will help me figure out what
has become of Cameron. I catch my breath and think about it
while I poke around. Part of me had not even really believed I'd
get this far. I'm no hacker. And now here I am.

And there's just so much information. The computer looked old
and battered but it's pretty close to state of the art, and the storage
capacity is a half terabyte with a lot of it being used. Sure: needle
in haystack, indeed.

I watch myself fall into an abyss of data. Information overload—
is that what they call it? It takes me a while to realize it, but when
I do I put it all aside for a bit, change into shorts and sandals,
slather on sunscreen, put on a hat, and head out for a walk.

There are plenty of cars on the street but not many people moving around, and I soon discover why: it's Tempe, Arizona, in high summer and so it's the city, but it's also the desert, and walking around the city streets at midday is like walking around in a blow dryer. It's so hot it almost knocks the wind out of you. It makes me think longingly of my home at the edge of a forest. I'd never realized before how green and lush it is there. I'd taken all that rainforest business sort of for granted. And now, quite suddenly, my heart misses it. As does my skin. It is dry and brown here, and hot, hot, hot.

Even so, Tempe is lovely. Today a bright blue sky is shot through with deliberate-looking clouds. So beautiful and perfect, it is as though they are constructed; an artful addition. And it may be hot out, but it's a college town, so there are interesting shops and restaurants strewn around and even little squares where fountains play.

I find a cafe where misters cool the patio temperature a full ten degrees. That means it's still super-hot, but bearable. Because it's so hot out, almost all the tables on the charming patio are empty. I choose one near the fountain and where the misters are actually hitting me with water and then I settle in.

I order an iced coffee and think about the challenge ahead of me. What is it I'm actually looking for? My instincts had guided me. But now that I have the computer, I wonder how it might be helpful to me. Should I have followed the man rather than grabbed the machine? I am filled with a sort of hopeless regret because I can't take it back. The computer is what I've got. I'll have to work with that.

I am so deep in thought that I don't notice two young women take a seat at a table near me. Maybe they're from out of town, too, and determined to take advantage of a sunny day, because they don't seem to notice the heat.

I'm lost in my own thoughts, so I don't try to hear their conversation, but snippets of what they say drift in my direction. Conveyed by the wind? Just about everything I hear them say is nonsensical to me—out of context—and I try not to listen, but then I hear one thing and for some reason it resonates with me so strongly, it changes the whole picture.

"Sometimes the thing you're looking for is the one thing you can't see," says one.

"S'truth," says the other.

And I just sit there, dumbstruck and considering. Have I been looking right at the answer and not seeing what I need? Am I doing the very thing they're talking about? And I realize: possibly.

I feel energized and ready to tackle everything in front of me. I finish my coffee and head back to my perfectly air-conditioned hotel room. No matter what else is true, I know I've got to take a leap.

So I jump.

CHAPTER TWENTY-THREE

THE ONLY MAIL program on Skeeter's computer is the native Apple email program, Apple Mail. That simplifies things, because at least I only have to find the files associated with a single email program.

I take a run at looking at messages because correspondence seems a good place to begin. However, I soon realize it's not as simple as it would be if the messages were on a computer that I was using. I have to figure out where the email messages are stored, then access user files. I'm not even sure about what needs to be done, and I'm stopping occasionally to google for instructions, so the whole thing is a bigger job than it would be for, say, someone who actually did understand what the hell they were doing.

I consult with Google and I ask YouTube and so I make my way one tiny step at a time toward my goal of actually being able to see what is in Skeeter's inbox. All the while I'm hoping he's one of those people who never deletes anything,

I spend another quarter hour with Google and come back with what looks like it could be the right answer. I have to search through the user files on a specified location on the computer that I am guided to by yet another online conversation found by watching a YouTube video after seeing something in, of all places, Pinterest.

I locate the file, drag it to the prescribed area, then open it as a folder in the main program of my own computer. Thinking of all the steps it seems like a lot, but making each discovery along the way has been so satisfying that it keeps me engaged, and the little successes keep me pressing forward. And finally, I discover that I have arrived.

Once I am able to start going through the mail files, I discover that Skeeter probably does delete some stuff, but I find some pretty interesting leads, anyway. For one thing, he's made a reservation on a hotel booking site for a suite in a hotel in Washington, D.C. The reservation began the previous night, even though I saw Skeeter himself in Lourdes this morning and then saw him getting ready to leave on a flight from an airport that doesn't schedule flights to Reagan National Airport in Arlington. Why rent an empty hotel room? Unless, of course, it was never empty at all. The whole setup gives me hope.

I am unsurprised at email exchanges between Skeeter and several special interest groups to do with range management. Some of the exchanges are strongly in favor of upholding and defending the rancher's right to grazing livestock on public lands. Some are vehemently opposed.

The correspondences include personal letters to high-ranking politicians as well as other ranchers. Some name specific amounts Skeeter is donating to them personally or through various lobby groups he is connected with. The money is earmarked to support political campaigns, but I see more sinister implications, and I don't think I'm jumping at shadows. I conclude that the money is actually meant to grease livestock grazing permits and even continue to support the whole system. One that, as interest in beef wanes and environmental concerns increase, I imagine would be more difficult to maintain and explain.

I find, also, correspondence with a Baltimore-area real estate agent about a piece of property in a town with a name I don't recognize. What's remarkable to me is that, though the thread of messages are between Skeeter and a realtor, the deal is being done in Cameron's name. I try to think what that might mean and how it's even possible, and I come up empty.

Are Skeeter and Cameron working together on something? The idea seems so unlikely, I dismiss the thought out of hand. And yet, the documentation is here. And I get this heavy feeling in the bottom of my gut: Is it possible they're in cahoots? Is it possible that all of that horse- and environment-loving talk was just an act Cameron had put together for the purpose of defrauding some-one/everyone?

Was what Cameron presented even real? The thought flits through my mind, but then I push it away. No. It's not possible. Cameron's love of horses is not only real, it's hereditary. He didn't create the work he does; his father did. I think that my instincts about people tend to be good and there had been nothing about Cameron that set off any alarms. I couldn't imagine that his love of horses and dedication to their well-being was anything beyond real and true. I put my head down; get back to work.

Digging deeper, I find links to a Twitter account. The email comes in the form of prompts to an account for @angryrancher that is apparently operated by Skeeter. Looking at the account on Twitter, it is absolutely anonymous, but it's clear to me from the email breadcrumbs in his inbox that Skeeter is, indeed, the *angry rancher* in question. As I scroll through postings over the course of a few months, the threads in the account becomes ever more angry—as advertised—and more and more unhinged, though I admit I'm not the most unbiased possible viewer.

Wild equines are the parasites that continue to be the plague of the American west. How long are we going to allow these interlopers from other lands to push noble American cattle from the range they have inherited by right?

Euthanasia is the only correct and longterm answer for the very serious threat posed by feral horses in the American west and southwest. The dangers they pose to all America holds dear can't be overstated.

Euthanasia. That seemed a very hard line. Before I began this whole adventure, I hadn't even imagined there might be people in the world who would advocate for something like that: killing wild horses to get them off the range. I had, I suppose, imagined that everyone thought horses were as beautiful and noble as I thought them. From these postings, though, and others they intersected with, it turned out that there were a whole cross-section of people who saw other radical solutions for getting horses off the range. Granted, I was a layperson, but the arguments seemed irrational. The numbers alone were staggering. The public lands were currently supporting over seven million livestock AUMs. In the same period, the horses were at about half a million, and the agency responsible for them was working to radically reduce that number. It didn't seem right.

Though comments like the parasite one seemed to have some support, the vast majority of the tweeters seemed either steeply opposed or else counsel a less militant approach. As I read, it interests me to find that, in the days leading up to Cameron's disappearance, these online discussions seemed to come to a fever pitch.

Then, on the day after the event—today—they stop abruptly. Though Skeeter seems to post frequently every single day, today there hasn't been a peep. It takes me a minute to realize two things: One, he is traveling. And, two, I have his laptop. There might be perfectly good reasons for him not to be posting today. But he likely still has a phone and possibly a backup of this computer. I know I'll be keeping an eye on this account for any action. Meanwhile, I've got travel plans to make and then, as soon as possible, a plane to catch.

CHAPTER TWENTY-FOUR

It takes me a little while to realize that, before I can possibly jaunt off to Washington, D.C., I have to go home. For one thing, I only brought enough clothes for a few days. For another, I was packing for a quick jaunt into the desert. And even though I wasn't planning on sightseeing, dressing for a visit to the nation's capital is a whole different thing. Plus, if I'm very honest, I have to admit that I miss the dog.

The first thing I do is decide to make use of that ticket from Mesa-Gateway that I'd never planned on using. Since I bought it less than twenty-four hours earlier, I am able to trade it in on a flight that will get me close enough to home.

In the airport and on the flight, I keep my eyes open, but I don't get a repeat of the sense of being followed and I'm relieved. Maybe it was all in my imagination, that feeling. Maybe no one has been following me at all.

From the airport I use something that is not unlike my usual route to get home. I travel from the airport via shuttle, then I take the shuttle to the distant parking lot where I left my car.

Once in the car, I take a circuitous and indirect route to my little house deep in the country. I have no doubt why I've really bothered to make the trip—but when I see his face it is brought home to me. He is standing on his hind legs, front paws on the yard fence, and he is barking joyously at my approach.

"Hey," I say, scritching his stomach when he calms a bit. "How are you? All good? Everything good?"

Slowly his joyous wriggles subside and he puts his soft muzzle into the palm of my hand and just breathes me in.

"I've got another trip coming," I tell him, but I figure it's possible he already knows in that empathic doggy way he has of knowing everything.

Dog greetings out of the way, I find it's good to be home, but somehow also it's different. I think about that. What has changed? At first when I look around, I think that nothing has. Then I register that this is not entirely true. I'm different, that's what's changed. I'm not the same as I was before. I've been touched by something unexpected. I realize it all with a sort of damp wonder.

The fragility of the feeling frightens me, but I can't shake it. It's like something in me has been strengthened by discovery, then weakened again by loss. I reflect on myself and what I've become. On who I am. It comes to me in one big lump of straddling realization that despite everything I have gone through and everything I have discovered about myself, I am someone who can love. That's new. And how that's even possible after all I've been through, I don't know. It shouldn't be, really. Yet there it is.

For whatever reason, I have discovered that I am able to let my guard down enough to love. I decide to like that about myself. I who have seldom given myself the acknowledgment—and love—I deserve am able to see this thing that I judge to be good about me.

At the same time, I recognize I am now being punished for my vulnerability. Even while I have this thought, I realize it is inappropriate. It is arrogant. Cameron's disappearance is not about me.

It's not about anything I did or anything in my background. Intellectually, I know all of this. Still. The feeling persists. I know that it isn't at all about me. Still. Somehow, I can't help but feel Cameron's disappearance is my fault. If I'd been able to ride better. Follow more quickly. Or, maybe better yet, if I'd suggested some other activity and we hadn't been there at all. And even while I attack myself with it all, I recognize these self-recriminations for what they are: regret for things seen and unseen.

And so I breathe with it. What else is there to do? I remember to breathe. Sometimes I have to remind myself. Now seems to be one of those times.

Other than breathing, there's little for me to do to prepare my home for another absence, but I set about it. When the phone rings I am so engulfed in these activities that I barely notice that the call is coming from Kuala Lumpur. I answer, but don't comment on the location. It doesn't really matter anyway.

"I have another job for you." I think back to a time when my assignments came anonymously. Was that a better way? I'm not sure, but when I reflect on it, a little wave of nostalgia floats along with the thought. Sometimes it truly *was* better when the assignments arrived disembodied.

"Wait . . . what? Another assignment? But the last one is not complete."

"I told you," she says, and something in her voice announces that she is aware of sounding patient. "The job has been canceled. For all intents and purposes, it's as complete as it's going to be."

"Can you tell me why?"

"Why what?"

"Why the job has been canceled."

"No," she says, and I understand from her tone that it's a ridiculous question. "It's old news. And it doesn't matter. It's beyond our concern. In any case, you won't lose your deposit, so it may as well have been done."

"How often does that happen?"

"Does what happen?" She does not ask me why we are still talking about this, but I hear it in her voice. The forced patience I heard a few moments before is wearing thin.

"A cancellation."

"Never. Almost never. But it's happened this time. Let's leave it alone."

"Okay, I'll leave it," I say, feeling dangerous. Feeling deadly. "Then no."

"No what?"

"I'm not ready for another job."

Then I terminate the call.

*   *   *

I can feel it. I am living dangerously. It puts every one of my nerves on end. It's a feeling, deep in my throat. Excitement mixed with fear. I realize that the choice I have made—turning down a job—can potentially cost me my life. I don't actually think that it will. I feel it is possible that I have, over time, built enough credit with those who manage my career that they will cut me some slack. But it's not like other businesses, so one never really knows. And if I'm wrong? Well, I'll never know that, either.

*   *   *

In the morning, it is raining. Really raining. Nothing ambiguous, but the type of rain that sounds as though a giant is standing above your house with a garden hose. A giant-sized garden hose. Movie rain. I stand at the front door and look at it. It is beautiful and everything smells fresh, but it is interrupting my plans. I had hoped for a walk in the forest with the dog. Maybe even the chance to paint. But no. Even I don't want to brave weather this ferocious.

Though I regret not being able to go for a walk, I am relieved to discover that I am still alive. It wasn't a foregone conclusion. Not that I think anyone knows where I am, but in my line of work, one is never quite sure what anyone else knows. It would be nerve-wracking if I were geared that way: to have my nerves wracked. But fortunately, I am not.

Because of the rain, instead of going for a walk, I pack my suit-case. I make sure I've included some business wear and I tuck Skeeter's laptop in there, too. Then I schlep all my gear out to the car in the rain, double-check that all of the dog's needs have been seen to. When I head out, I deliberately ignore the sharp pang I feel at leaving him home alone once again and the softly reproach-ful look I imagine I see in his eyes when I go out the door.

I've only been on the road for a short time when I once again get that familiar feeling. What's the expression? Like someone walking on my grave. Even though that isn't a thing, at all. It's more like a feeling. Of what? It's like a shiver. I check my rearview mirror and I peer into the forest next to the car as it flashes past. I watch the road ahead closely. All nothing. My imagination? I don't discount my senses completely. I've been looking over my shoulder for much too long not to listen to a strong feeling when it arrives.

Even so, when I look there is nothing to see, so I press on. And the miles fly by. And after a while, I put it out of my mind. And the road behind me stays clear.

CHAPTER TWENTY-FIVE

WHEN I GET to the long-term lot, I park behind a pickup truck while I watch the entrance. In the time that I am waiting and watching, I pick up my phone. I don't know whose hands Cameron's device might have gotten into, so I hit *67 before I try his number. I know that doing so will make my call show up as coming from an anonymous caller no matter who has his phone. And if no one does, or even if he answers, it won't matter.

There are a lot of rings and then voicemail. It was the same one I'd heard last week when I'd called. His voice, sure and strong and holding the trace of a smile. "Hi, this is Cameron. I'm sorry to have missed your call. Please leave your name, number, and the best time to reach you as well as what you're calling about."

I hang up. Then I dial again and get the same result. I listen once more, all the way through. I tell myself it isn't just to hear the sound of his voice. This time I prepare to leave a message, but I end up hanging up again at the last second. And I'm not even exactly sure why. The words just get caught in my throat.

While I'm musing about phone calls, a nondescript dark sedan pulls in. I slouch a little in my seat, but maintain my position: fairly certain that among all of these cars, I am hidden in plain view.

The car sets out to circumnavigate the lot, like the driver doesn't quite know what's being looked for. As the car slides past my position, I get a fast glimpse of a ballcap, sandy brown hair, and a youthful profile. I would guess a very young man, but I wouldn't be able to be sure.

As I'd hoped, the driver doesn't see me, here amid all these hundreds of cars, and, after a while, the car leaves the lot, presumably heading out to search still further. I sit there quietly for a bit, ruminating. The profile was not familiar to me in any way but I am perplexed. In this world, there are many people that might be looking for me, for many different reasons. But a very young man who does not seem particularly skilled at following? No. I can't think of any reason someone like that would be looking for me.

* * *

The flight is uneventful. Washington, D.C., is one of the hot spots of the United States. Where the U.S. goes to work. All sorts of people come from all over the country to spend time close to the center of the country's power, and they do it for a lot of reasons. Because of that, it's an easy place to move around in. If you ever want to be invisible, go to Washington, D.C. No one looks at you directly there. It's an eerie feeling.

It is not my first trip to the city. Flying into Reagan, I think about that. At the time in my life when I was someone's mother, and someone's wife, there were so many places I hadn't been that I have now been. Then I had never been to the nation's capital. That means I've never been there as a tourist, which I think is a shame. Everyone should go at least once. Every American. Visiting there makes you feel more . . . American somehow. More like you are part of this great collective we are signed up for at birth.

I know intellectually that the city is beautiful. The architecture is low and elegant, every building steeped in history and created by careful and loving hands. But honestly, I don't see much of that unless I really make myself look. To me it has always been a place to get some work done. It's always been business there for me. And I guess that's only to be expected because, after all, it's a company town. It seems that almost everyone you meet or talk to has some relationship to government. Either they work for some branch of it, or they work for some outfit that services some aspect of governing or some other thing that somehow connects them to the business of keeping the country running.

Today, though, none of that is my point of concern. Or maybe it is. Belle had told me that Cameron had been scheduled to take part in some hearings, though not for another few days. And I, myself, had heard him say he was here now on the voicemail he'd left for Belle. I'm thinking it makes sense for me to be here, too. Maybe not a lot of sense, but desperate sense, I guess. If I'm to find him, this is where I'll start to look. All roads lead here.

I have the Uber deliver me to the hotel Skeeter had booked. I've booked a more modest room in the same hotel. How certain am I that Skeeter has Cameron stashed there already? So certain. I'd be willing to bet my last dollar on it. Even more serious: I'd be willing to bet my *dog*.

The hotel is nice, though I've been in better. It's the sort of heading-to-seed operation that can trick online ticket sellers into giving four-star ratings. This was probably once an actual four-star hotel, but it isn't now. I don't think it's dangerous, though. Just a bit dodgy, so I settle into my surroundings and try to think about my next move.

It seems possible to me—even likely—that Cameron is in this very building. I try to feel excited about that, but it just doesn't take. I don't let the feeling psych me out, though. I don't allow myself to believe or even think that just because I don't feel his vibration, it doesn't mean he's not here. That whole feeling of vibrations thing can be vastly overrated. That's what I'm thinking now. And while I occasionally run down woo woo alleys, it's not my natural way of being.

My room is serviceable but unexceptional. At first glance everything seems perfect, but then you notice that the toilet roll holder is wobbly and there aren't enough hangers in the closet. The remote control has cellophane folded over it rather than a great cleaning in between guests, and some of the furniture is pitted with long use.

I'd hoped for some kind of view, and I have one: my window looks down over the closed and covered hotel pool and out across to the back of another building. I can see gray sky and a parking garage and, other than that closed pool, that's about it.

But I'm not here for sightseeing. If I were, I would have booked a better room. I haven't even unpacked when I use the house phone to call down to the desk. Before I even try it, I know it's going to be a lame attempt—not worth the time I'm about to take making a run at it—but you've got to start somewhere and it would be stupid to leave this simple stone unturned.

"Hi there," I say brightly to the front desk when someone answers. "I'm supposed to meet Skeeter Allaband in his room at five fifteen, but I completely forgot the room number. What room is he in, please?"

"I'm sorry. I can't give out that information. However, I can connect you if you like."

"I understand, but I'm afraid if I don't show up at five fifteen, there's a very good chance I won't get the job I'm applying for. It's just so silly of me. I should have remembered, but—"

"I'm sorry, ma'am," he says interrupting, though not unkindly. "I'd really like to help. But it just isn't possible for me to give you a room number. It's actually against several hotel policies. But I can try his room for you, if you like," he says again. Patient. Polite. He gets full marks.

"That won't be necessary," I say. "Thanks for your help." And to my credit, I don't say it with sarcasm.

After I've ended the call, I think on all of this for a while, and then I find I'm going around in circles and the walls start closing in. What am I even doing here, so far from my home and Cameron's? I don't even know for sure that he's in the city. Plus, I had an assignment and now not only do I not, I'm turning down perfectly good assignments, as well.

I decide a change of scene might calm my nerves and get me ready to see things evenly: light the way toward what my next move should be. I change into something slinky but comfortable—I'm in the city, after all—then I pop my laptop into my bag and get ready to head down to the lobby bar.

I am ready to leave my room when I have an odd thought. What if I were to run into him—would it seem as though I was stalking him? Though, if it did seem that way, it would only be because I absolutely was. And then I scoff at myself for the thought: I have believed from the first that, wherever Cameron is, he is being held against his will. It's just obvious from the way things went down. But my own insecurities force me to hesitate, even if I know that even thinking that is dumb.

After a while, I shake myself out of my room and drop down in the elevator to get to the hotel bar. Once there, I discover that this is where all of the aging hotel's remaining grandeur is now located. It's really pretty nice. There's a baby grand in one corner and some old guy is tickling the ivories. In the space of not very long I hear

"Sweet Caroline" and "Don't Stop Believin'" and "Livin' on a Prayer" and a bunch of other songs whose melodies and histories I sort of only barely know. It seems entirely possible to me that this same piano player has been doing what he does in that very spot since the 1980s, only occasionally updating his material to incorporate new piano bar songs as they emerge. A very specific kind of soft rock.

Once I take a seat, the music sinks into the background. I take a deep breath and welcome the peace.

The other occupants of the bar seem to be in the same headspace that I am. They want to be alone, but in company. I get that. That's not a bad place to be.

I take my place in a small sitting area: two small sofas with a coffee table between them. It's meant to feel as though it is in someone's elegant home, but of course there are other sitting areas, just like that, scattered through the space.

I'm still dragging my laptop out of my bag when a waiter comes to take my order. It doesn't take much thinking for me to ask for an Aperol spritz and some warmed olives: an easy, low-impact choice, but I don't know what I'm hoping for.

Sitting across from me, and at a distance of only about six feet, is a long, lean man wearing a cowboy hat and boots to match. I think he looks vaguely familiar, but I chastise myself about that. It isn't possible. What are the odds that this could be the man I'd seen driving when Skeeter arrived at Sam's Cafe? I try to put it out of my mind while I address my computer. After a while the drink and olives show up. The Aperol spritz is refreshing. It hits the spot and the olives are delicious. Another spot. And I didn't even know I was hungry.

As I sip tentatively, I shoot a look at the man in the cowboy hat from under my lashes. I'm certain I can't possibly be right about his identity. After all, there are plenty of regions in the U.S. where someone wearing cowboy garb could get the idea a Stetson hat and boots are proper business attire, aren't there? But the more I sneak peeks at him, the more I think I'm not wrong. It's Skeeter's driver. Even though it seems like too small a world. On the other hand, I know this to be the hotel Skeeter is staying at and I booked here for that reason, so maybe it's not such a coincidence after all.

From a distance, I look again at his gear: The hat. The boots. The belt. There aren't a lot of assorted lawyers and lobbyists around here who wear stuff like that. I wonder what, if anything, I should do. I could approach him. But what can I say? And what, really, do I want, other than being able to get into that hotel room to see if Cameron is there? Still. I'm pretty sure he has the keys to that kingdom.

Then an idea comes to me. I check the settings on my phone: the connections available to me. Aside from the hotel guest Wi-Fi and some of the secured Wi-Fi networks that aren't identified, I see that I can also try to connect to "Yvonne's iPhone" or "Terry's phone." I look around. There's an attractive blonde who could be a lawyer or a lobbyist or even a television anchor sitting one table away from me working on her laptop and sipping what looks like a martini. I'm guessing that's Yvonne.

Additionally, there are two men sitting near me, not together. Either of them could be the Terry from Terry's phone. That means I have a 50-50 shot. I've certainly been up against worse odds.

I approach the cowboy.

"Terry?"

"Yes," he says, looking up from his phone. There is no recognition in his face, but I can see him preparing to fake it.

"I thought that was you," I say warmly, sitting down at the table and propping my head on my hands, looking at him expectantly, aiming even for a touch of coquette, though that's never been my strong suit. "It's good to see you," I say, floating an invitation into my voice.

"I'm sorry," he says apologetically, and I can see he means it. "You have an advantage over me."

"Oh I love it!" I send him my best smile. "How often does that happen?" We both laugh. I've cast an old reel, but I can feel him biting.

"No," he corrects. "I meant I really feel as though I should recognize you. But I don't."

"It'll come to you," I say. "And when it does, I'm right over there." I point back in the direction of my drink and olives and smile before I walk back there and retake my original seat.

I can almost hear him racking his brain, trying to figure out how to play this, but life intervenes. I'm sitting in my seat, trying to figure my next move, when Skeeter shows up and starts talking to Terry, confirming my identification, even though since the time we'd started talking, I hadn't really felt it needed confirming.

I have a bad moment, thinking Skeeter might recognize me from Sam's Cafe or the airport. Then I talk myself down. The chances of him recognizing me are so small, they practically don't exist. I'm pretty sure he didn't even see me then. Certainly not before I took the laptop. And afterwards he would have had other things on his mind.

Skeeter drops down into the chair next to Terry and waves the server away. Then the two men chat quietly for a few minutes. At one point, Terry glances over at me and I wave back at him, trying to look cute, even though cute is not generally in my repertoire. It seems called for here. He gives a small wave back, then instantly turns his attention back to Skeeter.

After a few minutes of close talking, Skeeter gets up and heads out of the hotel. Terry appears to wait for a few minutes. I can almost hear him biding his time, trying to gauge the moment when it is right to approach me and also when his boss is no longer around. And just as I begin to wonder if it was either my imagination or wishful thinking, Terry gets up from his seat, grabs his drink, and saunters in my direction, super casual.

"I think I've got it," he says as he approaches.

"Oh yeah?" I say.

"I believe we met at Prada Del Sol. The Scottsdale Rodeo. Is that right?"

I sip my drink. I am as coquettish as I can muster and I smile. But I don't really answer.

"Something like that," I say. "But you're a long way from Arizona. What brings you here?"

"Hey," he replies. "I'm not the only one far from home. What are you doing here?"

"I asked first," I say.

"That's true. Okay: I'm here with my boss. You just saw him. He has business here. I just make sure everything goes smoothly."

"That's your job?"

"Yes." He kind of grunts it.

"You're his ameliorator?"

He looks at me askance. I wonder if I've overplayed my hand, but I'm relieved when he laughs.

"Something like that," he says. And then he grins. "If I knew what the word was."

I smile back and position myself so he has a clear view down the front of my not-particularly low-cut blouse. It's meant to feel like a secret. I am instantly aware that he's gotten the message.

"It's like a fixer, I guess. Ameliorator. Someone who has all the answers." I bat my eyes at him, careful not to let him see that I find it a loathsome game. "Answers to questions that haven't been asked."

He grins at that. I can tell he likes the description and the implication. He looks willing, but not that smart.

"I guess so," he says. "That pretty much sounds like me."

"I thought so," I say, but my answer is really in my eyes.

By now, both of our drinks are empty.

"Let's have another one, and then I have to run out and do an errand. Maybe we can meet up a bit later? For dinner?"

"I'd like that," I say.

He flags our server and we order another round. I get a second Aperol spritz. He gets a Manhattan. When the drinks come, he takes the check and signs for the drinks. I pay close attention and make a mental note when he marks 1582 in the place where the room number goes. I'm on eight. Somehow that makes sense to me: that Skeeter would have made sure he had a higher floor. And he signs it: "Terry Elrod." I make note of that, too.

We sip our drinks and talk about nothing for a while. Then he leaves and I sit there for a few minutes, perusing my phone and just passing time. I keep my face neutral and placid, but inside I'm thinking fast. I figure I've got one chance at this, and one only.

I go to the front desk. I make sure I am looking distraught. There's a young man behind the desk. He's wearing a suit. A sign on his lapel says his name is Dean.

"Hello, Dean. I'm so sorry to disturb you. I'm in 1582. And it seems I left my keycard—and my whole wallet—in the room."

"What is your name?"

"Terry Elrod," I say.

"Can I see your driver's license, please, Terry?"

"That's just it." I say it quietly, like it is costing me everything I have from losing my shit. "I'd left everything in the room. Including the keycard I'm thinking. I don't . . . I just don't know what to do."

The guy looks me up and down, then smiles sympathetically.

"These things happen. Let me get you a new keycard. Maybe you can stop by the desk a little later? Show me your ID?"

I nod and smile gratefully while he makes the card.

"Thank you so much," I say. "I really appreciate this."

As I head to the elevator, I know I'm projecting calm and cool and grateful but, in reality, I know I don't have much time. Terry had said he'd be back in a few hours to take me for a late dinner. And I don't have any intel on Skeeter's schedule at all.

Leaving the hotel desk, I take the elevator to the eighth floor. In my hotel room, and with the door firmly closed, I swap my laptop for my Bersa Thunder, though I know that the firepower from that handgun will be quite beyond what is needed.

While I'm back in my hotel room, I change from clothes meant to allure to clothes meant to move. A dark hoodie and tights and comfortable running shoes, and I pull on a pair of the flesh-colored nitrile gloves I bring with me everywhere. I don't dawdle, though. I don't know how much time—if any—I'm going to have.

I get up to the 15th floor easily, but I hesitate outside of 1582. What do I think I'm going to find? I don't even admit to myself that I'm hoping that once I get in there, I'll find Cameron and somehow be able to spring him from whatever shackles they have him in. Rescue him. And I want this chapter over. I want this man back in my arms. I want to be able to continue what we were starting so that we can see where it might lead. Is it really so much to ask? I don't think so.

And so, first things first. I tread the deeply carpeted hallway until I get to the door, wondering as I get there how it is possible that the carpet feels so much deeper on this rarified floor.

When I reach the door, I knock. Just in case. I don't even know what story I have in mind if someone answers, but I'm pretty sure no one will.

I'm not wrong.

When no one answers or calls out, I insert the keycard, half expecting that the green light that means success won't come on. But it does and I press forward, into the main room of the suite.

I find myself standing in a spacious living room. Big windows look toward the Capitol building. It's a much better view than the one from my room, I note. This view is much more appealing than the pool that appears to be closed for repairs that I see from my room.

I am standing in the suite's main room. From there, two doors lead off, one to the left, the other to the right. I'm guessing that they are bedrooms, though I can't tell because both doors are closed. It's quiet here, I notice, while I stand and decide to do what I need to do. The only noise is the subdued hush of the AC and my own quiet maneuverings.

Still concerned I'll run out of time, I press ahead, choosing to try the door on the left first, for no other reason than it's the one that is closer to me.

Inside, the room is in controlled disarray, not unusual for a hotel room, at least not for me. Clothes are strewn about, but not oddly. I have a peek in the bathroom—men's toilet products and dental products but nothing odd or off.

After that I cross the living room to check out the other bedroom. In this room, there is still no sign of Cameron, but I get a clue about who is staying here when I recognize Skeeter's battered briefcase. A shiny new MacBook is nestled next to it, I note. I suppress the urge to steal this one, too.

I check this bathroom, but so far nothing beyond the expected: toothbrush, shaving stuff, towels askew. I'm shocked not to find Cameron here. I'd been so sure. But it's clear that, if he ever was here, he isn't now.

I am about to head for the exit when I hear an unmistakable sound. Someone is using their keycard. I feel myself look left, then right, then left again, like a cartoon character that's about to get caught red-handed. I can almost hear the silly music, even though silly is the last thing I feel. And I'm hoping it's *not* the last thing I'll feel. But I'm caught and there is just nowhere to go.

There are a couple of beeps and then I hear the dead bolt slide back and the door opening. In that split second, I realize that I should have had a backup plan. But I didn't. I'd been so certain I'd find Cameron, free him, and get him out of there. Getting caught had not entered my mind, and now I'm stuck.

I think about sliding under and out of sight, but as is the case in many hotels, the base of the large bed appears to be a solid platform: there is no "under" this particular bed.

There's a closet. I searched it recently so I know that it is small, but it's not like I have any choice: it's the only game in town. I scamper over and pull the closet door shut behind me, then I slide silently down, so I am sitting on the closet floor. And then I just breathe as quietly as I can. It seems to me to be an actual matter of life and death because, if I'm halfway right about these guys, they won't hesitate to kill me—or see me dead—if I get in their way and—hell—I'm in the closet. I'm pretty much already in the way.

And so I meditate for a while, being conscious of my breath without being noisy about it. No box breathing today. I breathe in and out silently, focusing on a place in the dark just in front of my eyes. I try to get to a meditative state—it's hard at first, with so much buzzing around in my monkey mind. But after a while I settle in and my breathing evens out and I reach a state of something like calm. It's enough.

I have just settled fully and deeply into the rhythm of my breathing when I hear someone come into the room.

"I feel like I closed this door when I left." Skeeter says it quite loudly, perhaps talking to someone over his shoulder.

I could tell him that he did, but I figure I'm the last person he wants to hear from right now. I keep it to myself.

"Me, too," comes the answer from a distance. Maybe this is Terry, but between him being in the other room and me being in the closet, I can't tell for sure. I know it doesn't matter anyway: I'm in a closet, and the guy whose laptop I stole a few days ago in Arizona is on the other side of a flimsy closet door. If I sneeze or he decides to put a jacket away, I'm sunk. The one bit of reassurance: the strewn clothes I spied throughout the room make me think there won't be a lot of hanging stuff up.

I sit there quietly for a while, shifting my weight from one haunch to the other and not wanting to feel anything drifting off to sleep. Unlike my butt, the men show no signs of dozing off. I hear their voices. Idly I wonder what Terry will do when it's time for dinner and he tries to call me and discovers that the phone number I gave him was fake. That had been a risk. What if I run into him again? I tell myself it doesn't matter. I probably wouldn't be the first girl he bought a drink for who gave him a fake number. And, anyway, at the moment it's not even a sure thing I'll get out of *this* predicament alive, never mind some future one that I might not even reach.

Most of the time, while I crouch in the dark, I can't make out what's being said. I'm guessing they are in the other room, but I have no way of knowing.

After a while I realize that I have been in the dark for hours and it's only really getting to be a problem because I feel the need to pee. I curse the second Aperol spritz and hope I can find a way to get out of here before things get urgent.

In the dark, trapped in a closet, I toy with possibilities and run various scenarios to get out of there through my mind. None of them have good outcomes. Creeping out once the men are asleep is the only thing that looks like it has even the possibility of working, and that poses its own dangers.

The silence is broken when I hear the distinctive trill of a mobile phone ringing nearby. There's no mistaking the sound. And then footsteps. Heavy ones. Skeeter's phone, maybe left on a nightstand. I can't be sure, but it sounds like that to me because his voice, when he answers, seems very close.

"Hey." Skeeter's voice is a distinctive scratchy growl. And though I hope he puts the caller on speaker, he doesn't comply, and I am left in the dark about what is being said. And, of course, just in the dark, too. He doesn't hear my silent plea.

"Well, I'm not sure how to respond to that," he's saying. "I don't figure it's that tall an order."

More silence. And then. "Shady Side, sure. That's what I told you." A pause. And then, "You can't miss it, Mitch. The wood is so old, it looks gray. A sorta ramshackle look, I guess. But sturdy enough for these purposes. End of Columbia Beach Road. Okay, well, near the end." More silence, and then, "All right then, I'll see you there tomorrow after noon. We'll get this thing sorted."

Columbia Beach Road. Now bells are ringing. I'm certain that's where the piece of property Skeeter had somehow bought in Cameron's name was located: Shady Side, Maryland. It was an easy enough name to remember. I feel the familiar tingle of connection, even though I'm not sure yet what is being connected, and since I'm currently hiding in a closet, I'm not even free to properly think it through. Even so, before he hangs up, I've got my own phone out, shading the light from the screen but calculating distances. Columbia Beach Road in Shady Side. With those handles, I'm almost surprised they turn out to be real places. All of this is feeling imaginary. Can I actually still be trapped in a closet while a possible kidnapper chats on the phone? I think back to middle school. This was just not a picture I'd ever have imagined for my life. In truth, I realize, so little of what my life has become could have been forecast. Maybe that's true for everyone. Sitting in a closet, though, it just brings it all too close.

After Skeeter ends the call, things quiet down somewhat. Later still, the silence seems to deepen further. I am reassured when snores begin to rise through the silence. I know that Skeeter is asleep, and I have hope that Terry is asleep, as well.

I force myself to wait a bit longer, wanting them to be well and truly out of it before I risk making a move. That last half hour that I wait is the most difficult. My instinct is to bolt, but I fight that feeling, forcing myself to breathe evenly, inhaling through my nose and exhaling quietly through my mouth. A calming breath.

When I can't wait any longer, I open the closet door ever so slightly: just a single hair. Try to assess. Then a hair more. With the door open, the snoring is more pronounced. I move ahead an inch at a time. Being as silent as I can. A half inch. Skeeter has left the door between his room and the living room open, which gives me an immense break. It means I won't have to worry about the sounds that opening an adjoining door might make. Even so, when I reach the threshold, he stirs. My hand snakes instinctively into my purse, touching the reassuring cold of the Bersa. I flip the safety off, and I do all of this while never taking my eyes off him. Is he waking? I don't think so. I muse that an earlier version of me might have plugged him by now, just to be on the safe side. Somehow I don't feel like playing like that now. Not anymore.

In any case, after a heartbeat or two, he settles back down. The restlessness seems to have been an aberration because it sounds like he drifts back into deep slumber, and I continue my quiet shuffle toward the exit. I'm relieved to see that the door to Terry's room is closed, and I hear the occasional snore from that direction, as well. Stereo snores.

Away from Skeeter's room, I grow bolder, the inches turning to small but full steps. Finally, I attain my goal. At the door to the suite, I risk a glance back. It is full night now, and the Capitol buildings are illuminated as though for show. It *is* for show, I realize. Some of the most distressing performance art in the world has been executed within a few miles of where I stand. I take one appreciative look back and then I slip out the front door, feeling it close behind me with a soft "whoosh."

By the time I step inside the elevator I realize I have been holding my breath and I try to keep breathing regularly until I'm back on the eighth floor.

In my own room, I pull off the gloves while I glance down at the closed pool appreciatively. Capitol views are nice, but it's not what I signed up for. I check the app and book a car on Turo for just a few hours. Shady Side, Maryland. It doesn't sound very inviting. But that's where I'll head, even though I'm not totally sure what I will find. A walk on the shady side. I'm here anyway. I might as well push this thing all the way through.

While I wait for dawn, I clean the Bersa automatically. It pays to be prepared.

CHAPTER TWENTY-SIX

THE TURO CAR I've booked is a Mercedes. It's an older one, and relatively cheap. I pick it up a few blocks from the hotel, where I find it in a parking garage. There is a lockbox on the left back bumper, welded on, I imagine. I am texted a code, which I enter. The lockbox opens and the ignition key practically falls into my hand.

On first inspection I discover that the car is not quite as advertised. It has a big dent in the bumper and another on the right front quarter panel. And it is not perfectly clean. On the bright side: I know I won't look like a tourist in this car, not that it matters. But I will look like I belong.

Google Maps has told me that Shady Side is an hour away, and so I settle in. Rural D.C. is as stunning as can be, despite everything you've ever heard. You imagine the corruption of the Beltway, and while that's not wrong, it is important to note that rural Maryland is not far away at all. Somehow that changes everything.

It changes everything.

And so I push through.

It's a pleasant hour, too, that ride. I had owned a sort of west coast snobbery about what the country looked like, so I am surprised to find that, even here in the east, the country looks much the same. Horses graze on sparse plots and trees grow tall where they can and, sometimes, there are glimpses of water far away. It is beautiful. That, too, surprises me. Rural Maryland to me looks like rural Oregon or rural Washington State. There are differences, of course, and the ocean is on the other side. But some of the important things are just the same.

Near the end of my journey, I take the exit for MD-468, which gets gradually less busy until it turns into Columbia Beach Road, which loops and then twists me toward Chesapeake Bay. Despite what I'd overheard on Skeeter's call the night before, the address and the directions had made me think I would find something lovely: some high-end piece of real estate, view of the bay. But that is not what I find.

I get a pretty clear view from the street. The house is set back from the road in a copse of trees and it appears to be so much a part of the forest you almost wouldn't see it if you weren't keeping a sharp lookout. I park a short distance away wondering what I am going to do. Wondering, also, what I should expect. Will I find Cameron here? My heart tells me I will not, even though, to my mind, evidence has been pointing to the fact that I will. At this stage—and so far in—I don't know what to believe anymore or what I will find, so I proceed with caution. My feet are silent, my eyes are open, and the Bersa is in my bag, oiled and ready to go.

It is about nine a.m. Early morning by many people's standards. Even so, as I cross the yard it is clear to me that the house is still sleeping and not from any information that would be useful to share. That is, instinct tells me, nothing else. There is a stillness about the place. A quiet. One has the feeling of treading past something that is sealed. I do it anyway, pulling flesh-colored gloves on as I cross the lawn toward the side door. I'd hoped to find it unlocked, and I do, slipping in, determined to find Cameron. And if he's here, I tell myself, he's leaving with me. The Bersa's weight in my bag clinches the deal.

Once in the house, I find myself at the end of a corridor. I can tell the kitchen and dining areas sprawl off to my right. The sleeping areas fall to the left. But it is the smell that arrests my attention. I can't place it. Nor can I categorize it: bad or good. Burnt marshmallows, that's what comes to mind, though I'm not sure why. I'm not even sure I've smelled burnt marshmallows before, but that's what registers now: cloyingly sweet.

Since I've come in by the kitchen, that's where I begin. It's a mess. Every surface is covered with something. Empty packages. Dirty dishes. The sink is overflowing. A scarred table, mismatched chairs. An ashtray on the table contains ash, a piece of tinfoil, and a couple of straws. I'm not sure what it means but I suspect it might be the source of the sweet smell—it's stronger here, for one thing. Some deadly kind of incense. I don't understand it, but I feel I almost do. It's just out of my grasp.

In the next room, the curtains are drawn, and so the light is dim, but it is not so dark that you can't see that the living room is also in disarray. There's so much mess that at first I don't even notice the young woman settled among cushions on the sofa.

"Hey," she says when I walk in. She seems neither surprised nor alarmed at my sudden appearance. Now me, I'm surprised and alarmed. Where are my instincts guiding me this time? By walking in the door, I'm basically breaking and entering, and yet I'm also certain this is not that. Something is going on here. Something bad. I just have no idea what it is, but I also have no feeling at all that the stoned-looking young lady on the sofa is about to call the cops on me for breaking into her house, either.

My instincts are confirmed when she smiles at me unsteadily, but she doesn't get up. I have the feeling she couldn't even if she wanted to.

"Hey," I say back, not quite sure what's next.

"Did Terry send you?" I note that while her English is good, her voice is accented. Russian? Ukrainian? I can't place it. Something Eastern European, in any case.

"Something like that," I say. Glad that she has confirmed one thing, at least, when she mentioned Terry's name: I'm in the right place. Or the wrong place, depending—again—on your perspective. "Who else is in the house?"

"Kira was here before," she says, and I feel her stumbling over the words. It's like she's having trouble forming them. "But she's gone now. It's just me."

"And Cameron?"

She looks at me blankly and I doubt that she's faking it.

"I don't know that name," she says after a while, and it sounds like she's telling the truth.

"Mind if I look around?"

She gestures toward the other room. It's all the okay I need.

The first two bedrooms are empty, but not tidy. People have slept here, just not today. I hesitate with my hand on the door-knob of the third and final bedroom. Will I find Cameron here? I still don't really think so, but I've come this far, and not without reason.

Entering the room, I see that there is a form on the bed. At a glance, the covered shape is too small to be Cameron. And the form is still. So very still.

"Hello?" I say, just to let whoever it is know they are not alone. "Everything okay?"

And then I think of the condition of the young woman in the living room. Clearly half out of it. And also what I think is probably drug paraphernalia in the kitchen, plus the general dishevelment. Something is going on here. I just have no idea what it is.

"Excuse me." I say something one more time. And there is still no response. I cross to the other side of the bed, where I can see the face of the sleeper clearly. Only I see that it isn't a sleeper at all. I see the face of a young girl. I'm guessing this is Kira, the name the girl in the living room mentioned. She is very young. In this context I doubt myself, but I would say she is no more than twelve. I have to get close to her to even tell that she is still breathing. I touch a hand to her forehead. It is cold and clammy and her breathing is so shallow, it's hard to even see it at all.

She is alive, but every instinct tells me I need to get her out of there quickly. She is alive, but barely, and I don't even know where to begin.

CHAPTER TWENTY-SEVEN

THERE IS URGENCY, but I counsel myself, once again, to breathe.

There is an order to the steps I'll need to take as I once again dive into something that is none of my business. And I want to move forward, but I know that I'll first have to feel my way. If I knew, that's the thing. If I understood the nature of what I am dealing with. But I don't. I know it's a bad business, but I really just have no clue.

The child seems ill enough that calling 9-1-1 is the option that comes to mind first, but I discard it quickly. My instincts tell me I need to get these girls out of here, and fast. I have no idea what's going on—and the feeling of swimming in darkness isn't helping my mood any—but it's clear they need to not be here when Skeeter shows up. If I have anything to do with it, they will be long gone by then.

Back in the living room, I decide to see if I can back up a little bit, reasoning that it will help if I know what I am dealing with.

"I think I found Kira," I tell the other girl. "I don't think she's quite okay."

The girl looks at me with something like blankness. It chills me.

"I don't know her very well," she says, but I get the feeling she's not telling the truth.

"What is your name?"

Stoned eyes look at me benignly. With the light on I can see she is younger than I had at first reckoned. Perhaps thirteen.

"They call me Libby."

"Libby, where are you from?"

"It doesn't matter anymore. Nothing much matters." She says this absently. Without passion. She is focused on a spot behind me when she says it and then she shifts her eyes to mine. "Let's say Arizona. At least, that's where I ended up. For a time."

"How did you get here?"

"Flew."

"That much I figured. Let me put it a different way. How did you get here, like, what brought you here? Other than a plane, I mean."

"But the plane was cool. No one else was on it, just me and Kira. They gave us food and everything."

A private plane. That doesn't make sense to me, when Skeeter was flying coach. I don't say any of that.

"Ummm . . . cool. You and . . . ?"

She gestures toward the bedroom.

"Kira, yeah. Me and her."

"What do you do, Libby?"

"Smoke. Sit. Relax." She laughs. I don't get the joke.

"You know Skeeter?"

Do I see her eyes darken when I ask this? Do they travel back to that spot just over my right shoulder and just hover for a bit? I think so. Maybe. Either way, I don't need her answer after that. I know.

"Yeah," she says after a beat. "I know Skeeter all right." I can't gauge the thickness of her voice.

"And Cameron?"

"You asked me that already," she says, sounding irritated. "Do you think I'm lying? Or stupid? Either way, I don't know the name."

I ignore the outburst, but it seemed convincing. "Skeeter brought you here?"

"Terry brought us. But yeah." Her eyes seem to clear slightly. So much reality going on. "Wait: Who are you? Why are you asking this stuff?"

"Your friend, Kira, she . . . she's in a bad way, Libby. And I think we have to get you guys out of here."

"Where are we going?"

And truly, at that moment, I have no clear idea.

"Just away," is all I say. "I don't think you're safe here."

"What do you know?" I realize as soon as she says it that she's right. I don't know anything at all. But because she's right, I decide not to mince words.

"I'm not sure," I say honestly. "I just feel I've got to get you someplace safe. And I think Kira might need a hospital."

"I'm safe here." She says it defensively, but I don't think she believes it herself.

"You're not. I have no idea what's going on here, but I do know you're far from safe."

"You said Kira is unwell."

I nod.

"I don't know what's wrong with her, but she doesn't seem right."

"I don't believe you," Libby says.

"Go see for yourself," I say.

At first, I think she's going to decline my challenge. She had looked comfortable there, on the sofa, floating in whatever stoned realm she was presently occupying. After a while, though, I see her sigh and then start to unfold herself unsteadily from the couch.

Her legs are long and coltish and she wavers unsteadily when she first stands. I see her look at me quickly, as though wanting to observe what I saw, but I keep my face neutral and avert my eyes. Let her find her way.

It isn't long before she seems stronger. Strong enough, anyway, to move toward the bedroom. I give her a moment before I follow her, but when I do, I find her standing not far into the room and taking in the scene. For a while she just breathes it all in. I see her reaction float from disbelief in what I had told her to total attention. She takes in the shallow breathing and the fact that she can't get Kira to respond.

"We have to get her out of here," she says after a while, like it's something that's just occurred to her.

"Okay," I tell her without argument.

"You have a car?"

"I do," I say. I'm trying for calm, but really I just want to hustle both girls out of there, even without a clear idea about where we'll go.

Kira is wearing only a T-shirt and panties. I find a light coat and wrap her in it. While she is propped against Libby, the coat falls to her ankles. They stick out from beneath the coat pathetically, tiny little emaciated ankles. If she were conscious, I'm not certain they would hold her weight.

With Kira covered, I find an empty backpack, too, and pick up whatever looks like it might belong to her and toss it in there.

As I complete my self-appointed tasks, Libby rejoins us. She is fully dressed and looks strangely sober. A full backpack slung over one shoulder.

"Let's go," she says. Her eyes are dead and cold. Old.

I don't think about a reply. I grab Kira and am dismayed at how easily I can pick her up. Getting her out to the car is more difficult, not because she's heavy, but her dead weight makes her awkward. Libby and I manage to get her and the backpacks to the battered Mercedes. We lay her on the back seat and Libby covers her friend with a blanket that I hadn't noticed her bring out with her. Libby's every motion conveys concern for the mostly comatose girl.

Once we're locked and loaded, I head the big car back down Columbia Beach Drive, the same way I'd gotten there. We haven't gotten very far when Libby hits the deck. I look around and see a Range Rover Sport, black on black and heading our way. I recognize Terry at the wheel, Skeeter on the passenger side, both in their usual positions.

I gasp at first, feeling ready to duck and hide. Then I realize I am out of context. There's no way they would have noticed me and connected me with anyone they knew, and though a shiny new rental car might have looked out of place, the old beater Mercedes doesn't draw a glance. I drive calmly, slowly. A local mom heading out for groceries or Pilates. In no time at all, they're not even in my rearview anymore.

"They're gone," I tell Libby when she reemerges from the floorboards. "You recognized the car?"

She nods as she retakes the passenger seat.

"Will they come after us?" I notice that she's even paler.

"Possibly," I say. "But not right away. It will take them a while to sort it all through. We'll be far away by the time they figure anything out. And they don't know me or the car anyway." I don't bother telling her about drinks with Terry. It probably isn't relevant anyway.

Libby is satisfied with this answer. It makes sense to her.

I see her check on Kira in the back seat.

"She the same?"

"Yeah," Libby says. "You were right, though. In the first place. We need to get her someplace fast. I think she might be in danger."

By now we've traversed the complicated first steps of getting back to the city and we're on U.S.-50, which we'll take all the way back to D.C. I'm thinking hard, but nothing is coming. I know the kid needs help. On the other hand, I don't know what I'm dealing with. At all. Do I expose myself to save her? Plus, which of the various avenues open to me will get her the best care and best possible outcome? I wrestle with the answer, but I know I can't wrestle for long: we just don't have much time, either way.

When I see a rest stop, I pull over, grab my phone, and excuse myself. I have come to like the girl, but I take the keys with me anyway. Just in case.

There is a bench next to a lake, and I sit there and dial a familiar number. I feel grateful when he answers on the first ring. It's not always easy to get him.

"Curtis, it's good to hear your voice. It's me. I'm so glad to have gotten you. I need your help."

Curtis is a television journalist. I can count on Curtis. You could count on Curtis too, really. Anyone could. When you see him on the screen, announcing news from the field from his Los Angeles–based station, he looks both heroic and paternal. He could be everyone's brother/son/dad. And, maybe surprisingly, he is as reliable as he looks. Not everyone is. And Curtis is my friend. Not to sound pathetic, but sometimes I think he is my only one.

"You need my help? Is this the part where I'm supposed to sound surprised?" And though the words seem callous and uncaring, the tone is not. It is Curtis. He is reliable. There are a lot of people in the world, and you can wonder where you are with them. Not Curtis, though. He is always what he is. He is always what you imagine him to be.

"You will be surprised, though. You'll never guess where I am."

"The Riviera," he says seriously.

"No. Really. Don't guess. You can't."

"The Great Wall."

"Stop it!"

"I won't give up, though. You know that."

"I'm in D.C.," I say, feeding it to him so he'll just stop guessing.

"Oh, you're right. I would never have guessed that."

"Thanks."

"Telling me where you are is probably not why you called."

"Correct," I say. Thinking about how to even broach this subject. And thinking fast because there are places I need to be. I glance back at the car. And there are people waiting on me. I rush into what I've called him about. "I have stumbled upon something here that I just don't know what I'm dealing with. Let me describe the situation."

"Please," he says, all business. I'm glad. I knew I could count on him.

And so I do, without telling him what led me to them. I just tell him that I did. I describe the conditions of the house and of the girls themselves. The possible connection to a wealthy rancher. He asks a few questions. He asks about any smells I might have encountered. Any paraphernalia. I describe the burnt marshmallow sweetness and the ashtray full of weird things.

"And the kid is alive, you said."

"Yeah. I mean, I basically just took her, Curtis. Stuffed her into the back seat of the car and drove."

"Honestly, it sounds like an oxycodone overdose."

"Seriously?" Of all the things I had expected to hear, that wasn't one of them. For one thing, it's an area in which I have no expertise or experience.

"Yeah. Everything you've said lines up. Even that sickly sweet smell."

"How do you know all this stuff?"

"Is her skin blue?"

"What? No, she's not blue. She's not a Smurf, Curtis." I hesitate. Think. Then, "No. Not that I noticed."

"But you said she had respiratory depression."

"What?"

"Her breathing was shallow."

"Right. And she's totally out of it."

"Listen, you've got to get her to a medical professional, stat. What you're describing? She could die there, in the back of your car."

"Oh God."

"Yeah."

"I just don't know what I'm dealing with here, Curtis. Beyond the drugs, I mean. The whole thing. These two young girls in a house in the boonies. I'm completely out of my depth. Does any of what I've told you ring any bells for you?"

"Well, yes actually," he says and I feel an unexpected relief at the words. It isn't just me: it's not all in my mind. "But let me ask you a few more things."

"Go ahead," I say.

"You said the girls were from Arizona?"

"Yes. Well, one I don't know. That was their most recent stop anyway. Before D.C. The one I was talking with has an Eastern European accent. And somehow, she ended up in AZ. The other one hasn't spoken at all." I bite my lower lip as I say it. I am beyond concerned.

"That tracks," Curtis says.

"Tracks in what?"

"Well, Arizona is one of the top spots for human trafficking in the U.S."

"Human . . . what? No. That's not . . . that's not even really a thing, is it?"

"Seriously?"

"And Arizona." It was difficult to believe. I flashed on all that empty desert, cactus silhouettes at sunset and the beautiful mountains that seemed to rim almost everything. "That's unbelievable," I say, but not doubting him even as I say it.

"Were they held against their will?"

"I'm not sure. Maybe. I'm thinking that's why the house is in the middle of nowhere."

"Right," he says. "That makes sense."

"In the middle of nowhere and drugged up."

"Yes. That tracks, as well."

"But, Curtis, what do I do now? You have any suggestions? I mean, I can't just keep them with me. And there may be some danger involved."

"If I'm right about what you're dealing with, I would expect that, yes. Definitely danger at some level. Let me think."

"Think fast, please."

He laughs. He's kind of getting used to me.

"Okay. Well, here's an idea: there's a National Resource Hotline for victims of human trafficking. They have volunteers in every city. Resources and answers. Hang on: let me get you the number."

I see Libby in the passenger seat, looking in my direction with curiosity.

I raise a hand in a wave. Then a single finger: another minute.

"Listen," I say to Curtis, "can you make some arrangements, please? I'm maybe half an hour out of D.C. now. Can you call them for me, please? Set something up? I don't dare stop in one of these little towns with the sick girl, yet I know she needs help fast. But there will be questions. You know. And care for this will likely be better in the city."

"No, no. I hear what you're saying. You're not wrong."

"I'll be driving when you call back to tell me where to go. You'll be on speakerphone when you call, so be oblique."

"I'll see what I can do. But you owe me."

"Yes," I say. "Yes, I do."

CHAPTER TWENTY-EIGHT

WE GET BACK on the highway, but in a surprisingly short time, Curtis calls back.

"You're going to meet Abigail Myers. I'm going to text you the address."

"Okay."

"I told her who you are . . ."

"What?"

"Well, not who you are. Deal with it: I don't even know that."

I would have laughed had not everything been so dire. He was right. Meanwhile, Libby is eyeing me curiously. But there's really nothing for it.

"True."

"I told her the situation. She will have help standing by."

When I get off the phone, I can see that Libby is visibly shaken and I realize there was enough in the conversation to make her realize that her situation is about to change. Again.

"What's going to happen to us?"

"I'm not sure," I tell her honestly. "But it's going to be better than it was. I'm sure of that."

She looks at me dubiously and I try to reassure her.

"That was my friend Curtis on the phone." I realize as I say it that it's true. I don't have any friends, not really. Except Curtis. What a funny old world. "He's a newscaster. In L.A. He knows a lot of things and a lot of people. I told him what was going on and he made some calls." I'm guessing this part, but it sounds close enough to what he likely did. "The lady we're going to meet knows about Kira and what's going on with her—her breathing and stuff—and will know what to do." I hesitate, then add, "She will know what to do for both of you."

"You don't even know what's wrong with Kira." There is no inflection in her voice.

"She's overdosing on oxycodone." Curtis had diagnosed it on the phone, but I can see from the change in Libby's expression when I say it that he was right. I'm relieved. It means that whatever solution is right now being created will be the right one.

"How did you know that?"

"Curtis again. I told him what was going on and that's what he figured."

She bites her bottom lip again. Not hard, but I can see where it grows pale and then reddens up.

"What else did he tell you?"

"What do you mean?"

"About us." Does she look embarrassed? It's hard to tell while I'm driving. She certainly looks uncomfortable. Quickly, I think about how I should answer. Then realize there is only one thing I can say: the truth.

"He told me that what I was describing to him sounded like human trafficking."

She looks at me wide-eyed, and it is only then that it occurs to me she had not considered her situation in those terms.

"And is it?"

"I . . . I don't know," I say honestly. "I only know you were not safe where you were. And I'm sure there's a lot I don't know. But I do know this: you will be safe now."

"But what we were doing there was illegal. Terry told me if I told anyone, I would go to jail."

"You won't go to jail, Libby. I'm sure of it. You didn't do anything wrong."

"But I did." I have to strain to hear. Her voice is pitched so low I can barely hear. She looks at me wildly. "You don't know the things I did."

"You're a child, Libby."

"I'm not a child," she says defensively, somewhat making my case for me.

"You're underage. You weren't responsible for any of what you did. I promise. You won't go to jail."

We are pulling up in front of a large house—a mansion really—with a large sign in front announcing it be The Clear Center.

"We're meeting her here?"

"Yes. My friend said he thought it sounded like Kira needed immediate treatment."

I don't wait for Libby's rebuttal, but I pocket the keys as I leave the car and go to meet the woman who is waiting for us on the large verandah that fronts the house.

"Abigail," I say by way of greeting. "Thank you for being here."

"Who's this," she says, looking beyond me. She's says it kindly.

"I'm Libby." Libby has followed me out of the car. Her voice is cautious.

"Hello, Libby. Is that short for Elizabeth?"

Libby nods.

"Well, welcome, Elizabeth. Where is your friend?"

Libby jerks her thumb toward the car.

"Let's go get her, shall we?"

It's not that I have been forgotten, but it isn't about me. I'm grateful for that, and fairly certain Curtis had something to do with that, too.

Abigail takes one look at Kira, then sends a text. Two young men emerge from the house instantly, a stretcher between them. Abigail must have had them standing by. While we watch, Kira is whisked away.

"She's in good hands, Libby. Both of those two got here the same way. They know just what to do." And then to me, "Thank you for bringing them to me. Curtis didn't say why, but he made it clear you can't have an involvement. It doesn't matter. It just matters that they are safe now, thanks to you."

I feel a gratefulness well up inside me. I see so much in the world that is evil. It is reassuring to look at someone who seems wholly good.

"Can you let me know how they get on?"

"Of course," Abigail says. "Through Curtis. He's already set it up so that I keep him informed." And then to Libby. "It's going to be okay, you know? You're safe now. Those men can't hurt you here. Those men can't hurt you anymore."

CHAPTER TWENTY-NINE

WHEN I GET back to my hotel room, I fall on the bed. I'm so tired. And so much has been happening that my head is spinning. I'm not sure what I had expected to find out there in the wilds of Maryland, but—whatever it was—I hadn't found it. But I feel like I found so much else. Everything is connected, that's what they say, but if there is anything that connects that house to Cameron or Cameron to the girls, I can't see what it is. It's like I'm looking right at a thing, but I can't quite see it.

It's two in the afternoon, but I feel as though I haven't slept in a week, and maybe that's true. At the core of what I'm feeling, though, is disappointment. Of all the things I *did* accomplish, the one thing I didn't do was get even a hint of where Cameron might be. And the house. The house is in his name. The girls were there. Skeeter is, of course, also connected to the whole thing: I saw that with my own eyes. What does it all mean?

Before I dive in to try and get a few hours of much needed sleep, I decide to try and call Belle.

"You've got a nerve, calling me," she says. I sigh. Apparently, nothing has changed in the time I've been gone.

"Belle, listen . . ."

But she doesn't listen; she just launches right into me.

"You've got a lot to answer for. I can't even believe I picked up the phone when I knew it was you."

"Listen, I'm just trying to figure out where Cameron is. And I will let you know when I do. But I need some help. If you can just tell me when the hearings Cameron was supposed to attend will take place?"

A pause from Belle. And then, "Where are you?"

"Washington," I say.

"What? Wow. So"—she sounds completely taken aback—"you're looking for him?"

"Yes, of course," I say.

"Oh-kay," she says, and I just don't know how to read what's in her voice. "I didn't know you were going out there."

"I'm trying to find him, Belle. That's what I've been telling you all along. I had nothing to do with his disappearance. How are things at the house?"

"I don't know," she says, and I'm just glad she's talking to me again, even if it's a bit grudgingly. "When it rains it pours, you know? My mom had a fall the day after Cameron disappeared. She broke her hip. I came up to Las Vegas to look after her."

"Oh, man," I say. "That's hard. I hope your mom is okay."

"Yeah, it so sucks. She's, like, seventy-three, but she's really active. Like she's pretty healthy—she walks and stuff. Not generally unstable. But I guess you get to a certain age, right? Shit happens."

"And the hearings?"

"I'll text you the schedule," she says. It sounds like a concession. It sounds like maybe she is beginning to believe I had nothing to do with Cameron's disappearance. "They're taking place at Longworth House. Near the Library of Congress."

"Thanks."

"The first one is tomorrow afternoon."

When I get off the phone I reflect on the conversation. At least Belle sounds more ready to believe I had nothing to do with Cameron's disappearance. Still, I wonder at the timing of her mother's injury and then I chide myself for that, too. I'm jumping at shadows. Not everything is a danger situation or a reason for alert. Sometimes a broken hip is just a broken hip.

*   *   *

I brush my hair, then brush my teeth and generally get myself ready for bed, even though it is by now not yet three p.m. As I'm clambering into bed, my eyes fall on Skeeter's laptop where I'd left it next to mine when I unpacked. I'm tired, but I have a thought. I plug it into my computer using the Thunderbolt cable as I had the last time. Then I use the search function to search the computer as though it were an external hard drive:

COLUMBIA BEACH ROAD

I find links to some title documents on this computer. Cameron owns the house, as I'd already noted. Nothing more. I try another search:

LIBBY

Still nothing. But when I try . . .

ELIZABETH

I get identification documents. I see a driver's license, indicating that Libby is nineteen years old and a resident of Delaware. If there were not also a driver's license photo to go with it, I would think it was some other Elizabeth, because Libby is certainly not nineteen. But I see the license with my own eyes. And far be it from me to doubt the possible strength of a fake ID. So she's not nineteen, and she's not a resident of Delaware. I realize I need to probe further, see if there are also IDs here for others. Doing that might provide some answers. Right now, though, I find I am completely out of steam. I can barely think straight. Barely, even, keep my eyes open. Tomorrow, maybe after the hearings, will be another day for searching and finding. For now, though, I just really need to get some sleep.

CHAPTER THIRTY

I WAKE UP with one of those totally disoriented hangovers that can happen when you sleep during the day. Is it morning? Is it night? Have I slept through a whole day cycle? Have I maybe even not really slept at all?

Then it all comes back to me in a sort of terrible rush, and I realize that the worst part is still that I have no idea where Cameron has been. How long can this go on this way? Me following terrible leads as far as I can and ending up with Pandora's boxes of outcomes and everything still more terrible every time I look.

I sleep a few hours more. When I wake again, I order oatmeal and coffee from room service. As I shower and prepare for my day, I can tell that things seem more approachable than they had been before enough sleep. Yesterday afternoon I was lost and confused. Today I feel as though I am encountering something that will be difficult but that I can get through.

I will see Cameron today. Finally. That's a foregone conclusion. I will see him at the hearing. I resolve that I will find a way to talk with him and make sense of everything that has happened or at least figure out what is going on. I feel sure that finding him will provide the missing piece.

Belle had said the hearings are being held at Longworth House. I look that up and discover that it's walking distance from my hotel. It's a long walk, but still. I feel as though I need it; as though stretching my muscles will stretch my spirit and my heart and, besides, my actual muscles have finally recovered from my long horseback ride. There's just the ghost of a twinge left, in my buttocks and my quads. Pain almost not remembered. I try not to let that be a metaphor for my life.

I leave the hotel even earlier than I need to, intending to get a coffee along the way. With coffee in hand, I window-shop and I ramble, feeling that this, too, is fueling my soul. Healing me in some way I can't quite explain. And why do I need healing? That's something else I can't explain. For a moment I had belonged again. And now I am cut loose. Again. Does Cameron hold that key? Or is he, too, a fantasy? Is he the shadow of the ghost of what belonging can even mean?

At the end of my walk, I discover that Longworth House is huge and impressive. The sort of building that looks like a place where all state business should be done. Business of state. I arrive ahead of almost everyone, treading up the stone steps alone. But I arrived early on purpose. I want to choose my position and hear all the angles and discover what everyone has to say. And most of all, of course, I want to see Cameron when they bring him in. I want to be in a place where I can judge his condition and also the state of his mind.

When the hearing room door is unlocked, I am the first one inside. I position myself so that I can see the door. I'm anxious to get a look at Cameron as soon as he comes in. Will he look all right? Will he have been well treated? What kind of pressure will be put on him, and will he be strong enough to take it? And who, if not Skeeter, spirited him away, and how are they holding him? Though this last does not seem like a question I will get an answer on today, I remain hopeful.

Before Cameron shows up, a lot of people speak. If I weren't so anxious about Cameron, I'd even find it all interesting. There is discussion about the control of herd size: spaying of mares versus birth control that can be administered by dart. The pro-horse groups are vastly against spaying, which is permanent. And I learn that birth control hormones administered via dart are much cheaper, easier, and safer than spaying. It seems a no-brainer to me, but the governmental powers that be have their own reasons for not doing it—reasons that the pro-horse groups argue against instantly, with science to back their claims. Although there is a splinter of the pro-horse group that wants neither spaying nor darting, maintaining the horses must be left natural and darting is a pharmaceutical cash grab that will hurt the horses over the long run. I get a sense of why this has been ongoing. There aren't even just two sides to any aspect of the story of America's wild horse; there are many, and so there is even squabbling on the two main sides. And everyone is very passionate and the stakes, to all of them, are high and real.

Of all the issues, though, the big one—and the one that everyone keeps getting back to—is the management of the publicly owned lands that make up the range. Some of the speakers, the ones that are pro-livestock, say that horses rip up the range. That horses erode it. The pro-horse folks, though, claim the opposite. They arrive with verifiable charts and information that indicates that horses help the environment. That it is the eating habits of the sheep and cattle that rip up the range. It's like watching tennis. The volleys are hard and fast and after a while I don't know where to focus my eyes.

Then there is the other side. From the sidelines, it sounds like the current agency plans are directed toward guiding the extinction of the American mustang. No one says that but, from the things they *do* say, that is my take. At the current rate that the wild herds are being rounded up and thinned, the powers that be will rapidly bring the mustangs to a place where they will no longer be genetically viable. The genetic pool that is left will be so small that they will be even more likely to move toward extinction. It all seems obvious to me, and I'm not an expert, but still the discussions go on.

"Next to speak will be Cameron Walker."

My head swivels around in surprise. I had been watching carefully and had not seen him come in.

"Mr. Cameron will be joining us electronically today."

And then there he is, on the big screen, and I am riveted to see him. I am looking hard for changes in his appearance, but that takes second place to the thing I notice as soon as he appears onscreen: his location. A stiffness grows in my throat and my chest as I recognize the furniture. I recognize the piece of art on the wall behind him; there can be no mistaking it. The mountains, the cacti, all of the details I had committed to memory when I stayed there. He is in his bedroom at the Flying W, something so startling to me it confuses me at first. Then, once it all settles in, it makes me mad as hell.

When he starts to speak, though, even that is forgotten, or nearly so. I just can't believe what I'm hearing.

"I would like to begin by saying that recently facts and research have come to my attention that have proven to me without doubt that my assertions of previous years were incorrect."

Something like a gasp ripples through the assembled. It's quite theatrical. I'd think it was funny if I was not already so concerned and confused.

He continues.

"I had been erroneously led to believe that great damage to the range was occurring due to overgrazing by livestock. However, I have now seen convincing evidence that it is, in fact, the horses themselves who are responsible for this erosion of the range."

"Mr. Walker." Even the moderator of the proceedings looks confused. You can tell this was not what she was expecting. "This is a huge reversal for you. You have long been a staunch defender of wild horses on the range."

Does he look pained? Does he look pushed to breaking? He should, but he doesn't. He looks like he's sharing a conviction, and somewhere, in all of that, I feel my heart break. He had told me things—a lot of things—and I had believed all of them. And there he is, sitting in his room like nothing ever happened. Like I hadn't fallen in love with him. Or almost fallen in love with him. Or whatever it was that I had been feeling. It's like a different person is sitting there, one I'm not sure I want anything to do with.

"Yes, ma'am," he says by way of reply.

"What has brought about this complete change of heart?"

"Science," he says after a hesitation. "And evidence that I had not seen before."

"What do you now feel the outcome should be for the wild horses of the west?"

The way she phrases the question doesn't leave him any wiggle room. She is directly asking for the outcome he desires. I wonder if there is anyone in that room who is not surprised by his answer.

"It is my feeling that they should be removed from the range, entirely. And as soon as possible. The environmental damage done by them is almost incalculable. It needs to be stopped as quickly as possible." It does not seem to me that his voice changes as he says this, but I see a pulse in his throat bounce, even on the video. I don't know what that means. "They are not wild. They are feral and so contribute to the loss of suitable environment for the truly wild animals who roam there."

I try hard to think back to what he had told me when we first met. I was certain he had told me that he believed that those that said horses were an introduced species were wrong. That he thought horses had been in North America since prehistory, even though the more popular belief was that the Spanish colonizers had brought them in the 1400s. But now? Everything he is saying is contradicting the things he told me he believed. And me? I didn't know what to believe anymore, but at the top of the list of things not to believe was Cameron, repeatedly saying things that I knew were opposite to values and thoughts he had said he believed just days before.

After a while I feel as though I've heard enough, but I continue to listen and watch and internally weep while Cameron speaks out against everything I know he believes in. To hear him tell it, he would like to see the extermination of the animals he has championed his whole life.

After Cameron has said goodbye and the screen goes dark and the next live speaker is being brought in, I sit there for a while processing everything that has been said. A little while later I leave the hearing. It's like everything Cameron said continues to buzz around in my brain even after he's gone.

The first thing I do when I leave the hearing room is go out into the courtyard and dial Belle. I realize I don't expect her to answer, but I'm surprised when I get an out-of-service message. I had let my phone dial the number, so I know it can't be wrong. I redial it again anyway with the same result. I'm confused. What does it mean? What does any of it mean?

I sit there in the pretty courtyard and digest the whole thing. The surprise and shock at what Cameron said in the hearing takes a while to wear off. When it does, I find that I am angry. Really angry.

If he'd been at the hearing in person or even with the background of some anonymous hotel room, I would have had a different take. But the way things played out, I know that I've been conned. I feel it in my gut; my throat. From the first I had believed in him. Had even come to briefly believe in a possible future with him. And it had all been, what? A game? An act? I feel taken for a fool. I feel had. It has been a really long time since I have allowed myself to feel so exposed. No, that's wrong: it's been a long time since I'd allowed myself to feel at all.

When I've breathed myself to calm, I find that there is a familiar burning in my gut. I know what it means. I have never before killed for personal reasons. There has always been a price tag attached. Always. I have a sense that is about to change.

CHAPTER THIRTY-ONE

SO MUCH IS swirling around in my head. More questions than anything else. With all of those queries still to be answered, I discover that there is only one thing I know for sure: my time in the nation's capital is done. As soon as I can get out of the hearing room, I make a beeline for the hotel and then from there to the airport. I don't even think about going home, but also, I make no effort to book a flight for Phoenix until I'm heading there. You can always get a flight to Phoenix. It's a hub.

As soon as I land, I grab a car and head back into the desert. There is a shallowness waiting for me there.

I didn't really have a plan when I left D.C. Just go. But by the time I land, pick up the rental SUV I'd reserved while on the flight, and head south, I pretty much have an outline. And while some of the desert scent manages to break through the AC and the hot desert sun bakes the car's finish, I think it all through. Refine. Mentally prepare.

How sure am I that it was Cameron's room on the video call? So sure. When I stayed there, I'd stared at the picture when I'd woken in the night. I'd seen the play of light and shadows in that room and I'd noticed the furniture and everything that was on the walls. I had to entertain the idea that I was mistaken. And I did entertain it. But I knew I wasn't wrong. Something solid in my heart. It feels like granite. But colder and darker still.

I am deeply focused on all of these thoughts when, half an hour out of Phoenix, I change lanes and notice a red sedan three cars back do the same. And this time I'd been so focused on everything else I was feeling—that loss of belonging, that feeling of being had—that I hadn't had a sense of the follow. Yet here it is, so obvious I couldn't ignore it even if I wanted to.

I make another lane change just to confirm the follow. The red sedan makes the same change. I pull off the highway at one of those dreary shopping mall towns that line the I-10 and am unsurprised when the red sedan follows suit. What to do now? There are just so many people who could be tailing me that I don't even know where to start. With that in mind, I head into a Starbucks drive-thru and am amused when the red sedan follows me, but three cars back. I can't tell anything about the driver from my vantage. A ballcap, that's all I know. Oh, and he's an amateur—I can tell. The fact that I'd been so engrossed in thought and still noticed him tells that story. Another part of the story: no professional tail would have followed me *into* the drive-thru. It's too dangerous. You could get trapped. And also, he's clearly going to get left behind. What was he thinking?

It takes me a while to think about what to do with all of this. On the one hand, he's such an amateur I figure I'd be able to lose him easily once my latte gets handed over. While I wait in line, I try to think if that's the best move. Do I confront him? Find out who he is and what he wants? I've had success with that before. Or do I just blow out of here and put the whole thing out of my mind?

In the end, I decide to do neither of those things. The line is moving slowly and so I get out. Walk back the three cars. I'm surprised to see a kid who looks sixteen. He doesn't look the least bit dangerous and he's obviously not old enough to be a professional, so I can't imagine why he'd be tailing me. His expression catches me off guard more than anything. He's not looking at me like he's a stalker. Or he's out to find me for some bounty I don't even know about. His expression is one of reverence. It confuses me, that look. I don't understand it. I've never seen a look like that directed at me before. I don't know quite what to do with it.

Despite the look almost of veneration I see on his face, he watches me warily as I approach his car, but he does nothing. Wary reverence. It's an odd look. I indicate he should open his window and he does, but just a crack.

"Hey," he says.

"Hey," I reply. "Are you following me?"

He tries a grin that emerges more like a grimace.

"I guess, yeah." He doesn't say "caught," but I hear it, just the same.

"Why?"

"Why am I following you?"

"Yeah."

"It's a long story."

"I've got time. You wanna talk?"

"Okay."

"After I get my coffee, I'm going to park and go sit at a table over there." I indicate an attractive outdoor seating area. It's hot enough out that no one is sitting there right now. We won't be overheard. "You come join me, OK? Tell me what's up."

He nods anxiously and I stroll back to my car just as the line starts to move.

I'd ordered a hot latte, and now I'm wishing I'd gotten it iced, but I hadn't known a sit in the sunshine was headed my way. I have them add an ice water to the order in the hopes it will keep me from overheating, then I head out to meet my follower.

I am perplexed. I can't imagine what this kid is following me for. It is out of my experience. I run through possibilities. Something to do with a former hit maybe? Though in that case, maybe I'd already be dead. No. The way he was looking at me didn't make me think this is a vengeance thing, and I just can't imagine what else it might be.

By the time he approaches, I have just gotten settled. He's got a giant-size cold drink in his hands. Maybe a Frappuccino. Condensation drips down the sides of the plastic cup. I feel myself start to salivate, wishing again I'd gotten something cold, but I dial it back. Stick with the program, I tell myself. But just what is the program? What could this fresh-faced kid with the giant icy drink and a Chicago Cubs ballcap possibly want with me?

"Sit," I tell him when he gets close enough. He drops into the nearest chair obediently. He doesn't say anything right away, just sips his drink and watches me with a disturbing intensity. After a while, I call him on it. "What? What are you looking at?"

"I'm looking for a resemblance."

"A resemblance between what?"

"A resemblance between the two of us."

I'm perplexed and I'm pretty sure I show it. "Why would that be?"

He seems both hesitant to speak and anxious to tell me, like he's been holding it back, but now we've come to it and it's going to bubble out.

"Because," he says, borrowing the timing from maybe every suspense movie he's ever watched, "you're my mother."

CHAPTER THIRTY-TWO

IT'S LIKE SOMEONE has punched the wind out of me. I just look at him. I don't know what to say.

My son was a child when he died. This young man is about the age my son would have been now, had he lived. Some teen number with a lot of hard edges. And if I look at this young man very closely, I can make myself think I see . . . something. I'm not sure what. I only know that looking at him hurts my heart.

I see the way his hair folds over his collar, in much the same way my late husband's did. And there. On his nose. Are those freckles? In just the way they occupied my nasal region when I was a teen. I see these things and I feel such a longing. Such a wishfulness. I feel things I've never felt before. Things I haven't allowed myself to feel. And I breathe. For a moment I just breathe and observe. And maybe, even, I wish.

He is neither attractive nor unattractive, just a normal-looking kid. Right now, he is wearing a hopeful expression. I think I see fear there, too. And who could blame him? If he's being honest, there's a lot here to unpack.

I want it to be true.

I wish it to be true.

I wish that he belonged to me. That I belonged to him.

I wish—more than anything, I wish—that I was, in fact, his mother.

Could it be true? Could I let it be true? What would it mean—to me, to him—not to be alone anymore?

To belong. As I once belonged. As maybe he once belonged. How hard would that be? Maybe not difficult at all. Maybe.

Maybe I could let it be true.

I think about all of those things in the space it takes to draw a half dozen breaths. I think about it, but I don't express it in any way. Instead, I say what I know to be accurate. What can be the only truth. And even while I think it through—and know the truth very well—I still wonder: Why? Why could I not let this thing be true?

I skate near it, but then I find I can't do it. It would be the biggest lie. Even if the largest part of the lie was only held in my own heart.

I take a deep breath. Close my eyes. Open them again. Take another breath.

"I'm not your mother," I say at length. I hear my voice. Low. Measured. Filled with regret. "It's impossible. What's your name?"

"Jaxon," he says.

"Jaxon," I repeat. "That's a good name. Strong."

"Thanks. My gramma said you chose it."

"Wasn't me, kid. I'm sure of it." I catch his eyes. Make sure I hold them. "I saw my boy in the ground."

"Wasn't me," he says in just the same tone, and I smile despite myself. Despite all of this. The kid is charming, I'll give him that. Whoever his parents are or were.

"So what's the story?" I've said it quietly. Without demand.

"Story?"

"Of how you came to be following me. I'm sure there's a reason you chose me and not someone else."

"Sure there is," he said. "I was real little when my dad got picked up."

"Picked up?"

"He went to jail. Stupid stuff. He was maybe not the brightest guy. Anyway, before he went . . ."

"When you were little."

"Right. He told me that you had died when I was born."

"Not me," I say. But it feels like rote. Jaxon doesn't seem to notice he is deeply invested in the story. His story. Our story. And what he thinks is his own creation story. I have no choice but to shatter it. I can't help it. I do the math quickly, but there's nothing I can say that will make this right.

"He told me you had died, but he lied about everything. To everyone. His whole life. So I kinda figured it followed he would have lied about you, too. And it didn't really make sense to me. I'm not sure why. Just the way he would talk about you made no sense."

"All right," I said, just adding words so he'd keep talking. "Okay. So then what happened?"

"I searched on your name."

"My name."

"You know, your name. And I found a few leads. You weren't the only one with that name. But there were age differences, you know. Situation differences. A few people—not a lot—with that name. And no one with the same full name. Katherine Eveline Ragsdill." He says it like a prayer. And suddenly more things make sense. "But then I found the title on your house and all the numbers were correct." He looks at me earnestly then. And that reverence is back. He looks at me with something like love. "Your name, your birth date, everything. When all of that fit, I knew it had to be you."

He had found me. Even though I was unfindable, he had ferreted me out. Only I wasn't who he thought I was. Even though, in some ways, I kinda was.

"I'm sorry, Jaxon. I really am terribly sorry. But I'm not your mother. I think, you know, that maybe this time your dad was telling the truth."

"But I've watched you. I followed you. I've been following you on and off for weeks. I know what you do."

I feel myself pale at that. How long had he been following? And what had he seen?

"What do you mean?"

"We're alike, you and I."

"Explain."

"We like our own company. We don't like to listen to people saying a lot of stupid things. I've inherited that from you."

There is a part of me that wishes, more than anything, that this could be true. Wishes it so badly I am tempted to just lean into it. To just go along. This kid needs a mother, right? I could be that mother. Sure, I could. Why not?

So many reasons, really. But then again. Why not?

There is about him something like a neglected pup. Someone who hasn't been loved enough. I can just feel it on him. And even from the very few words he's said, I can build a picture of a life. And it's not a pretty picture. Mother dead, perhaps at his birth. Father ends up in jail. Maybe he was raised by brokenhearted grandparents—and whether paternal or maternal, they had lost a child. Lost everything, either to death or jail, which can amount to the same thing. And I look at him and I know he is not mine. But I wish he could be. It would be a lot for both of us. But maybe it would be enough.

And I also know it can't be. You don't fix a lie with more lies. Oh, you can start out that way, lots of people do. But in the end, it will always come back and bite you on the ass.

I reach out across the table for his hand. It's metal surface is hot enough that he pulls back, but I hang on.

"Listen to me, Jaxon. And I'm so sorry to say this to you. But I am not your mother. It isn't possible for me to be. I . . . I had a son. And he would be about your age now. Had he lived. But he died. It . . . it was not a good death. I . . . I witnessed it when they . . . when they put him in the ground."

These are images I had packed away a long time ago. I thought for good. But revisiting them now brings them back, and it's all I can do to keep on holding it together.

"How do you have her name, though?" He is suspicious. I don't blame him. I'd feel the same. And we have already established that he is somewhat like me. "How is it you have the same name? My mother's name. And her birthday?"

"How do you know all that?"

"There are sites. Online. All you need is a name. The rest comes up."

I curse myself then. Silently. How had I been so careless? Of course: You get a driver's license, a credit card. You buy real estate. You leave a trace. And even if you are trying to leave a very small trace—an invisible trace, let's say—it's still there. And if some desperate kid is looking for his mother, maybe you get found. Because love and a broken heart? Those things can find a way.

"It's a coincidence, then. It must be," I say, even though I know it is anything but that.

The hurt on his face is bald. He looks as though I've hit him. I can almost see the red shadow of a slap.

"It's not a coincidence." His voice is even quieter now. "And my dad did lie to me. But I see now that he did it to protect me." He starts to rise. "You didn't die. But he knew the truth and he didn't want me to know: you just didn't want me."

"Jaxon," I call out to him as he heads back to his car, but he doesn't turn back. And I'm in such a dilemma. I can't tell him the truth. The truth begins the unraveling of everything: the tiny bit of safety I've created in an angry world. But how can I let him think his mother just left him behind? The thing I know I *can't* do is rush into things here. I have this sense that anything I say might now change my life forever. And his.

So I keep my mouth shut. And I feel my eyes grow heavy as I watch him drive away.

CHAPTER THIRTY-THREE

AFTER A WHILE I get back on the road.

With the unexpected delays, by the time I arrive at the Flying W it is deep night. I leave my car far enough from the ranch house that my lights can't be seen as I park. And I've gotten lucky: it's not a pitch-dark night, and there is more than a sliver of moonlight behind me. It lights my way.

I'm carrying a light pack as I move into the desert. The Bersa is in my hand. I am anticipating trouble and I don't know what form it might take. Like a Boy Scout, I'm feeling like I need to be prepared. And I don't know the whole story and I don't know fully what's going on, but at this point I'm only thinking one thing: Cameron is going to die.

I creep through the darkness and discover that it is not the desert itself I am afraid of, though I know I probably should be: there are lots of frightening things out there. But there just seems so much more to be afraid of, quite beyond the natural world. More than I'd ever imagined.

I follow the road because I know the last thing I want to do is walk into a cactus in the dark. Another last thing: I don't want to step on a snake, but I try hard not to think about that. In any case, I reassure myself, wouldn't a snake be off sleeping in its den right now? Do snakes even have dens? Maybe whole hordes of them are out there, just beyond where I can see, waiting to take me out. Or in their dens. It becomes obvious that I need more clarity on snakes and their habits if I'm going to be skulking around the desert at night, though I clearly don't plan on it.

As I creep through the night, it comes to me that none of these thoughts are productive, and I move on. Sometimes you just have to breathe deeply and trust the universe. I have always trusted the universe somewhat less than I trust myself, though in all honesty that hasn't always served me well. There have been times when the universe was pointing at an outcome very clearly, and I resisted and pushed back and finally got my way, only to discover that the path the universe had mapped for me would have been simpler, after all.

But the desert. It envelops me completely. I push my mind from the possibility of big cats or wild dogs and all of that in addition to that original idea of snakes. Even without the human factor, there is just so much that can go wrong.

As I'd experienced on previous visits, the ranch house is large and it rambles. I have an idea of what part of the house Cameron's suite of rooms are in—it's one of the few things I know—and I move in that direction. At one point I feel a branch snap underfoot and a dog starts barking, then another. I freeze in place and reduce my breathing to a silent, shallow pant. There is more barking, but I am grateful when it doesn't come any closer. I guess that the dogs are confined someplace. An idea that is confirmed when I hear a woman's voice shout, "Shaddup, you doofus dogs—it's the middle of the night!" At the admonishment, the barking subsides.

I can't help but smile at this. The dogs are right, of course. There is cause for concern. Me. And I wonder at how many times an overly complacent owner has shushed a dog's barking, only to discover the following morning that they should have listened to the warning of their canine best friend.

As I approach Cameron's room, I see that the lights are on. I creep, ninja quiet, to a window. Peer inside. Nothing, though I recognize the piece of art that was on the wall when he testified at the hearing and when I stayed in the room a few days before. A few days. So much has happened, it feels more like a month.

I move cautiously to the next window and there he is, on his bed, on top of the covers fully dressed, one arm over his eyes as though shielding them from the light or his thoughts from the air, but I can't tell if he is awake or asleep.

For a while I just watch, and while I watch I feel. I'm not certain I had even acknowledged to myself that I had been falling in love with him before all of this madness began. I mean, I'd maybe mentally toyed with the idea. But truly acknowledge it? No. I hadn't gone there. Maybe I hadn't really believed it was possible. That someone like him would want someone like me. Him: beautiful, powerful, even wealthy. Me: broken, on the run, hiding. If you knew anything at all about both of us, the two of us together made no sense.

So I had imagined myself falling in love with him. And not just his beauty. Or his power. Or his wealth. But the whole of him that I had imagined included this passion for the horses he so professed to love and protect. And was it all a show? Well, it had to have been, because there he is, sprawled under the same piece of art I'd memorized—cow-faced with love and concern for him—when I'd spent the night alone in his room. And he had disappeared, then reappeared in peril, and all of it makes me realize he is more evil than all of the evils he had professed to loathe. I had thought maybe we belonged together. And all of it was a lie.

And, yes: by now I am fully aware that I have come to kill him. That's what dragged me all the way back here, through the heat and encounters with overly earnest young men. Cameron has lied to me. He has been disingenuous. He has put children at risk. He has taken what I offered and judged it incomplete. And I realize, even as I think this, that there is a scenario where we go through all of this and no harm befalls him. But at this moment, I can't imagine things happening that way.

I feel the tug of the Bersa. Through the cloth of the backpack, I feel the heft and readiness of the handgun. I am prepared for whatever outcome awaits.

I am prepared, but am I ready? Every minute I stand here makes someone discovering me there more likely. And yet. I bring out my phone. Dial his number. It rings for a long time before it goes to voicemail, and I don't hear a corresponding ring coming from inside. Does that mean anything? I don't think so. Now the only thing that needs resolving is how I take him out. Do I do it, gangland style, right here, through the window? There are a couple of downsides to that, of course. There is danger from noise and also breaking glass. The violence of all of that matches my rage, but it won't serve me in real time. Do I wait for him to go somewhere and pick him off from a distance? Or do I go in close and finish him?

I am pondering all of these possibilities—and more—when the picture changes. Someone enters the room carrying a tray. I recognize the cowboy: dirty blond hair poking out from all sides of a felt Stetson. And he's armed. It's such a cliché. A sidearm is plainly visible on his right hip. He says a few things to Cameron. I can't hear the words. But his face looks cold and unfriendly as he says them. Cameron sits up and regards the cowboy as he speaks. I'm too far away so I can't hear what is said.

Cameron's shoulders look tight to me, like he's holding himself stiffly, or maybe holding himself back. I can't be sure which. But the cowboy is weedy and bandy and Cameron could take him with a single fist, I'm sure of it. Why then does Cameron seem almost to cower in his presence? As I watch the two of them through the window, something comes clear. Cameron may be in his own room, but he is a prisoner. I had been thinking he had orchestrated something huge, something that included his own kidnapping and changing his public opinion on the matter of the horses. But as I watch this interaction between Cameron and the yellow-haired cowboy, I realize there is a very different dynamic going on.

Inside the room, the discussion is heating up. I see Cameron shake his head emphatically. See the cowboy snarl more words in Cameron's direction. At those words, Cameron starts to rise. With a couple of easy movements, the cowboy throws a casual backhand into Cameron's face. The fact that Cameron doesn't fight back is telling. Cameron isn't manipulating the situation for his own benefit. He is not the criminal mastermind I had been imagining him to be. He is a prisoner.

And suddenly everything makes so much more sense.

CHAPTER THIRTY-FOUR

NOT EVERYTHING MAKES sense.

After the cowboy in the Stetson hat leaves Cameron's room, I stand for a while longer in the moon's shadow. I'm still standing there, outside the window, and I see Cameron fall back onto the bed in a defeated heap.

It takes me a while to figure out what to do, but when I do, I move. Still undetected in the shadows, I sidle up to the window nearest to the bed. Then I tap-tap-tap quietly on the frame.

After a while he raises his head. Looks in my direction. Then he looks again as though he can't quite believe his eyes. He holds a finger to his lips. Motions me to wait, then gets up. I watch while he secures the perimeter of his room. If, as I now believe, he is captive, there will only be so much he can do. Still. He does it now. Then he crosses to me.

He opens the window. In silence, he reaches out, carries me through. Sets me down on my feet inside of the room. Puts his arms around me. Squeezes me tightly enough that it causes some concern. Tips my head back. Kisses me full on the lips. I don't know if it's fear, but what I taste: something has changed.

"I was afraid I'd never see you again," he says in a hoarse whisper, close to my ear.

"Me too," I say.

"How did you know?"

"I didn't," I tell him. "I watched at the window. Figured it out. Maybe figured it out."

"There's more here than meets the eye."

"I figured that out, too. Look, I have a car. And a gun. Shall we go?"

"It's not that simple," he says.

"It never is," says me.

"No, really. They've got my kid."

Of course they did. Of course they do. I'd forgotten he even had one. I feel myself sagging against him. The sag feels like defeat. For a moment I'd been thinking it was all close to over. I thought I just had to get him out. Him and me. I had seen it, in my mind's eye. The two of us, darting back through the desert forest, to where I'd left the car. Getting into the car, heading down the road, the headlights out until we were back on the highway and screaming back toward the city.

At the mention of his child, though, the vision pops out. Suddenly it feels like we are starting over again.

There is so much I want to ask him. I realize there is no time just now for any of it. Only this.

"Where is he?"

"I think they have him here someplace."

"Who are *they*?" I ask.

"It feels like I'm not even sure anymore," he says. "Was I ever sure?" I don't say anything, because I can tell he's asking himself. "But I'm not sure now."

"Where is Belle?"

"I don't know," he says. "She just seemed to disappear the first day."

"Last time I spoke with her, she was in Vegas. With her mom. Her mom broke her hip."

"Oh!" he says.

"Yeah. I talked to her when I was in D.C."

"D.C.? What were you doing there?" He asks it, but I have a feeling he knows.

"Trying to find you."

"But I was here."

"I know that now." I think for a minute. "But you weren't always. I spent that first night here."

"Here in my room? Or here at the ranch?"

"Room," I say. "That's how I finally knew where to find you. I saw you at the hearing. Recognized the stuff. From your room, I mean. What I don't know: Where were you that night? When you disappeared. How did you get here? How long have you been back here?"

He reaches out. Strokes my hair. "I'm sorry. Someone could come at any moment. We don't have time for all of that now."

"You have to tell me one thing: The stuff you said. In the hearing. Why?" I ask it, but I already know, now that I have a picture that is more complete. Somehow, though, I need to hear him say it.

"They threatened my son's life."

"And you feel he is here."

"I know he was. I haven't seen him for a few days. They brought him to me, just after they brought me back here."

"They."

"I don't even know that, I'm afraid. They didn't tell me who they were. It's just, what I gather. From how it's all unfolding."

"And what did they say?"

"They told me if I didn't cooperate, they would kill him."

"You know they probably intend to kill him anyway?"

He nods. "Yeah. But what choice did I have?"

What choice did he have? There is always a choice, isn't there? Though I don't say that. But there is always a choice. Do you compromise the things you hold dearest for the one you love best? Is that ever the call? Or always. Or is it at those times when choices are forced that what you are made of appears? Where the rubber hits the road, as they say.

Life is always about choices. I've seen that often, and I haven't always come out of it well. Do you sacrifice your only child for your own highest principle? Especially when you suspect that the sacrifice would never be enough. It's a conundrum, for sure. Faced with those choices, I'm not certain what I would do. But I have an inkling. Life has shown me that, too.

So now I have this small piece, but there is so much more. His disappearance on the trail. The house in Maryland. The human trafficking. Belle's absence: her mom. And the horses—the poor, dear horses—who will have to defend themselves from all of this evil if he bails on them. And he *has* bailed on them. Plus, they are horses: they are vegetarians and prey animals; they're not built to defend themselves.

Time is too dear, that's what he said. They could come back at any time. Whoever they are. And so I ask none of it. And I don't answer his question. I figure it was rhetorical anyway. Instead of answering, I slip back out the way I came in, forging ahead, because the only thing I know how to do is move.

CHAPTER THIRTY-FIVE

THE SLIVER OF moon that guided me to Cameron's quarters helps me in navigating the grounds now. The other thing that helps is the Bersa. It is good to know that, even if I am caught, there are other ways out.

So I creep into the night.

The fact that I have only the most rudimentary idea of how the house is laid out does not help me. And it's a very big house. Some eras and areas might have deemed it more lodge than house. And it rambles. And I am unsure of how it fits together.

I know where Cameron's room is. I have a pretty good understanding of the location of the kitchen and the dining area. Beyond that the structure is a mystery to me and I know I'll have a lot of windows to peek in before any hope of success. And that, of course, means a lot of opportunity to get it wrong and get caught in the process. It's not a good situation no matter how I examine it. But I'm in pretty deep already anyway. I feel I have to try.

Once I get back out into the night, I put some distance between myself and the house. I am hoping for some kind of break, I guess. And the opportunity to view the whole from a distance. Assess. Plus, a chance to catch my breath. This day has been filled beyond capacity, and there is no end in sight.

From a distance, I assess the ranch buildings again, but in a whole new way. I have not seen it in the light dark of early evening, while illumination still burns at many windows. In this context, a new profile begins to emerge.

It's easy to see the space that contains the main lodge of the ranch house. I have a good idea about the stables and other farm outbuildings beyond the house. But then I notice for the first time that there is a small house behind the house. A casita they would call it in these parts. On earlier visits I hadn't noticed; had perhaps thought it was part of the house itself. In the gloaming, though, I can see it is a distinct dwelling, unconnected to the larger house. And there are lights on. I realize that, if I were going to hide a kid, that's where I'd put him: close by but away. I have to be wrong, of course. It won't be as easy as that. Still. I skirt the edge of the compound and head in that direction.

When I get near the casita, I get a hint that my hunch may be correct. A couple of cowboys are chatting near the front stoop, rifles resting easily in the crooks of their arms, as though they are comfortable holding them. They are not expecting any action—we're in the middle of nowhere, after all—but they are ready, anyway. Just not right this second. Though in their defense, they don't know that I'm creeping up on them. In any case, I can't be certain about what they are ready for. And why.

I do a wide loop around the house, mindful not to walk into a cactus, and come at it from a different cowboy-free angle. There are a couple of windows here, and a back door. The room beyond window one is dark. I try to peer inside anyway, but can really see nothing at all. In the room beyond window two, a television is on and broadcasting. I can't tell what is on the screen. Nor can I tell if anyone is watching, so it all means nothing.

I try the door, but am unsurprised when I find it locked. It's not some crappy old lock, either, like one you what might expect on a door of the same period as the house. Rather it is some fancy-looking dead-bolt contraption that I have zero chance of picking, so I don't even bother trying. Instead, I go back to the darkened room. I try the window, but it is locked, though I notice that, unlike the lock on the door, which has been updated, the window is single pane.

I fish in my bag for my nail clippers. It seems a long shot, but I use the end of the file to score a large square into the thin glass. Then I take off my hoodie and wrap it around the Bersa. I brace myself before I hit the window with it. I know it will make noise, I'm just not sure how much. It's the only game in town, though, and so I move.

When I hit the window with the hoodie-wrapped gun, it makes a sharp crack, almost like a branch breaking in a forest. It seems unbelievably loud to me, and I freeze for a moment to see if there will be any action in response. I'm something like amazed when there is not. Rather a neat square breaks raggedly out of the center of the pane and I both marvel at my ingenuity and am grateful for my luck.

With the hoodie now wrapped around my hand, I pull shards of glass out of the frame, looking to make a hole big enough for me to climb through.

Once inside the dark room I stay where I land, as still as I can be, for a full minute. Then I push it out to two. What I'm listening for: first of all, I want to know if my less than silent entrance has attracted any attention. But there is no answering racket that lets me know guards with guns have been alerted and are on their way and after a while I breathe slightly easier. But I keep listening. Is the house making any noise? It doesn't seem to be.

After a while, I get my courage together enough to creep down the hall toward the room that holds the television. The door is open, so no stealth is required there and I enter, quiet and hopeful. But the room is empty, though the TV is still on. Some bright, light police show, all garish colors and too many breasts. Who even watches shows like this? At the moment, no one. So there's that. I turn the television off and move more deeply into the room.

Further inspection delivers much of the same: there are signs of recent occupation, but no one is here. The whole house is empty. I can tell someone has been here recently, but I can't tell who it was and I'm certain no one is here now. It seems that I banged up my favorite hoodie and wrecked my nail clippers and have absolute zero to show for it.

I try to think back to what Cameron had said about his son, both tonight and during that first dinner together. Twelve years old. Living in Phoenix with his mom. That's the total sum of everything I know. But mom in the city seems like a pretty good lead. Better than anything I've got. It seems to me she would either know where the kid was or be frantic. How to find her? I've got to get myself out of the broken house and back to civilization, so that will be my first challenge. But I figure if anyone is going to know where the kid is, it's her.

CHAPTER THIRTY-SIX

I MANAGE TO get back to my car without tangling with a cowboy, a cactus, or a snake. I feel lucky on all three counts.

At first, I'm just concerned with getting back to my rental car and out onto the highway without detection. By now it is the deepest section of the night and there is no traffic on these roads so near Cathedral National Park. I wind my way slowly along the deserted highway and feel again the shadow of the place that Cameron would have occupied next to me if things had gone a different way. Where would we have ended up on this night? But it's not worth thinking about. Fate had other things in store for me. It still does. I bow my head; move on.

I find myself heading back to the casino hotel where I'd spent my first night in Arizona. The casino feels like a safe zone. I know it will give me a place from which I can do some research, but also my body desperately needs rest by now. And sustenance. I need to fuel myself so I can process everything I've learned.

After I check into the hotel, I decide to go downstairs to see what I can I rustle up in the way of food. I find a restaurant that spills into the casino called Cibo Matto. I squint at the stylish sign, doubting my grade school Italian. Who would name a restaurant

"crazy food"? But then I look around at the location and the nature of the establishment and think: Why not?

I plunk myself down and order a steak. Rare. People watching,
yes, but mostly resting. Regrouping. And the location is absurd
enough—not to mention the name—and there is enough to
look at that it keeps me from thinking. That feels good for a
while. Not thinking. I have to figure out how to make a practice
of that.

The steak ends up being a good call. After all, we're in ranch
country out here. There will be the expectation that they can get a
steak right. And they do, dumb name notwithstanding.

Back in my room I don't waste time doing anything other than
falling into bed. I sleep in exhausted luxury, my body taking all it
feels it has coming to it, and maybe a bit more.

I wake up with the usual disorientation that comes with being
in a strange bed. And then I remember: Cameron is alive and at
home. His son has been threatened. Nothing is at all how it had
seemed to be. I'm not yet sure how I feel about any of that.

At first I have no idea where to begin looking for Cameron's
ex-wife. But then I get an idea. Cameron had told me his son was
twelve. With that information in mind, I put together a search for
twelve to twenty years before now and I'm looking for marriage
announcements. Cameron had told me his family was fourth gen-
eration Arizonan and the family had wealth and status. It makes
sense that the wedding would have been held in the state and that
the nuptials would have been announced here. And so I do a simple internet search knowing that, if this doesn't work, I'm pretty
much out of ideas. No pressure.

"Cameron Walker" + "marriage" + "lourdes" and I know, even
as I type it, that it's a long shot. With that in mind, I'm a bit

astonished that the thing I'm looking for comes up first on the first page of search results:

Cameron Allan Walker II and Eloise McMartin Walker of Lourdes, Arizona, and Bryan and Mercedes Tuffin of Scottsdale are pleased to announce the marriage of their children Cameron Allan Walker III and Andrea Azalea Tuffin on March 6th.

There was more, of course, and I barely glance at it, other than to ascertain what field the bride had studied in, because I'm trying to find her now, not when she was my lover's bride. The announcement said she had a degree in zoology from the University of Arizona, so that's a clue.

But when I do a search for Andrea Azalea Tuffin, I find nothing, and on Andrea Walker, I of course find a lot, but nothing matches. The sensible thing for me to do, of course, would be to just go to Cameron and ask how to get hold of his ex-wife, but even trying that seems like too dangerous a proposition as it involves once again getting past deadly cacti and men with guns. Instead, I call someone I know will be able to get me an answer.

"I'm trying to find someone," I tell him when I get him on the phone.

"You called the right guy," he says and he already knows I know it. He had found me once before, then let me get lost again when I didn't want finding.

"I think this will be an easy one for you," I say. I figure I could have found her myself, but it would have taken time. Cody is a private investigator, and so he has access to the kind of records that turn things up.

"I'll pay," I tell him.

"Damn straight," he replies.

I feed him what I want. He tells me he'll call me back as soon as he knows anything. I figure that will be soon. On the scales of things Cody can find, locating the ex-wife of a wealthy rancher should be a piece of cibo matto.

While I wait, I go down to the gift shop, buy a bathing suit.

When I get to the pool, I start to do laps strenuously enough that after a while I'm just about seeing stars. The thing is, right now I can't figure out if I'm trying to remember, or if I'm trying to forget. Either way, the strain on my body feels good. Right. It feels like what I need.

To my surprise, though, I'm not thinking about the business at hand. Rather, I keep thinking about Jaxon. His eyes. So like mine. And that tenacity. Like me, too. He is not my son. It isn't possible for him to be. And yet. In different circumstances, he could be, couldn't he? Isn't fate just a sliding door? I don't like how I've left things with him. Left him thinking that his mother—Katherine Eveline Ragsdill—didn't love him. That she walked away. He's been thinking that his whole life, I tell myself. What difference does it make now? What difference? But I know it does. A thing like that can lay on your heart. On your life for your whole life. It can lay on mine, too.

And I find myself also thinking that I've let myself be a target, hanging onto that handle. Of course someone was going to find Katherine Eveline Ragsdill if they went looking. It's not exactly a Kate Smith or Jones. Stupid. I shake my head at the stupidity. Like hiding in plain sight in a fright wig. Of course that one was going to catch up with me. Of course. It was only a matter of time. How did I not see it before it got here?

I took her name—I *bought* her name—but I had not bargained, also, on buying someone's life. Their hurts and troubles. I had imagined—what?—that the name was somehow detached from anything. I should have known better. An identity as solid as the one I bought is not manufactured. It's borrowed from someone who doesn't need it anymore. I never calculated the strings. I didn't pay for them, either.

After a while, Cody gets back to me with the location of Cameron's ex-wife. I write down what he tells me, but for the moment it's not at the top of my mind.

"Before I let you go, Cody," I tell him. "There's someone else I'd like you to find."

After I give him the name, I check out of the hotel and get back on the road. There's still so much more to do.

CHAPTER THIRTY-SEVEN

Amanda Walker and her offspring, Cameron's son, Mason, live in a very nice townhouse in North Central Phoenix on Maryland Avenue. I sort of grin a grimace at the name as it makes me think of the house in Shady Side, though this one is nothing like that: the word "Maryland" is the only thing they share. The townhouse looks tidy and affluent, but in a quiet way. Understated. It's not even gated, but it still doesn't invite you in.

I don't need to be sitting outside in visitor parking to make the call, but that's how it works out anyway. Being there help me put the pieces together. I drive by the school, then I drive to the house. Then I make the call. In this case one wouldn't have worked without the other.

"Hello, Mrs. Walker," I say politely, warmth in my voice. It surprises me sometimes that I'm good at that: sounding warm. "This is Constance White calling from Phoenix Groves Middle School. I'm Mason's nutritionist and I thought we could have a chat."

"Umm . . . hello, Miss White. I'm well . . . I'm sorry. I didn't even know Mason had a nutritionist. To speak of. That is . . . how can I help you?" She sounds nice. Interested. Maybe a bit concerned, but that's all right.

"Well, I've had Mason's whole class doing an experiment. We called it a fat finding mission."

"Oh. Well, haha. That sounds very clever."

"I've had everyone eating walnuts and a special green supplement every day. In a month, we're all going to retest our blood sugar levels. And see what we learn from that."

"That's . . . Well, that's super interesting."

"Isn't it, though? The thing is, Mason seems to have left on a vacation without his Fat Finding Kit. I wonder if I could drop it off for him?"

"I'm sorry, that won't be possible. He left on a trip with his father a few days ago."

"His father picked him up?"

"Well, an associate of his father's did." She sounds like she's considering. "An assistant of some sort, I guess."

I'm working very hard here. I'm working so hard I can feel sweat form on my forehead; between my breasts. How to get information without looking like you're fishing for it. How to get it volunteered without asking. Sometimes it doesn't work. And usually it does work only with some finessing. You can only get the info you want with subtle work. And so I sweat.

"Would that person have picked Mason up from school? Someone on the school's pickup list?"

"No, I don't think so. It was a young woman I hadn't met before. She said she was kind of like my ex-husband's assistant."

"Kind of?"

"That's just what she said."

"I see," I say as though thinking about it. That's the other thing about pulling information. You have to saunter toward it. Like you don't even really care.

"Did she say where they were going?"

"Well, it's funny you should ask that, because it didn't make much sense to me. But maybe his dad has something going on there. We've been missing each other, on the phone I mean, for the last few days. But she said they were going to Washington, D.C."

CHAPTER THIRTY-EIGHT

I ASK A few more questions, but I know I'm not getting anywhere. Did her husband have permission to take Mason across state lines? Yes, he did. Both parents travel frequently and Mason would come with. They'd made easy out-of-state travel part of their custody agreement. Did Cameron have to report about every address Mason would stay at when out of state? No. He did not. Neither parent did. What about the assistant picking Mason up from school? This also was not unusual. Both parents had people who worked for them who sometimes got delegated to pick Mason up.

"Actually, Miss White, the tenor of your questioning is beginning to cause some concern. If you have something to say, I'd appreciate it if you'd just come right out with it."

I hang up quietly. Politely. But really, I want to howl at the moon. Something is happening. Something just out of my grasp that I can't quite see. It's like looking in a kaleidoscope. All the pieces fit together somehow, but when you hold them up to the light, you just see prisms and shapes. You can even detect some sort of a pattern, but you can't quite sort out what it all means. That's how I feel right now.

My first instinct is to book another flight to D.C., just go screaming back there, but as soon as I have that thought I realize it would be a stupid idea. And for so many reasons. Stupid and counterproductive and—maybe worst of all at this stage—a useless waste of my time. I have the ability to direct things from here. If I'm careful and mindful and keep my eyes on all of these moving parts, my energies will be more useful here, too.

The trouble is, I'm deeply confused. That kaleidoscope image rises up again. I close my eyes, still sitting there in Amanda Walker's guest parking area, and try to make sense out of everything. There must be something that I'm missing. Some loose thread I can pull to make it all start to unravel.

I book another place to stay. The closest one is a Frank Lloyd Wright–designed hotel with four swimming pools not much more than walking distance from where I'm parked at Amanda Walker's. I make the reservation sitting right there. And then I roll over and when I arrive I am entranced by the starkly beautiful design.

I've booked a room poolside. It's so expensive for a second it makes my eyes sweat, and then I breathe and let it go. I don't know why I felt I needed it. Or maybe I do understand the urge. I suddenly feel the need for self-indulgence. It's like, out of the blue, I have a clear view of where I'm heading and there won't be comfort there. Not for a while. Or booking nice hotels. So now I want to think—conjugate?—in peace. And the Biltmore Hotel will do just fine for that.

As I check in at the hotel, I ask to use the business center and then I catch two big breaks: a good-looking gentleman of a certain age is leaving as I enter. He holds the door for me. Which means I don't have to swipe my keycard. The second break is that there is no one in there as I arrive. It's all smooth desktops and workstations and phones. I have given a lot of thought as to where to make this call. There are almost no pay phones left in the universe, I've noticed. I mean, I've looked. And my cellphone won't do. A simple Google search had told me that even if I use *67 when calling the police, they have some kind of enhanced call display that sees the number that's calling anyway, like they've got some sort of miraculous superhero laser vision. Now at the business center I use a house phone and I use *67 anyway, thinking that maybe it will slow down the process of looking for the caller, but I really don't know and it probably doesn't matter anyway because when they look, they'll just find a hotel and there will be no connection to me.

The call I place is to the police station in Shady Side, Baltimore. And this is what I say: "I'm calling about 697 Columbia Beach Road. Please listen closely as I'm going to hang up very soon. That address is being used for human trafficking and drugs. Children are in danger there. Please investigate." And then I hang up. And I know that, despite the *67, they will be able to trace the call. But I reason that it's a large hotel with a lot of occupants, even in the off-season. They'd have a tough time narrowing it down to me. Meanwhile, even if I don't know quite what I'm doing yet, I've put something in motion. If he's there, it's possible Cameron's kid will get saved before something terrible happens to him. And that seems like my biggest goal right now. Sure: I want to get him back. But if we can also avoid terrible things happening, it would just be so much better.

Calling the Shady Side cops seems like a start, but before I even make that call I know that it's not enough. I sit, almost slump, down into one of the fancy office chairs, and I call Abigail Myers. It seems like a long shot, but short of charging out there on my own—something that I know will take two days to organize and execute—Myers will know what to do and get it done.

"Hello, Ms. Myers," I say when I get her.

"Abigail, please."

"Abigail. All right. We met a few days ago." I hadn't given her a name then; there seems no reason to do it now. "I brought a couple of young girls to you. I found them in Shady Side."

"Yes, of course. I remember you. Hello."

"The girls are okay?"

"They are, yes. Kira is recovering. And Libby . . . well, she's making plans." There's a smile in Abigail's voice as she says this. I feel like asking about it, but I've got business in hand.

"I'm calling about something else today, Ms. . . . Abigail. Something related."

"Yes." She is instantly alert. I hear it and something inside of me breathes. This had been the right call.

"I'm not certain, you understand? But I have reason to believe another child has been taken to the house, or maybe *is* being taken. I'm back in the west, so I don't know what to do . . ."

"Yes. No," she says quickly. "We have resources for this, too. Give me the address."

I do. And I tell her that I've anonymously alerted the police. "I have to be honest: this is all so far out of my experience," I tell her.

"Thankfully," she says, "that's true for most people. What can you tell me about the child?"

So I give her Mason's name and pedigree. I even tell her that the kid's father is currently being made to do stuff against his will in order to save the kid.

"But I don't think the people who have Mason are playing fair."

"That would be par for the course with this type of situation," Abigail tells me. "These aren't community leaders, generally."

I laugh at that, though not unkindly. It's just so close to the mark. "In this case, the guy actually *is* a community leader. We've just got to stop this, Abigail."

"I'm going to go out there myself."

"Not by yourself, though."

"I hadn't planned on it," she says. "But I'll let you know if we turn anything up. Can I call you on this number?"

And I curse myself because, this time, I forgot *67. It's like I'm falling apart.

"Sure," I say. "That would be great."

And then I end the call. And I sit there. And I just try to breathe.

CHAPTER THIRTY-NINE

OUTSIDE OF THE lobby, on a lanai between the hotel and a fancy courtyard bar, there is—yet another—gift shop. I buy a sun hat. Go to my room, unpack my case, and put on my bathing suit. Then I wander poolside, and find a chaise under misters and in the shade because it's hot. Really hot. Hardly anyone is out there, and somehow that makes it better, not worse. The hot season is the off-season and so I have this whole luxury hotel with a full staff carting drinks around poolside practically all to myself. When I try the water, I am delighted and astonished to find it cool and refreshing. Later when I ask one of the servers how that's possible, I discover that all of the hotel pools are cool—or heated, depending on the season—to a perfect eighty degrees, year-round.

I have brought Skeeter's laptop with me poolside, even though I'm paranoid enough to cover the distinctively bashed computer's outer skin with a towel while I swim. Once I'm back in my shady spot and settled, I order a Bloody Mary. It arrives double-time and with condensation dripping down the side of the glass. And I figure that, in this venue and with this backdrop and accoutrements, if you can't think a thing through, well, you'd better just give it up.

Everything keeps coming back to Skeeter. Hence the laptop. But throughout this whole thing it has been his name, again and again, that keeps cropping up. I don't know for sure that's who placed the hit on Cameron in the first place, but considering how things have gone down since, it's a pretty good bet. The kids in Shady Side that I'd brought back to the city with me. I'd seen Skeeter there, heard him talk about them. Clearly his involvement is key. I don't know for sure that's who organized that first helicopter roundup, but few people would have the resources and motivation to do that on their own. Just about everything has Skeeter's fingerprints on it, and suddenly it seems to me that taking him down will be the key to almost every other point under contention.

So the laptop. First, I have to scoot back into my suite to get my own computer and the Thunderbolt cable, because I'd forgotten about the special connection. When it's made, I resolve to comb through the whole thing and find whatever I might have missed on earlier passes. And the computer has a lot of storage, so that could potentially be quite a bit.

What I hadn't looked through before was Word files and possible business hierarchies: however Skeeter had his business files organized. When I find them I get that dull thud of satisfaction again, because there they are. I can't personally see the organization of them at first, but at least I think to look this time, so we're getting someplace. There are files labeled "Ranch" and "Hearings" and "Pedigrees" and "Eleana" and so on. When I come to one marked "Personal," I expect some special login will be required, but it just turns out to be a file with that name, so I roll through. The folder proves to be a real hodgepodge of stuff: not necessarily highly personal, but all to do with him. Personally.

I see a file labeled "Walker" and think I might be about to stumble across what I had been looking for. Just then, the computer makes a loud pinging sound. Loud enough to be irritating. I turn from my own computer, where I'm going through the files on his, and turn to the battered laptop. There's a message on the screen: "This computer belongs to Skeeter Allaband." And a phone number. I'm sitting there pondering what to do about this message, when the box disappears and another that says "Remote Wipe" pops up on the screen. There is a dialog box there so I can stop it, but pressing the box and outlining the dialog all do nothing. And then another message pops up on the screen. "This computer is the property of John Sebastian Allaband," and I realize it makes sense that he wasn't born with "Skeeter." The name is followed by a phone number and the advice to return the computer if found. Then "Remote Wipe" again.

I sit there dumbfounded for a moment, and by the time I recover, the computer has basically turned into a brick. I try to chastise myself but stop it: it's perfectly reasonable to think there was probably nothing I could do. Other than having the presence of mind to look at the files sooner, of course. But I've been busy. And, also? It's water under the bridge.

Despite the bridge analogy, there are no words to express my disappointment in this moment: my hopes dashed by a minor technological marvel. I feel a bit like swearing. A bit like crying. I do neither. Instead, I motion to my server to bring on another Bloody Mary. While I wait for it to show up, I drop my floppy hat onto the chaise and plunge back into the pool.

CHAPTER FORTY

I DO LAPS in the beautiful pool. And then I splash around some. As usual for me, exercise lifts my spirits somewhat. Honestly, if I had no way of accessing endorphins, I probably would have not survived as long as I have. I don't quite understand it, but I don't question it either. I just move.

Back in my room, I shower, put myself together, wander to the better of the two restaurants in the hotel and have dinner. All the while I know I'm going through the motions. Outside I probably look like a teacher from the Midwest, out here for a conference and enjoying some time alone. On the inside everything is swirling. I'm trying to put it all together. Trying to have it make sense.

After my dinner I wander the beautiful grounds, look at all of the pools, have a drink at yet another fabulous bar, then head back to my room where I fall asleep easily. All this thinking, it seems, has tired me out.

In the morning, it's the sound of my phone that wakes me.

"I've got an address for you," is the first thing Cody says when I answer.

"Thanks, Cody. I knew you'd come through."

"You okay?" Was it something in my voice? I hadn't been aware. But his hometown concern touches me. I know it's real.

"Yeah, no. I'm okay. Just a lot going on. Thanks again for this. You're the best. You always make it look easy. I'll stick something extra in the payment."

I write the address down carefully, then fold it up and put it in my phone wallet, which is the safest place I have. It's not something I can deal with right this minute, but it's something I want to deal with, for sure.

I have just put my phone down when it rings again. After so long with basically no phone calls, I'm suddenly feeling like a switchboard. And I'm not loving the feeling.

It's Abigail.

"We have him," she says by way of hello.

I let out a breath I hadn't even known I was holding.

"Mason?"

"Yeah." She sounds slightly breathless. Like she's been running, but I recognize it as excitement and a job well done. She's happy. It's taken her breath away.

"That's amazing," I say. "I can't tell you how relieved I am to hear that. Tell me."

And so she does. How she had driven out there herself with a couple of colleagues—as she speaks, in my mind I'm imagining the two burly guys who had brought Kira in on a stretcher when I dropped her off. Abigail had gotten there just behind the police. A man had answered the door when the police knocked. Abigail was standing right behind them. I ask and the guy doesn't meet Skeeter's description, so maybe it's Terry or maybe it's someone else, but it doesn't really matter because the upshot of all of it is that Mason and a couple of other little kids are now safe, and partly because Abigail had bulldozed in when the police began to demur because they didn't have a warrant or whatever. I smile at that. Considering the agency that backs her, she has probably less to lose and fewer rules to follow than a police officer might. More at stake, too. As a result, the kids are safe with Abigail, and the guy—whoever he is—is in custody for transporting a minor from out of state.

"He had IDs for all three kids," she tells me. "But since we had Mason's backstory, we were able to identify him. We called his mom. She was able to absolutely identify him. She backed up everything you'd told me. She's on her way to D.C. now."

"I told you yesterday that the kid was being used as a pawn by a bad guy, right?"

"Yes," Abigail says. And she doesn't press further. I understand it. It's partly the business she's in.

"Is there any way you could convey that to the mom? And maybe help keep both her and the kid safe for a couple of days? That's all it's going to take to clean up this end, I think."

"I can do that," Abigail says solemnly, like she's making an oath.

"Thank you. I'll let you know when the coast is clear, so to speak."

"Sounds good. Meanwhile, you're a hero," she says. "You maybe saved this kid's life."

"Me? No. That's all you Abigail. I wish I'd been there to see it."

"It's my job," she says. Then, "Yeah. I'm happy, too. Best of all, I think we got there soon enough—the kids are all fine. A little shaken up, but unharmed. It all could have been so much worse."

CHAPTER FORTY-ONE

It all could have been so much worse.

After I hang up, the words echo in my head. I'd been there myself. I know how true they are.

With Mason safe and Abigail keeping both the kid and his mother under wraps for a few days, I need to figure out how to shake Cameron loose. With Cameron freed of confinement and also the reason he was being forced to cooperate out of the way of danger, I will have a better idea of how to deal with Skeeter.

It's first thing in the morning, and I know I won't want to go back to the ranch to tell Cameron the good news and try to break him out of there until after dark. Beyond that, there is a lot of stuff I need to do, important things maybe I should be focusing on, but I find I can't bring my mind to stillness. I know I need to find a source of calm. And then I think of one.

I check out of the beautiful hotel five minutes ahead of the required time and then I head out to Cathedral National Park again. It's too hot by half, but I push that thought away. I have this day.

When I get there, I follow one of the roads that lead to a trailhead. It happens that the one I choose at random is close to a bend in the Salt River. With my new hat shading my head and a few bottles of water in my bag along with the Bersa and with my painting gear on my back, I traverse my way to the river's edge. There are a few people there, taking advantage of the cool of the water. They don't let my arrival disturb their play. I just want to be alone, though, so I follow a path next to the river upstream until I find a shaded, pretty spot and I break out my paints.

I'm feeling stronger now. I feel like all the noodling I've been doing is making my art happen. It all feels like it's starting to come together. How I know: the mixing of color is starting to be muscle memory. I no longer have to think about how to get a vibrant purple. I just squeeze out some cool red and add some warm blue and I know pretty much exactly what I'll get. And it isn't just a growing command of color. The framing of a scene: where I begin, where I follow through. I'm getting to a place where it's suddenly all coming together. Where it all finally makes sense. The feeling is exquisite. Sublime?

Can life be like that, I wonder? Can you reel through it and then suddenly—or even, not so suddenly—you get to a place where it all makes sense? I suspect not. I suspect that living life may not just be about doing a thing until you're good at it. That maybe you get good at life by leaning away from trying to get it right. By observing. By being. By doing it all without thought of the result. By being kind. I suspect there is no muscle memory for getting good at life, and that by doing the best we can and being the best we can be, we win at life, whatever that looks like.

This day no horses cross my path, hunted or otherwise, and the landscape I sketch and then paint is barren and beautiful, the signs of life subtle but present. This is how I will remember Arizona, I think, in some near future when I am no longer here. Dry and rich. Hot and varied. Empty and teeming with life.

When the light starts to run out of the day, I find I am hungry. It is too early to try and get Cameron out of there and so I feel lucky when I am able to get a table at Sam's. I will eat, and more of the day will run away. It's all coming together, I think with satisfaction. Everything is working out.

Sam recognizes me right away.

"Hey, kid," he says by way of greeting. "Good to see you again. Did you find what you were looking for?"

"Thanks, Sam," I say. "It's good to see you, too. And yes. I think I did find what I was looking for."

I order a burger and fries, then munch thoughtfully when they arrive, carefully observing the room while I eat. Looking for familiar faces or connections. And while they might be there, I don't manage to put anything together. Or maybe the thing is just to be, I realize suddenly as I tuck the last French fry away. Maybe my being there is enough. Sometimes it isn't about all of the things you accomplish, I realize, as though this is a new thought. Sometimes it's just about eating the food, breathing the air, sipping the wine. It's not about being first or fastest, it's just about being. The thought floors me and I have to sit with it for a while.

By the time I leave the restaurant, it is late, but maybe not late enough, but I just can't hold myself back anymore. I want to get on with it. I know that at ten thirty p.m. not everyone will be asleep, but it's ranch country, and so I have a hope that most everyone will be in their rooms and getting settled for the night, rather than out here somewhere quarreling about pricing and livestock strains.

Once again, I park at a distance, then navigate the cactus and try not to think about snakes while I creep to the house.

By now I know my way to Cameron's part of the house. I make my way there with no wrong turns. I am not surprised to find his room in darkness. I imagine that being held against your will would be stressful. I'd probably try to sleep away a time of confinement, too.

I get close enough to tap the window as I did last time. No response. I tap a little harder. While I'm tapping it hits me with a start how little I know about this man. How could I have come to care so much about someone when I don't even know if he's a light or heavy sleeper?

I tap a bit more, but after a while, I find I am tapping with less conviction. It's becoming apparent he is so deeply asleep he can't hear me. I check the windows nearest the bed, where he brought me through. They are all locked up tightly. But it's a big room with a lot of windows, and I set out to check them all. I don't have to get that far, though, before I find one that is open and I am relieved that it is not one of the ones that is high up. I can clamber through it easily, and I do. Then I stand in the dark, trying to catch my breath from both excitement and exertion. As I stand, though, I realize that something has changed. The room has a feeling that is absolutely dead. With a sinking heart I ignite the flashlight in my phone. Beam it around the room. My instincts were correct: there is no one here. I am alone.

CHAPTER FORTY-TWO

Since I'm already here and there really is almost nothing left to lose, I scan around and try to see how long the room has been empty. There are no conclusive clues for me, but I have a sense that he's not just down the hall. The room is his so it's difficult to spot where the holes might be—and what might not be there. But I have a sense that he has himself not been there for a while.

Once again, I feel defeated. There have been some successes, sure. But the key things—one after the other—have come up short. Like each time I am almost there, and I can taste victory, it is taken away. I feel like crying, but I don't, of course. Instead, I suck it up and head back the way I had come in. I feel like I am nearly intercepted a couple of times along the way, but I am glad when I reach my car without incident because there's a part of me—a very small part, but still—that just wants to throw it all in. That part of me would welcome interception. That part of me just wants it all done.

I am frustrated and I am alone and I am filled with a grief I can't even begin to understand. It is by now the dead of night, and without being fully aware of where I am going, I start driving in the direction of Skeeter Allaband's ranch. I haven't been there before, but I have a pretty good idea of where it is, a more or less direct line through the thinnest part of the park, fifty twisty miles away. And so I head out and the dulcet tones of the map app in my phone give me all of the specifics I need.

As I drive, I think. Why am I heading to Skeeter's place? What am I hoping to find? And the answer is: I'm not quite sure. I only know I have just one lead left. If it doesn't pan out, I really don't know where to go.

By the time I arrive it is still deep night and as much as I want to just jump into action, some better instinct guides me, and I cool my jets for a few hours until the thinnest sliver of first light pushes its way over the horizon. It's not a lot of light—at least, not at first—but I will at least be able to see where I'm going.

I leave the car a little way up a service road off the highway about a half mile from the ranch entrance. I've used my map app in satellite mode to get a sense of where the ranch buildings are in relation to the road. It's a visual from space, but it still tells me that, from the highway, there will be another ten-to-fifteen-minute walk to get to the ranch buildings. It's not a huge distance, but it does mean that I need to get everything right: I won't be able to just make an easy jaunt back to the car if I forget something or I need to get away. Also, though the buildings can be seen from space, it's difficult to determine exactly what they are. This big rectangle might be a house, but it also looks as though it could be a barn with an indoor arena. And this small cluster of outbuildings? It might be casitas, for ranch hands or guests. But it also could be barns. There is just not enough detail for me to tell.

The walk is unpleasant. Where at the Flying W there had been some verdant growth—desert forest all around—the Allaband Cattle Company is a barren burr on an arid backdrop. And from what I'd learned, maybe it hadn't always been that way. And maybe—just maybe—the development deals Skeeter had done with his land had contributed to creating it as an arid wasteland.

As I begin to walk, I feel desperately unprotected and I recognize that comes from how little I know about Skeeter's operation. I know it is a working cattle ranch, but I don't even have an idea of the size, though, in all fairness, even if I had those numbers, they wouldn't mean much to me.

As I narrow the distance between my car and the ranch, it occurs to me it would not be unreasonable for some erstwhile cowboy on his way to work to come across me heading toward the ranch. And then what would I say, I wonder? Even while I admonish myself for having the sort of thoughts that can make things come true, I realize there's not much I can do about it. The closer I get to the ranch, the more vast and imperious I find it to be, and the worse my thoughts get.

And then I'm there, thankfully with no cowboy encounters.

Up close, the buildings begin to have sense and meaning. What I had thought might be a horse barn when I looked at the satellite images proves instead to be a multi-car garage attached by a breezeway to a house that is not merely large: it is huge beyond my wildest imaginings. A castle or shopping mall–sized residence that probably only houses one or two.

Not far beyond this huge mansion, I come across a normal-sized ranch house, which means that you could only fit about three of my little houses in it, instead of the ten or fifteen that would fit into the big one. This one has its own pool, too, though smaller and less palatial.

As I skulk around in the shadows, two things become very clear to me: 1) There is no way I can discover if Cameron is here by just sneaking around in the pre-dawn. There is simply too much ground to cover. And 2) While I had suspected that Skeeter had piles of dough, nothing I'd seen before had hinted at the level of ostentation I see here now. I know I'll have to process what that means in the total picture I am building, but such noodling isn't for now. Right now, I have to focus on what is known, and also on what can be in my control. So much of what I've seen here is not.

I am hesitating, trying to think where to go. Where to begin. The mansion, with endless rooms and anterooms and other rooms whose names I can't even imagine. Or the normal-sized ranch house? Or one of the casitas? Or the barns? Really, it's all overwhelming and an argument could be built for any. Or all. But I am momentarily petrified by indecision. And just as I have settled on heading toward the larger house, I see headlights flick on not far from where I stand. My reactions are thankfully fast. As soon as those lights come on, I hit the ditch, rolling out of sight of the car that rolls past the very spot where I had been standing not three minutes before.

The adrenalin is racing through my veins so sharply that I don't initially feel the jolt of pain that runs in a swath across one shoulder and down my back. I don't stop to self-evaluate, though: the experience has confirmed what I suspected. There are better ways to approach what I have come to do.

I manage to get back to the car without being seen though I am in so much pain, I'm not sure how I keep going. Back at the car a new sea of pain explodes when my shoulder touches the back of the seat, and I suspect I know what I have done. It's not a sprain or a cut, I think, but maybe the cactus I have been trying so hard to avoid.

Without giving it too much thought, I head back to the casino hotel, which, even while I do it, feels like an approximation of tucking my tail between my legs and running.

Even though it's barely seven a.m. by the time I get there, I am in luck—plus it's a weekday in the off-season. For a few extra bucks they give me early, early, early check-in, and I get up to the room with as little time passing as possible. I strip off my clothes almost before I'm in the door.

Once I'm naked and standing in front of the full-length mirror in the bathroom, my suspicions are confirmed: I must have rolled over a couple of small cacti and some very sharp rocks because my back and shoulders are a desert scape of angry flesh, jutting here and there with quills, as though I'd done battle with a tiny porcupine. I fill the big tub with hot water and try to soak the cactus spines out. When I'm done, I feel somewhat better, but I can feel that there are many—hundreds?—of little barbs still under my skin and I just don't know what to do.

I feel like I probably need to see a doctor, but I'm just not in the mood. I do an internet search instead—which I know is always a bad idea with health stuff—and I read how you can get cactus needles out with glue. This sounds simple enough, and so I set out to try it. Calling housekeeping and asking them to bring me some glue; happy when they say they can do it.

After it arrives, spreading the glue on the impacted area is a terrible challenge, and then waiting around still enough for it to dry. I feel foolish while I do it, but I don't have a better idea. Do I really expect this to work? I'd laugh, I guess, except I'm in quite a bit of pain and feeling like an idiot, to boot. After all, I have places to be. Things to do. And here I am on my belly on a hotel bed waiting for glue to dry. I just couldn't imagine anything more stupid.

I wait as long as you're supposed to, and then I wait longer still, for good measure. I know it all would be so much easier with someone to help me, but I realize that I can't, for instance, just trot down to the casino and ask a croupier to peel the dried glue off my back. While I'm thinking about that, though, I get an idea I realize I should have started with and I call down and make an appointment with the spa.

When I get there, I'm wearing a hotel bathrobe and a grimace. I'd booked a massage, but now that I'm there, I tell the girl behind the front desk what I really want and get to see her well-sculpted eyebrows arch up like twin question marks.

"Excuse me one minute," she says. Her voice is calm, but those eyebrows tell a different story.

She crosses the spa to confer with another girl, this one in a very professional-looking white smock, as though she is a doctor. I see doctor spa lady shrug and smile, then cross over to me welcomingly.

"Forgive Brenda: she's from the northeast. I grew up in Arizona. You did the right thing, with the glue. Now let's see if I can help you."

She seems competent, confident, and completely unfazed. I feel so relieved I fairly sag with it. She guides me into one of the massage cubicles and goes to work on my back and shoulders. The glue I've already had drying does pull out some of them, but then she goes to work with tweezers.

"What the hell," she says as she plucks. "You're not supposed to *roll* in cactus, don't you know that?"

"Yeah. I know. It was an accident," I say.

"I figured," she replies. "Got some road rash back here, too."

"Thanks for taking a run at this."

"Oh, you're welcome. I wanted to be a doctor before I took up aesthetics, so I'm actually kinda having fun."

When she's done, she lets me know that there are still a few needles below the surface of my skin. "I just couldn't get them out safely. You'll need to see a doctor or just plain wait. After a while, your body will just reject them. In the meantime, you'll probably want to sleep on your stomach for a few days."

I pay for a deluxe massage, then tip her extra well. Back in my room I lick my wounds, feeling miserable, sorry for myself, and still somewhat in pain. I also know I'm losing valuable time, and I worry that I might lose track of Cameron. What if they take him away and stash him someplace new? But there's really nothing I can do about it. I still feel a burning need to get into Skeeter's estate, but I can tell I'm going to need to be a little more ingenious. Clearly, the full-frontal approach was not going to work this time.

CHAPTER FORTY-THREE

I HAD SEEN Skeeter briefly in D.C. Or rather, he had seen me, though I was not sure if I'd made any kind of impression. Terry was another matter. If he was around, he'd remember me for sure. I manage to buy plain glasses from the gift shop and a blonde wig from the salon. With that and some frumpy clothes and an apron filched from a cupboard near the casino kitchen, I figure I'm sufficiently disguised to storm the castle.

Back at the Allaband Cattle Company the following morning, I drive right up to the front door. Knock. I don't recognize the woman who opens the front door. I'm just relieved it is neither Skeeter nor Terry.

"Lawrence sent me," is what I say.

She looks at me quizzically.

"I'm sorry?"

"Lawrence," I repeat. "At Who's Cooking Catering? You requested a chef."

"I did?"

"Well, someone did." I paste an annoyed look on my face, cross my arms, and stand as though I'm going to wait her out.

"Okay, ummm. Okay," she says. "Wait here. Let me see."

It's my single shot and I'm hoping I haven't blown it. My thought is that an operation as big as this will have many hands who won't know what the other hands are doing. Someone ordered a chef? Okay. Well, go cook something. She's back shortly and that's pretty much how it goes down.

"Sorry," she says, "I couldn't find . . . whoever ordered you. But . . . ummm . . . well, the kitchen is in there. I hope you'll find everything you need? And we'll figure it all out later."

"Okay, thanks," I say. I have brought everything I need to make scones for two dozen people. And I've got clotted cream and jams, too. The operation and then the serving will take a few hours. By then I hope to have some inkling of what I'm doing. But poking around from the inside should provide an advantage. I'm also fairly certain there will be no cacti inside the house, so I should be safe from that, too.

I'm relieved when I see the kitchen. It is gorgeous, fully equipped, and absolutely derelict, as though no one has actually properly cooked here for a while. It's clearly amateur night in this kitchen all the time, likely with everyone fending for themselves and heating up the occasional packaged meal. It might take them a while to discover that no one on the ranch hired a chef, but there's no doubt in an operation like this, someone might have. I'm hoping they keep wondering long enough that I can do what I came to do. Which is *not* make scones, but that will be a start.

First, she watches me for a bit. I make sniffing noises at the counter and set about looking for cleaning supplies. It's legit. You wouldn't need to be a professional chef to see this wasn't a place cooking should be done. Not in this condition.

"What's your name?" I say to her as I work. I'm hoping for more than a name, and I get it.

"I'm Muncie," she says. "I'm Mr. Allaband's assistant."

"You are?" I say, pausing in my scrubbing of the counters. "It's weird then. That you didn't know I was coming."

"Yes," she sniffs. "It was."

I shrug. "Sorry. I can't help with that. I just know what Lawrence told me. Which was nothing. As usual." I kinda grin at her and she grins back. We're connected now. We both have bosses who don't tell us everything.

"Well, I'll leave you to it, I guess. I'm going to be in the barns for a while." She scratches something on a piece of paper. "Here's my cell number. Call me if you need anything."

I sketch her a fast salute, then drop back into my work. After a while I hear the front door close and a car engine start up. I drop my rag and head down the nearest hallway, which is a risky business, because I'm still not certain if I'm alone in the house or not. With that in mind, I trot back and get my cleaning rag and a bottle of surface cleaner. At least if someone questions me I can pretend to be cleaning something. Or looking for the bathroom. Or both.

It's a big house, and there are grand spaces for gathering and entertainment, and there are additionally long hallways that lead to other rooms, many of them with closed doors. I tell myself those closed doors don't mean anything. What is the likelihood that Cameron is being held here, waiting for me to find him? I push the thought out of my mind. This is simply the only idea I have. If this doesn't work, I can't imagine what my next move might be.

The large grand spaces are easy for me to clear. There are no doors, only a formal living room leading to a dining room leading to a less formal living room leading to the kitchen, where I'm centered, which has its own eat-in area separate from the cooking space. I head off down the nearest hallway. The first door I try is a laundry room larger than my bedroom at home. Across from it is a pantry. Logical enough. Then a large guest bathroom. Also logical. Next a large bedroom, almost like a master suite because it has its own bathroom, but since the next room also has its own bathroom, I realize that might just be the theme of the house: large bedrooms with their own bathrooms. And since both of these are closest to the kitchen, and then bracketed by a garage, it seems possible to me that this whole wing is intended to accommodate service people. The one closest to the kitchen looks to be unoccupied and I'm relieved at that. At least I'm probably not going to get accosted by some angry chef thinking I'm trying to steal their job.

With the whole wing closest to the kitchen taken care of—and no sign of Cameron—I move more deeply into the house, realizing as I do so that the farther I get from the kitchen, the less excuse I have for being out of that area.

Quickly I realize that the house has a lot of unoccupied rooms. They are made up, as though for guests, but hangers in closets and drawers are empty. A lot of space, no one home.

When I finish one whole wing, and with at least four more to go, I figure I should get back to the kitchen and make some semblance of scone preparation.

I find a large metal bowl and mix dry ingredients—flour, baking powder, baking soda, sugar, salt—in lieu of sifting. If I actually cared about the outcome, I would sift. But I don't. So I don't. I know they'll still be okay anyway.

I was prepared to cut the butter into the flour with two knives. And I'm feeling pretty smug, too. Like all that time stuck in the forest didn't completely go to waste. But then I find a food processor, so decide that will work even better. Especially since, again, I don't care. Additionally, I find some large baking sheets—apparently, I'm not the first caterer in this space. I set the oven to preheat and then—with all this strong evidence of work-in-progress strewn about the kitchen—I head off into the second wing.

A few more unoccupied bedrooms. An office. Then a locked door. My heart leaps. For all I know it just might be where Skeeter keeps his sex toys, but I have a feeling it isn't that. I knock. Firmly. Nothing. And so I knock again. And then a voice.

"Really? Knocking now? Is that a joke? Why would you even bother?"

And I can't even believe my luck. I'm only—what?—fifteen doors in and there he is, because I'm certain it is Cameron from the first.

"Are you able to open the door?"

Dead silence, and then: "Is that you?"

"It is," I reply.

"No," he says. I can tell he wants to ask me what I'm doing there, but he holds it for now. Clearly, we have more important fish to fry.

"Hang tight," I say. I feel like I've heard a noise from the direction of the kitchen and I've forgotten my cloth and cleaner. "I'll think of something." And then I scurry back to the kitchen where Muncie is having a good look around herself.

"Where did you get to?"

"The house is so beautiful," I say. "I was just having a look around."

"Well don't, okay? Just . . . just stay here and do whatever it is you're doing, all right?"

"Sure," I say blandly.

"And I've had an ask around. No one knows who hired you."

"Yeah," I say, "me neither. Just Lawrence said—"

"Yeah, yeah, okay. Lawrence. Skeeter's out on the range, or I would have asked him myself. He should be back within cell range within the hour, though. We'll find out then."

"Perfect," I say, addressing my creation and ignoring the hot oven. "Meanwhile, scones," and I spread my hands wide in a visual *ta da*.

"Seriously?" There is a visible softening.

"Of course. Honestly, it would have been done by now, but the house is just so pretty."

The flour ingredients are in the food processor now. I toss in the butter, a chunk at a time.

"Oh, that's awesome," she says. "When will they be ready?"

I'm running the food processor now. The butter chunks up like small pebbles in the flour mixture. I dump it back into the big metal bowl and pour in the milk I'd premeasured and had sitting out for this moment.

"Twenty minutes, give or take," I say. While she watches, I mix it with a few strong strokes with a spatula. I don't want it well mixed. Just hanging together. "Maybe give me half an hour. That will give them a chance to cool when they come out of the oven."

I turn the dough out on the clean counter. She watches while I form it in a large circle with my hands, never pressing too hard or making the dough too thin. Then with the edge of a drinking glass, selected earlier, I start to cut out perfectly circular scones and carefully toss them onto an unoiled pan, one at a time.

"Goodness," she says. "Well, this is just fascinating." I keep working while she talks. There's getting to be more and more circles. "I actually have to run a couple of errands. I'll be back in forty-five minutes," she tells me.

"That'll be perfect," I say, looking up from my work and beaming at her, while I slide the baking tray full of scones into the hot oven. "I'll see you in a while." I'm setting a timer for twenty minutes as she heads out the door.

As soon as I hear her car leave, I go to the kitchen junk drawer I'd spotted earlier. There is a small hammer there. I leave the scones to bake and go to the room where I'd found Cameron. Hoping there are no repercussions, I smash down hard on the handle with the hammer. It is not a security lockset. It disintegrates under pressure. The door pops open. Cameron peeps out.

"Holy shit," he says looking at me, but whether it's my new hair or my costume or the fact that I have essentially rescued him—am in the process of rescuing him—I'm not really sure.

"No time for details, but Mason is rescued," I say, tasting the sweetness of the surprise on his face. "Follow me," I say. I have the Bersa tucked into the waistband of my jeans. I whip the wig off as I go. Drop it. There's not much point to the disguise with this lug trotting along behind me: he blows my cover just by existing.

I'm relieved to see there's no one in the kitchen. I turn off the oven, grab a kitchen towel, and pull the scones out as Cameron grins. "Seriously? You're stopping to bake?"

I grin back at him. "Sorry. Can't help myself."

"They look fantastic."

"They'll be all right." I wrap a couple in the tea towel and stuff them in my bag.

"Who are you?"

"Right?" I reply.

And then we're moving again.

"Where are we going?"

"We have to get out of here. After that I don't know. You're not safe anywhere right now, are you?"

I look back at Cameron and he seems a little wild-eyed, but he doesn't respond. We're heading down a corridor toward what I hope is the front door, when I hear another door open in a different part of the house. Footsteps coming toward us.

"Damn," I say. There is a closed door to my right and I open it, pulling Cameron in behind me.

"Damn," I say again, when I realize what I've done. I'd expected yet another empty bedroom—so many in this house. Instead, we have stumbled into Skeeter's office. The man himself is seated behind a huge oak desk, his back to a window that looks out over the Superstition Mountains. When we practically skid into him, his face lights with surprise.

The office looks like a set designer created for some TV show featuring a cowboy mogul. Everything is there, right down to a Remington bronze sculpture—cowboys on horseback. There are steer horns and framed animal paintings on the wall, lots of burnished leather, and a wall of leatherbound books with perfect spines.

For just a moment, time is suspended. I feel caught. I *am* caught. Both of us—Cameron and me—are caught.

Skeeter is the first to speak, "What the hell?" he says and I see his right arm snake out toward his desk drawer.

"Don't!" It's me, and the Bersa is pointed at his head. Cameron looks at me as though I've sprouted horns.

"What do you want?" Skeeter's voice is deadly quiet. I have the feeling it wouldn't take much for it to turn into a roar. It's a natural enough question, though at this point things are so nuanced I'm not even sure anymore.

Until this moment, all I'd wanted was to get me and Cameron out of there safely. But suddenly, the encounter feels like a metaphor for everything. Sure: I can get Cameron out, but what of the future? This man hired a hit on Cameron, I'm quite sure of it. Then he kidnapped his kid. And did so many awful things, both to Cameron and his own community.

In the split second I contemplate all of these things, I wonder, also, how Cameron will ever be safe again. He won't, that's the answer. And if I hadn't known it before, I do now, here surrounded by all of Skeeter's wealth and power.

"I want him safe," I say, indicating Cameron with a nod of my head, while never taking my eyes off Skeeter's face. "Trouble is, I don't know if that can happen if you're alive."

"You have a dilemma then," Skeeter says, the faintest trace of a smile on thin lips. He leans back slightly, maybe waiting for me to relax. I don't though. I stay taut and poised, secure in the knowledge that, however he is calculating the situation, he's underestimating me. That's not a bad thing for this moment.

"It was Skeeter?" Cameron sounds bewildered. "Skeeter, it was you who grabbed me? Grabbed my kid. Threatened us. It was you all along?"

There is a rage growing in Cameron's voice as he says this. I hadn't realized: However all of this had been done, Skeeter had kept his face out of it. Having others, not people Cameron would recognize, handling him and making their demands. That only made sense, when I thought about it. Why would Skeeter make himself known to his captive? Better to have distance, in case something went wrong.

And something had gone wrong.

Now the tables have turned and, much to my surprise, Cameron advances on Skeeter. I might have the gun—and no one doubts that if I intervene it will be deadly—but Cameron is just mad as hell. He advances at his old foe. Skeeter sees the younger, stronger man coming and the grin drops off his face while he pushes his chair back and starts to get up. Cameron reaches Skeeter just as he rises. Cameron matches Skeeter's momentum and catches the older cowboy on the jaw with his fist. Skeeter is knocked back into the large glass window. For an instant, it groans under the weight of the large man, and in my mind's eye, I see it shatter and him falling through. But in the end the glass holds, and Skeeter crumples in a heap on the floor behind his desk.

Cameron is over him in an instant, gathering him up by his shirt collar, and I hear ripping, but nothing comes apart.

"Explain yourself, man," Cameron demands. "You've gone too far."

But Skeeter is anything but remorseful. "You privileged little shit," he says. "Born with a fucking silver spoon."

"What?" Cameron looks genuinely shocked.

"You heard me, boy. Your whole life has been a goddamned picnic. You've never had to work for a single thing."

"What?" Cameron says again.

"Spending your time running around trying to *save* those goddamned horses, when all they have ever done is cost me money. Time and money."

Cameron has let go of Skeeter's shirt. The older man falls to the ground with a low "whuff" sound. He looks defeated. I wonder if it's true. While they're breathing, guys like Skeeter aren't ever defeated. Like a rattlesnake, they can look like they're done but until you've cut 'em in half and buried them in two separate holes, they might come back to bite you.

"There are things I could say to you—" Cameron's voice is low and deadly—"but I'm not going to waste my breath. You've scared my kid, scared everyone close to me, and *held* me against my will and endangered my life, and God knows what else you are responsible for."

"What shall we do with him?" I've been putting the pieces together, but this is Cameron's call. I defer the endgame to him now. It's his show.

"Let's get him out of here. Run him to the cops. They'll know what to do with him."

I wish I agreed with Cameron. Guy like Skeeter: he's going to have friends. He probably has influence. I'm not sure the police is the right way to go, but the alternative? *My* alternative? That's not something someone like Cameron could understand or condone. That's why I loved him. That's why I can't love him now.

I don't agree, but I support his desired outcome. With a modification.

"Okay, Cameron. We'll give him to the cops. But we'll have the cops come here."

"Fair enough."

The police station is a solid forty-five-minute run, so we know we're not expecting them to come in under an hour. We barricade ourselves into the office with him, just in case any of his men get some ideas.

We leave him sitting on the floor. It's undignified, sure, but it seems like a safe place to watch him.

"I'm thirsty," he says after a while. "Get me some water."

"Aw, you'll live," I say, not bothering to tell him that I don't want to risk going out where someone in his employ might get the idea to rescue him.

"That's cruel and unusual," he says.

"What am I? A cop? Call my union. And pipe down."

Since it's clear he's not getting anywhere, he does what I've suggested and pipes down. Cameron and I settle in on the opposite side of the room, though I keep the Bersa uncocked and ready. I've got the idea I need to watch him like a snake. I take the scones out of my backpack. Pass one to Cameron. He takes a bite.

"Hey," he says quietly. "This is good."

"Oughta taste it with jam and clotted cream."

"You don't have any in there?"

I laugh. "I did, you know. But I left it all in the kitchen."

"Bad planning."

His turn to laugh.

"So much of this has been that."

"Why did he take you in the first place?" I want to know. I've got the gun trained on Skeeter at the other side of the room, but we're pitching our voices low so we can't be overheard.

Cameron shakes his head. "I knew it was something about the horses, obviously. Because when they grabbed Mason, they told me what to say. That was really all I knew."

"There's more to it," I say.

"There is?" Cameron is looking into the rearview quizzically.

"Yeah."

"Hmmm. Well, let's ask the source." He raises his voice in the direction of the snake in question. "The lady wants to know why you took me in the first place."

"Screw off, Ritchie Rich."

"Now that's not very nice," Cameron says, rising to his feet and crossing the room. I follow, watching Cameron's face. It's not a tone I've heard from him before. Or a look. "But you get another chance."

I see Skeeter pucker before Cameron does, but it happens too fast to warn him. Skeeter spits something vile and thick that lands on Cameron's face, which is close by.

Cameron takes out a bandana and wipes his face with it. And his face. Though I don't know him well, Cameron's face is like thunder. While he wipes, he looks like he's thinking. That's how it seems to me. It looks like he's thinking about what his next move should be. When he decides he strikes quickly, like a snake, chopping viciously across the side of Skeeter's neck in a way I figure is meant to disorient the old cowboy's vagus nerve, but do no real damage.

Skeeter responds with a sharp strangled sound. There is silence for a few minutes, the only sounds gargled breathing from Skeeter, heavy breathing from Cameron. And me, no sound, but I'm gripping the Bersa so hard my knuckles are white.

"Okay. Let's try that again. And keep in mind before fucking with me? The lady has a gun. It would be a pretty simple matter to just finish you and dump you in the desert. So give me what I want: why did you grab me."

"We had to," Skeeter says, his voice weaker now than it was. "We were rounding up those parasites." I hear a loud whack and then a sputtering and then Skeeter continues. "Horses. We were rounding up those horses. Illegal."

"Damn straight."

"We thought it was safe. Because we thought you was dead."

"What?"

"Why would you have thought that?" I ask it, but I know the answer.

I hear another whack, though I'm not sure what part this time.

"Answer," Cameron says by way of punctuation.

Skeeter mumbles something.

"Say it again. Say it so we can hear it."

"I'd put a hit on you."

"A hit," Cameron prompts.

"You know: I'd hired someone to kill you. And I thought it was a done deal by then. It was supposed to be. So I figured you was dead. Figured wasn't nothing you could do about me taking the horses then."

"You'd put a *hit* on me? Like . . . a contract killing?"

"Yeah."

"Why aren't I dead yet?"

"When I nabbed you, that day you came careening into the corrals after the helicopters when we was having our little roundup, I canceled it."

"You canceled a hit when you kidnapped him, you mean?" I say.

Skeeter arches a brow. "I guess you could look at it that way."

"You can do that?" Cameron looks at me. "Cancel a hit?"

I just shrug. How would I know? But, of course, I know.

Then he looks at Skeeter. "You can do that?"

Skeeter had the answer that I did not. "You have enough money? Turns out you can do anything."

Somehow the words chill me, but Cameron is just getting started.

"So you figured I was dead, then you found I wasn't, so you *nabbed* me. That wasn't super smart, was it?"

"Sure it was. It was perfect. Would have been. It was a good plan."

"It was stupid. It was crazy. You can't just go around hiring people to kill people. Then kidnapping them."

I clear my throat. "There's more, too."

"More?"

"This I really don't get. There's a house in Maryland in your name."

"What? How do you even do that?"

"I don't know that either."

"You can do anything with money, son."

"He was using the house for some kind of human trafficking thing. I don't fully understand that part. There were drugs involved," I say, remembering the paraphernalia and poor Libby. "And that's where he sent Mason."

"You sent Mason to . . ." Cameron's voice is choked in rage. I'm wondering if the police will even get here in time to see Skeeter alive. Part of me doesn't even really care.

"He wouldn't have been hurt." Skeeter is double-talking now. Both of us can hear it in his voice. He's talking fast, trying to save his life. I don't blame him, but I'm also not sure if it's going to work. "We were just going to . . . to keep him there. For safety. Get him out of the way, you know?"

"Did you even ever intend to release him? Or me?" Skeeter doesn't answer but he doesn't need to. We don't quite have all the pieces yet, but things are coming clear. And it seems likely to me that neither Mason nor Cameron would have made it back alive.

"So you were preparing to hang the human trafficking on me. Why? In case you ever got caught?" And right there, Cameron had figured something beyond what I had. But it made a mad and perfect kind of sense.

"It wasn't quite like that, Cam—"

"And you get my kid involved to somehow strengthen the connection to me? Never mind. Don't answer. Everything you say is lies. But I'm getting the picture. The police can get the full story out of you. I know enough that it's everything I can do right now not to kill you."

It's been about half an hour since we called the cops and I know I have to get out of there before they arrive.

"I'm sorry, Cameron, I can't be here when they arrive."

He looks at me curiously but he doesn't ask any questions. By now there are probably a lot of things about me that he's wondering about.

"All right," he says. "The gun?"

"I'm thinking he's got one in his desk drawer. I saw him looking for it before."

Cameron checks and sure enough, it's there.

"Loaded, too," he says. He doesn't ask where I'm going. "I'll call you later?"

I nod. "My car is close by. Let me know when you're clear."

CHAPTER FORTY-FOUR

I LEAVE THE house by a side entrance and start hoofing it toward my car. When I hear a vehicle headed in my direction, I duck into a copse of trees, and then another. In some ways, I don't even care if someone sees me. In other ways, though, I just don't want a conversation. It's been a rough enough day already.

When I get back to my car I decide to just stay put for now. I run the air for the AC, but I don't listen to music, because I want to be able to hear if anyone approaches.

About an hour later, my stomach lurches when a familiar green truck pulls up in front of me, but I am only half surprised when Cameron pops out of it. He's wearing a grin, like he's pleased with himself. For finding me, I guess, but maybe also for dispatching Skeeter. I still figure he'll be out in no time, but for the moment Cameron is relieved and happy. He's believing justice will be done.

"Where'd you get the wheels?"

"It's Skeeter's," he says, getting into my car. "I figured he wasn't going to be needing it today."

"I hope that's right," I say.

"Damn straight," Cameron replies, and I'm not quite sure about the nuance of the words in this context and I don't ask.

"We're leaving the truck here?"

"Sure," he says. "Why not?"

Why not indeed?

When I start driving, I don't know where I'm going, and then I do. I know I can't just take him back to the Flying W. He will have work to do there to secure it for himself and to get Skeeter's people out of there.

While I drive, I find that I am sipping on adrenalin, so I give him the skinny in heady gulps. What I know about Mason. About Belle. About the whole setup over there right now.

"Who are you?" He isn't the first person to ask it.

I am aware that he is looking at me with something like awe. And it's not a good thing.

"What . . . what do you mean?" The hesitation is real. I'm not quite sure how to answer.

"You just . . . what? Rescued me?"

I laugh self-consciously, carefully keeping my eyes on the road.

"I guess I kinda did, didn't I?"

"And you say Mason is okay?"

"Yeah. He's with his mom and his mom's place is under surveillance. I'm taking you there now."

After I say it, I realize I hadn't asked him. Hadn't consulted him. Hadn't included him in any of this decision making. And then I realize another thing: that's where we are now. For me, somewhere between the time where he decided to give up on the horses in order to soften the blow on his son, he lost me. Somehow. In a way I really don't even understand. Because, your son, right? That's super important. But his sacrifice would not, ultimately, have saved the kid. And he must have known that. How could he not?

I shoot a sidelong glance at Cameron, lost in his own thoughts on the passenger side. *I* am what saved the kid. And have now saved Cameron, too. And there is in me an anger at all of this that I don't even fully understand.

An anger. No. And then I recognize it for what it is.

A grief.

I had thought for a moment that I belonged somewhere. Maybe in this beautiful man's shadow. Maybe at his side. And then life happened. And now I see him differently. He is imperfect. Flawed. Okay, but is that so bad? It is not so bad. We are all imperfect. But I needed him to be better. At least better than me. And he was not.

CHAPTER FORTY-FIVE

FROM THE TIME I take the Glendale Avenue exit off the 51 and head toward Maryland Avenue, I'm keeping my eyes sharp. As I approach Amanda Walker's townhouse, I have two hands on the wheel and I'm scanning left and right, looking for things that don't look as they should be. You just never know who's watching, but I'd been led to believe there was going to be protection at her place, keeping an eye on the kid. Now I'm thinking they can keep an eye on Cameron, too.

Against my better judgment, I drive right in and stop in front of her garage.

"You should be safe here."

"At Amanda's?"

"Yeah. It's a long story. She can tell you parts of it. I have someplace I need to be."

"Will I see you again?" He looks kind of forlorn when he says it. I feel pretty bad about that. Like this last week or so has just been hell on him. His world is upside down, and I'm not helping any.

"I'm sorry," I say, and the regret he probably hears in my voice is real. "But I don't think so."

And then I feel kind of dumb dumping him at his ex-wife's, but I know he'll be safe there. And the rest of his life? I think about it as I drive away. My body reaching back to the place where I belonged, if even for a moment. That sense of connection. Of mattering. The thing I thought I felt.

I think about it, but then I force myself to shut it off. Cameron has a lot to sort out, but he's just going to need to figure that all out on his own. The belonging I felt was fleeting and never real. Plus, I've got to deal with my own stuff.

CHAPTER FORTY-SIX

BECAUSE CURTIS HAD supplied me with an address, it doesn't take me long to track Jaxon down. He has, after all, the same distinctive last name that I've had for the last few years. It's just that he came by it honestly.

When I find the address, I am unsurprised that he lives in a small house with his grandparents, his late mother's parents. I watch the house for a few days before I reach out. If Jaxon's father has ever been in the picture, he doesn't seem to be now. And it isn't that I'm waiting for anything in particular. I'm just not quite sure what to say.

I watch long enough to get a sense of his schedule. He has a job at a place called Burger Dee-Lite that doesn't look like it has too many Michelin stars. I don't know what Jaxon does there, but when he leaves, he looks smaller. Diminished. Beaten down somehow.

On the second day, when he leaves his shift, I follow him for a bit, and then I intercept him.

"Hey, Jaxon," I call out.

His head lifts as he swivels around, but when he identifies me, his face darkens, and he shoves his hands more deeply into his pockets.

"You," he says, not meeting my eyes. "What do you want?"

"I just want to talk," I say. "I have some things . . . some things to tell you. Is there someplace where we could sit quietly for a bit?"

He half shrugs, but points to an Italian restaurant across the street. The place is empty—too early for dinner, too late for lunch. Jaxon appears to know the kid working the bar, and we are told it's a go for us to just take whatever table we want in the back room.

"Jus' holler if you want anything, a'ight?"

The décor in the back is even more dark and dreary. Framed cheap prints of saints on the wall. It's possible the place looks all right at night, when it is full and the candles on the table are lit and there are people here drinking wine and eating food. But right now, it's hard not to see the poorly painted plasterboard or see the gouges in the tables. It is perfect for my purpose: I'm certain we won't be disturbed.

"I'm going to tell you the whole thing," I say once we're settled. "You won't like it all, but it will be the truth."

"All right," he says. And he's not looking right at me, but I can tell he's listening, just the same.

"I'm not your mother," is how I begin.

"Same old story. I thought you had something new to tell me?"

"Pipe down," I say. "And just listen for a spell. Okay?"

He looks like he might say something. Argue with me. But I give him a look, and he settles down. I may not be his mom, but I've been a mom. The look. It never goes away.

"Okay," he says, only wriggling faintly in his seat.

"I'm not your mother," I say again. And then I soften my voice. Lower it. "But your mother is certainly dead. I'm going to tell you something that I swore I would never tell a soul. Telling it puts me in grave danger. It jeopardizes everything."

"Are you going to tell me or not?"

I smile. The energy between us. I have not had a teenage son. But if I did, I imagine he would be like this.

"I am," I say. "But I'll do it in my time."

He sighs and sits back in his chair.

I smile and sit forward in mine.

I take a deep breath. And I begin.

"There was a time when my life, as I'd known it until then, had ended. And I was doing things that required me to have a life that I no longer had claim to. And so . . ." How to tell it. That was the thing. "I found someone who could . . . sell me an identity."

There. He was sitting forward ever so slightly. I had his attention now.

"Sell it?"

"Yes. You already know that the identity I bought belonged to Katherine Eveline Ragsdill."

"My mother." His voice is soft. Barely above a whisper.

"Yes. Though I didn't know it at the time. I didn't know anything. I still don't really. And until I met you, I never thought very much about where the name had come from. It was . . . it was just the identity I'd purchased. Do you see?"

He is sitting quietly. Maybe his face is slightly red, though he's trying hard for me not to see it. This was not the outcome he'd been hoping for.

"You bought it from my dad?"

"No. Not your dad. Just some guy I found who . . . specializes in deals like that. I would say your dad had nothing to do with it."

"So my mother is dead."

"Yes. I'm sorry. How did your father say she died?"

He hesitates before answering. And then, "In childbirth," and the words are very quiet.

"She was young?"

How do I know this? Well, I can do math, for one. But also, there had been nothing about her when I'd searched, when I'd first tried to find out if she had ever been. That's not true for most people. It had not occurred to me that it was because she hadn't really gotten her life started when she died.

"Yes," he says. "She was seventeen."

"Crikey," I say, though I'm not generally one for genteel cursing. "That's a real shame. I'm sorry to hear it. One thing, though, Jaxon: I'm certain she loved you very much. Don't think otherwise. Please."

He looks at me fully then: his eyes meeting mine in a way they haven't before.

"Why?" He wants to know.

Why indeed? Why do I care? I'm not really sure. And then I know.

"I know what you are feeling. That loss of something you don't even know you had. That connection, I guess. The connection of belonging to someone, without question. I had that, also, with my son. You would have had that with your mother. So, yes. I have a sense of what you have lost. Because I lost it, too."

I can tell from the way he looks at me that he doesn't know quite what to do with that. What maybe it means. I don't know, either. I only know that he fits into a spot that is empty. I've felt that without being able to name it from the very first.

He looks at me for a while without saying anything. Then, quietly, "I believe you. But tell me this: Why did you need to buy an identity?"

How much to say? Though really, what's to lose now? It's all lost already.

"After . . . after I lost my child, I wanted to hide."

"Was it your fault? That he died, I mean."

It's a good and valid question and I'm not sure how to answer. And then I do.

"Nobody thought so. Nobody would have blamed me. But I guess I did."

"You did?"

"I guess I do," and I find I'm crying. Lightly. Just because it's there. And also here I am, exhuming all these places that I have kept covered for so long. It's a lot. "Yeah. I guess I still do."

"I'm sorry," he says. I can see his face is more open now. Less guarded. "I don't really know you at all, but I think maybe . . . I don't think it was your fault. You loved him so much. I can see it all over you. You would have stopped it if you could. Whatever it was."

And I'm still crying, but now I'm nodding, too. Yes. Yes, he's right. I would have stopped it if I'd known. If I could. I would have done anything for it not to have occurred.

"I've done bad things since," I say. It feels like a confession. The darkness of the room, the saints on the wall, all add to that feeling.

"I know," he says. Forgiving me. Benediction. And yet there is nothing for him to forgive.

And we nod at each other, understanding things perfectly. Neither of us knowing anything at all but understanding that is a piece of that, too.

CHAPTER FORTY-SEVEN

WHEN WE PART, it is without the expectation that we'll see each other again. Even so, I know in my heart that it isn't the end of the story.

And then I go home, where it feels like I haven't been for a long time, and where the dog lets me know he had noticed my absence.

I'm frightened, at first, when I get out of the car and he is not at the gate to greet me. When I enter the house, though, I understand. He is on the sofa, and he keeps his back to me.

"Really?" I say. "You're cold shouldering me?" And he turns still farther away.

I sit on the edge of the couch, nudge him over, scratch his belly. He responds by rolling slightly onto his back. Begrudgingly. As though he is allowing me to scratch his tummy.

"I'm sorry, bud," I say, still scratching. "It was kind of an emergency. I don't think we get one of those again in a while."

When I get up, the dog does, too. He pads behind me into the kitchen and through the whole house.

"You've forgiven me," I say. He turns his head, but I grin at him. "Ha!" I say. He likes the tone and wags his tail.

I'm relieved to find that everything is in order. There was, of course, food and water available to him, so at least I know his icy treatment had nothing to do with that. And his ability to go in and out is unhindered. I spend some time cleaning up the yard; cleaning what he left behind. And once I'm done, I invite him to walk with me in the forest. He comes gladly and I can tell all is forgiven. He's not one to hold a grudge.

It was raining when I left, but now it is beautiful out. Perfect. We walk into the forest in the golden hour, the dog at my heel until he hears something scampering in the forest. At those times he takes off, but he comes right back. His prey drive is not significant. He's not one of those dogs that feels the need to chase a creature until it drops. He just wants it to run away. It's like he's insulted they presume to lollygag around in front of him. He requires them to show that they understand his superiority by running away from him. And then he's happy and the chase subsides.

I've missed my forest. Missed these walks with the dog. Missed, even, my painting sessions. Like the plein air masters of old: how many ways to paint *that* tree? I'd looked forward to getting there.

But things are changing; shifting. I can feel the earth moving under my feet. Things feel altered now. And the situation leaves me too exposed. Fully exposed, really. I could just change my number. I could change my ID. But it feels to me that more is called for. A lot more. I'm not quite sure where to start, but I'm getting there.

When we get back to the house, my phone is ringing. I glance at the call display. A number from Whale Bone Alley, Siberia. I roll my eyes. Let it ring. I'm not in the mood. I make some tea. Feed the dog. Start to unpack my bag. And the phone rings again. Fly Geyser, Nevada. Is she just going to keep doing this? Rotating through some crazy Rolodex of anonymity?

"Do you pick these places," I ask when I answer. "Or is it some kind of randomizer?"

"Fly Geyser struck a chord, eh?"

"So you pick them."

"More or less. It's complicated."

"Of course."

"I didn't call about that."

"I know."

"The hit. With the cowboy." She hesitates, but I already know where it's going, but I don't know yet how I'll respond. "It's back on."

"No."

"What do you mean 'no'?"

"I mean 'no.' I'm not going to do it. And you shouldn't allow it, either. We're not some . . . some crazy jack-in-the-box service where things are on and off again in a heartbeat."

"That isn't actually how jack-in-the-boxes work."

"I *know* how they work," I say. "I just couldn't think of a better example. What I mean is, you can't just on again off again at will. There are real people involved. Hell, *I'm* a real people."

"So it's like that, is it?"

"No. It's not like that. Whatever you're thinking, it's different than that. It's just, you ended the assignment. If I were to take this one, it would be a new assignment. And I'm not taking it."

There is a silence so deep, I feel certain she is going to argue with me. Make some point that is probably valid. But she doesn't.

"Okay," is all she says. That and "if it isn't you, you know it'll just be someone else." And then she terminates the call.

"Fuck!" It's all I can think to say.

CHAPTER FORTY-EIGHT

I SLEEP ON it.

I sleep on it and then I live with it. I go through the day thinking about all that has occurred and what my next move should be. The whole puzzling out of everything isn't as simple as it sometimes seems it should be.

Toward the end of the afternoon, I call Cameron.

"Where are you?"

"Back at the ranch."

"How did it turn out?"

"About like you figured, I guess. Skeeter's got friends. But he did some seriously bad things."

"Provable bad things," I add.

"Yeah. For sure. He's got friends. But so do I. It's an awful situation. I'm going to get a lawyer today."

"You are. That surprises me. What for?"

"Well, just all the stuff you said, for one. The house in Maryland. The human trafficking stuff. Even some of the kidnapping stuff: me and Mason. The way he set it up, no one actually saw *him* do it. Do you see?"

"Yes, actually. I do."

"So did he kidnap me? Or was I simply being weak on my convictions? And did he kidnap Mason? Or was it me all along? You see what I'm saying?"

"Unfortunately, yes."

"I mean, fortunately, there are a few people who witnessed some of this stuff. You for instance. You'd be able to vouch for me on several fronts."

As he says this, I bow my head into my hand and just feel the pulse at my temple. And the soft place where my hair touches my forehead. I feel the things that are incontrovertible. Beyond a shadow of a doubt. The things that are real.

Vouching for him is, of course, not a thing I'll be able to do. I don't say that. What I actually say: "Yeah. Of course. You're right. There's that."

"Like, if I don't play this right, I'm the one that might actually end up in jail."

And I want to reassure him, and I nearly do. But then I realize, of course: he's not wrong.

*   *   *

After I get off the phone, the dog and I take a walk in the near twilight. Another walk. The dog is in heaven after I've been gone so long.

The walk is necessary though. I have a lot to work out. It's late in the day, but the light is still strong. And it's a beautiful light. It dapples through the trees, turning what in Arizona was a marauding sun into gentle, radiant warmth and light. It is beautiful here. I have loved it. As much, I reflect, as I can love anything.

And the walking, that's the thing. It feels good. Right. Something I miss when I don't get enough of it. When I don't do it right. I walk hard enough that it makes me aware of every portion of my body. I feel the flow of energy to my thighs, my glutes. Feel the strength I'm forcing into my core. My legs pump, but after a while my arms pump, also. I'm not even aware of it at first. But I'm pushing myself to a point of deeper breathing, higher velocity pumping of blood. And I'm pushing myself because why? Well, that I'm not really sure of, but it feels like something that has to happen. Something to clear the cobwebs—to get me to see things as they are and/or need to be.

If the dog notices any of this extra effort, he gives no sign. He's just happy to have me there and to be out of his little compound. Even gilded cages get tedious after a time.

After I'm back at the house and I've caught my breath, I call Jaxon.

"I'm doing something crazy," I tell him. "I want you to be part of it."

"Ummm . . ." I can hear the hesitation, but also the curiosity. "I mean, I'm supposed to work. Not much else going on, I guess."

"I'll Venmo you some money for gas. This will be a good thing for you, I promise. Please say you'll come."

"Where am I going?"

"My house."

CHAPTER FORTY-NINE

AFTER ALL THIS time keeping my forest home absolutely secret, it's funny opening it up in this way. Funny as in strange. It feels like some new corner has been turned. And I know it's not a corner I'll be standing on for long.

Jaxon arrives two days after I call and request his presence. He had to borrow a car, and it was a long way to come.

"You live here?" He looks shocked or surprised at the surroundings. I'm not sure which.

"That's right."

"It's beautiful," he says. Surprising me. "Like," and he looks embarrassed at the admission, "kinda magical."

"Thanks. I'm actually glad you feel that way." I realize that's a cryptic thing to say, but I can't help myself. Fortunately, he doesn't seem to notice. He's busy looking around in delight at the forest. And the dog. The dog has met us at the gate, of course.

"Nice dog," he says as he walks. "What's his name?"

"Don't ask," I say. "It's a long story."

He shoots me a look, but he does what I requested and he doesn't ask.

"He looks like a cool dog," is all he says.

I show him around the place. It's a small house, so there's not a ton to show, but what there is is nice. I've made it a home in a relatively short time. I made it a home after beginning from below zero.

After I give him the ten-dollar tour, I take him out to the garden where I serve us iced tea plus some scones I'd made for the occasion. The dog curls up between us, easy, like this happens all the time. There's a soft breeze rolling through the forest. It kisses the branches, makes them sing. It is easy to pretend we are what he wanted us to be. It is easy to pretend we are mother. And son.

"I have to go away," is how I begin. It's not what I meant to say. It's not the other half dozen or dozen things that would have been better to say. But it's what comes out.

"Where?"

"I'm not sure yet. But—suddenly—none of this is working for me anymore."

He just squints at me.

"It's like everything is closing in. I got careless, I guess is what I'm saying. I let . . . I let too many people get close to me. And I made some big mistakes. One of them was your mother. No. Let me finish. The name—your name and hers—they're too distinctive. I should have been more thorough around that. I didn't . . . I guess I didn't really think it through."

He shrugs at me helplessly and I curse myself. He's eighteen. What do I think I'm asking of him? But also, what am I giving? I think it still has a chance, so I press on.

"So, okay, listen: the house is in your mother's name. You are your mother's son."

"Are you trying to tell me something?" he says. "Because I feel like you are? But I'm not getting it."

"I'm going to give you all this stuff," I say, gesturing all around. "I mean, it's not like it's a palace. But it's paid for. And it's real."

"You're going to give it to me?"

I nod.

"Why?"

"I can't keep it. I can't keep any of it. I did it wrong before. Maybe I can do it right some other time."

There. He's squinting at me again. I can tell I'm not making a whole lot of sense.

"But a house . . ."

"It's not just a house, either. There are several acres. And there's lots of . . . stuff. There's a bank account, too. With money in it."

He shakes his head. "What? You're not even making sense."

"But I am, Jaxon. Truly. Life has lined up this way, do you see? We both lost someone dear to us. Maybe the most important person in our lives, ultimately. And we can't ever be that person for each other. But maybe, at least, I can give you some of what your mother would have wanted to give you. Security. A home. A feeling of having been looked after. And me: I get to give, in a way, to a son I never got to see come to this age."

"That's nuts," he says, but with less conviction this time. "That's a crazy plan."

"Oh, now that's not even an argument," I say, but I'm smiling. He smiles back. "But we're doing this, Jaxon. I've already had power of attorney drawn up in your name so you can have access to everything. So you don't even have to switch anything. But I won't be back."

"Not ever?"

"No. There's one thing though."

"What?"

"The dog."

"You can't leave your dog."

"I know," and I feel suddenly near tears. "I know. But I don't know what the future will bring. And this is his home."

"Like I said before, he's a cool dog. Sure, I mean, I'd keep him for you if you wanted. But I don't think that's the call here. It would be . . . it would be like leaving a kid."

"We'll decide in the morning," I tell him. "Let me show you where you'll bunk down."

*   *   *

Obviously, I very nearly just leave in the night. There are so many reasons for me to do that. In the end, though, there are more reasons not to, not the least of which is Jaxon, who has felt abandoned his whole life. I have this one gift. I want to do it right.

CHAPTER FIFTY

IN THE MORNING I make us espressos and this time pancakes, and then we walk. He tells me about his plans. What he's been hoping for his life. I laugh out loud when he tells me he had a dream of becoming a landscape architect. I laugh because there are times when life can seem shitty and mean and pointless, but other times it all comes together and everything is perfect. Everything turns out as though there is some guiding hand.

And I tell him right away—to take the sting out of my laugh—that he'll have this beautiful property to play with—to architect the landscape, if that's what he wants. But also, there will be more than enough money for him to pursue that very dream.

"More than enough?"

I nod.

"Yeah, sure. Start planning it now."

There is more of this. More of this bittersweet connecting. I could give you more details, but you know what they look like. He is not my son. It's impossible that he is my son and that I am his mother, though I have borne her name. But we are connected anyway. One way or another, life put us together. And now what I had is his. All of it. I hope he does right by that gift, but that isn't my concern. My concern: that he understands his mother—the woman who died while giving birth to him—loved him very much. And that somehow her love has come through me, who coincidentally lost someone who might have grown to be very much like him.

Everything is connected, do you see? Everything is connected until it is not.

There is more food. There are more walks. There is some planning. I decide to keep my Volvo for the moment, just because it makes things easier. I have him sign the pink slip. And sure, I could have done it myself, but there is something symbolic in that.

I load the car up. It's not a lot of stuff, but maybe it is enough. There is bedding. There is clothing. There is quite a lot of cash. There are some electronics. The Bersa, of course, plus a twin of that gun in a hidden compartment in the trunk. At the very last I decide Jaxon is right: even though I think it would be in his own best interest, at the last I decide I cannot leave the dog.

Darkness is just falling as I prepare to leave.

"You're really doing it," he says as I shlep the last of my things out to the car.

"Yeah," I tell him. "I really am. And I'm mixed about it, because I'd love to hang here for a while with you, watch you grow into it, you know?"

"I do," he says.

"But yeah. That's part of it. I really have to go."

We do that for a bit longer. Hang around. Even have a few laughs. Before I get in the car, I tell him that I love him. The way a mother might. He hugs me tightly, bending down from his height, and he says it back. Then I pop the dog into the car. And the dog and I? We just drive away.

CHAPTER FIFTY-ONE

As I DRIVE, there are moments I wonder if I'm doing the right thing. But at the same time, I know absolutely that it is correct.

This time I'm driving straight toward the desert. It takes a longer time to get there than when I've flown, but my base is in my car now—at least *for* the now—and so the patina that everything takes on is different than it was.

It's a long drive and it's an old car, so it's not like it has Sirius radio or fancy electronics or anything that would help me pass the time. All I have to occupy myself with are my thoughts. And so, as I drive, what I think about is what I already know: as long as Skeeter is out there conniving and weaving his nasty webs, Cameron and those he loves will never be safe. And Cameron had said he was going to get a lawyer, but I don't believe that, in the end, a lawyer will be able to help with this. Skeeter has *friends* and *cronies* and others that will protect him when he does the wrong thing. Not only that, he's skilled at covering up the things he does and even making it look as though someone else did it. He can distance himself. He can create false scenarios. And Cameron—pure, sweet, honest Cameron—he doesn't stand a chance against all of that.

And so, I drive until I get to the desert. And then I drive some more. And while I do, I think. I think it all through. By the time I get to where I am going, I have something like a plan.

I park again near the entrance to Skeeter's ranch, and I watch. It turns out I don't have long to wait. When he leaves, I follow him. When he slows, I follow him at closer range. He stops, eventually, at a gas station. I don't see any cameras at the pumps, but I pull on my hoodie, with the business end on my head. And even though it's dark, I put on my dark glasses. Then I pull up to the pump opposite where he is. There is no one around. I plug him efficiently right in the temple. I'm skilled enough he won't have known what hit him. There have been cases when I care about that, but I find that I don't. Not this time.

CHAPTER FIFTY-TWO

Though I'm in his neighborhood, I don't tell Cameron I'm here. It would just complicate things, that's what I think. And it would bring questions where none need to be. He's safe now, that's all I know. He would never have been before, and now he is.

I have one more call to make before I ditch my phone, and I'm not looking forward to it. But first, of course, I have to anonymize my call. I come to it with a sort of reckless abandon. I'm thinking about all the weird places I could make the call be from. When I've done about two minutes of research on it, though, I realize it will not be quite as easy as that, and I settle for a *67, which, of course, she doesn't answer—what was I thinking anyway? I settle for a text, and then I head for Sam's while I wait for her call.

"Hey, kid." Sam sounds enthusiastic. "Good to see you. You drinking tonight?"

"No thanks, Sam. Maybe a burger. You do burgers, right?"

"Best in the state," he brags.

"Bring it," say I. "Fries, too."

"Girl after my own heart," he says as he heads for the kitchen.

With the burger ordered, the call comes, as though on cue. I head toward the door so I can take it outside.

"What's up?" she says. The bonus of not ever having called her needlessly. She knows when she hears from me, something is going on.

"I just killed Skeeter Allaband." There. I've said it. And it's bald.

"Ah. Let me think." A bit of silence while I do what she asks. "Okay. You've killed the client. That's what you're telling me."

"Yes."

"That wasn't part of the deal."

I laugh at that. Then, "I should think not."

"And what was your thinking?"

"Are you sure you want to hear it?"

"Try me."

"Okay. Cameron is a good and honest man. He's trying hard to do the right thing. Skeeter Allaband is . . . well, he's kind of evil. And I'm pretty sure he's the client. So I figured, if I took the evil client out, maybe you'd leave Cameron alone."

There is a deep silence then. Deep enough to drive a truck through. I'm not sure what to do with it, so I keep my mouth shut, let her figure.

"You're right on one count. Wrong on the other."

"Tell me," I say.

"Well, okay, yes: Allaband was the client. You tell me he's dead. I'll have confirmation soon. But in the meantime, I trust you: I'll take your word on it and call off the hit."

"Thank you."

"No one to report to. No one to check to see if we got the job done. No worries—it's over."

"Thanks again."

"You, on the other hand, I'm not quite sure what to do with. Your handling of this whole business was erratic and put us at risk."

"Yes," I say quietly. "I know."

"Under the circumstances, you are not a good fit for us right now. One could say you're on a different page. I wish you luck, but . . ." And then I realize her call had terminated. And I know I should feel rejected or upset, but all I feel is relief. She's said she was going to leave Cameron alone.

I go back into Sam's. He's a pro. He had noticed me absent myself for a call and had held my order. It shows up in a minute, though, piping hot. I eat the burger and realize Sam was right: it probably is the best in the state. Maybe it's the best in the world. The fries are great, too. As I eat the delicious food, I think about what I had and what is now gone. I think about belonging and the grief that comes when that belonging is a thing of the past. I think about all of the love I've had in my life and then what I traded it for.

When I'm done eating, I pay my bill. After that, I go out to my car and give the dog some water, then take him for a fast spin around the parking lot. Then I get in my car and begin to head away from the desert. We skim out of there. We just drive away.

AUTHOR'S NOTE

Dead West is a work of fiction. All of it. Entirely made up. Here's the thing, though: the plight of America's wild horse is real. A few years ago, I set out to write a nonfiction book for kids about wild horses. The book I pitched was light and lovely. Horses. They're wonderful, right? Beautiful. Who doesn't love horses?

I know a lot about horses: their care and feeding and all that. Colors. Breeds. Backgrounds. I thought I knew a lot. And then I got a close-up view of the political arena that determines the fate of wild horses in America, and I came to understand a very different picture. In this book, I only hint at the political corruption and finagling that goes on in this space. And I only hope that, by the time you read this, there are still wild horses in the West, because there are dark forces against them. And the odds? They're not good.

Anyway, somehow—and it was entirely against my will—all this research and passion around wild horses crept into the third book in the Endings series, *Dead West*. I honestly didn't see it coming, but here it is. Again, there were no individuals in my mind when I crafted these characters, but I will say that—fortunately—there are more than a few beautiful people like

Cameron Walker out there, creating sanctuary and trying to forge the way for a more stable future for the American mustang.

The wild horses in this book are entirely fictional. There are a band of Kiger horses, who live pretty much as described in *Dead West*, but they roam at the wonderful Return to Freedom sanctuary in Lompoc, California, an organization that continues to be a strong force for mustangs in America. And no one gets near them with helicopters.

Also, there is a Salt River band of horses, but they are entirely unlike the ones in *Dead West*. How and where the ones in the book live and roam are entirely my own construction. And I didn't just fictionalize the horses. I completely moved Arizona park geography around to fit my purposes and my story, so please don't follow in any of these paths because you will surely get lost!

I made up parks and towns, too. Cathedral National Park and the one-horse town of Lourdes, Arizona, don't exist at all—though if Lourdes did, I'll bet you'd find a fantastic croque monsieur. In short, everything that seems real has been altered in this book. I'm not sure why. It just happened that way.

As always, I didn't get here alone. The fabulous team at Oceanview Publishing—Bob, Pat, Lee, Faith, and Christian—have been so supportive of this series and character. It continues to be such a gift to have this amazing team.

My wonderful agent, Kimberley Cameron, continues to be a real champion for my work. She knows the publishing industry as well as anyone, but she loves books and reading, too. I'm so grateful to have her beside me. Through Kimberley I have met Mary Alice Kier and Anna Cottle of Cine/Lit Representation and Whitney Lee of the Fielding Agency. Everything is better because of you guys.

Dead West got a lot of help from first readers Anthony Parkinson—aka my husband—Sarah Entz, and Will Bass. Their observations were always delivered with love and sometimes laughter but—man!—so much was bang on. The book is oodles (oodles!) stronger through their contributions.

My family team is incredible, as well. In addition to my husband, Tony, my brother, Dr. Peter Huber; my son, Michael Karl Richards; my brother-from-another-mother, Roger Chow; and my beautiful daughter-in-law, Kristen Hauser Richards are always standing by with support. I am lucky to have so much love in my life.

Other friends, family, and colleagues have been likewise deeply supportive. Kathleen Benton and all the VGs continue to astonish me with their caring and cheerleader-like support. Stephanie Parkinson Briguglio, Michéle Denis, Sheena Kamal, Laura-Jean Kelly, Jeannie Lee, Chris Newell, Jo Perry, Diana Welvaert, and Carrie Wheeler are always there with caring, laughter, and appropriate words of wisdom. I love you guys.

And you, of course, dear reader. I cherish every letter—not to mention tweet, Instagram tag, and Facebook poke. You are a big part of this partnership. I feel your presence. Thank you for caring.

BOOK CLUB
DISCUSSION QUESTIONS

1. Prior to reading *Dead West*, what did you know about contract killers? How did you feel about being introduced to an assassin-for-hire? Did your insights or feelings change as you learned more about the protagonist?

2. Is the reader meant to identify with the protagonist? Feel sorry for her?

3. The protagonist of *Dead West* is a complicated character and clearly an unreliable narrator. Do you think the story would have been told differently in the third person? Perhaps told by Cameron?

4. At what point did you realize the narrating character was nameless? Did that enhance the story or detract from it?

5. Did the narrating character in *Dead West* remind you of any other fictional character? If so, who and in what way?

6. What feelings did this book evoke in you? Were you surprised?

7. Were you surprised at the appearance of Jaxon? At the protagonist's reaction?

8. If you got to ask the author one question, what would it be?

9. What do you think the author's purpose was in writing *Dead West*? What ideas or themes was she trying to get across?

10. What did you learn from *Dead West*? About the mustangs? About human nature?

PUBLISHER'S NOTE

We trust that you enjoyed *DEAD WEST*, the third book in Linda L. Richards' Endings Series.

While the other two novels stand on their own and can be read in any order, the publication sequence is as follows:

ENDINGS (Book 1)

Redemption from the darkest of situations— An exploration of the costs of reinvention, questioning motivation, and if ever the ends justify the means

"Provocative and powerful, *Endings* by Linda L. Richards sweeps the reader from leafy suburbia into the strangely seductive underworld of a woman who teaches herself to kill for a living. Page after page, Richards ratchets up the tension, weaving tradecraft, disguises, and psychology into a riveting tale that peels back the layers of the soul."

—Gayle Lynds, *New York Times* best-selling author

EXIT STRATEGY (Book 2)

A shattered life. A killer for hire. Can she stop? Does she want to? Her assignments were always to kill someone. That's what a hitman—or hitwoman—is paid to do, and that is what she does. Then comes a surprise assignment—keep someone alive.

The tension, the psychology, the disguises—and Richards weaves it all together with often lyrical prose—creates an evocative protagonist, who is trending toward the dark side. And the assignment in *Exit Strategy* offers possible redemption. She's faced with instruction to protect this time—not to kill.

We hope that you will read the entire Endings Series and will look forward to more to come.

If you liked *DEAD WEST,* we would be very appreciative if you would consider leaving a review. As you probably already know, book reviews are important to authors and they are very grateful when a reader makes the special effort to write a review, however brief.

For more information, please visit the author's website:
www.lindalrichards.com.

Happy Reading,
Oceanview Publishing
Your Home for Mystery, Thriller, and Suspense